BINDI

BINDI

A Novel

PAUL MATTHEW MAISANO

Little, Brown and Company

New York Boston London

Little, Brown and Company
Hachette Book Group
1290 Sixth Avenue, New York NY 10104
littlebrown.com

First Edition: August 2018

Little, Brown and Company is a division of Hachette Book Group, Inc. The Little, Brown name and logo are trademarks of Hachette Book Group, Inc.

The publisher is not responsible for websites (or their content) that are not owned by the publisher.

The Hachette Speakers Bureau provides a wide range of authors for speaking events. To find out more, go to hachettespeakersbureau.com or call (866) 376-6591.

ISBN 978-0-316-50948-0
Library of Congress Control Number: 2018931938

10 9 8 7 6 5 4 3 2 1

LSC-C

Printed in the United States of America

For my grandmother Ruby Lee, who,
warts and all, taught me a love
"as whole as the sky"

Mother is putting my new secondhand clothes in order. She prays now, she says, that I may learn in my own life and away from home and friends what the heart is and what it feels. Amen. So be it. Welcome, O life!

— James Joyce

BINDI

Varkala Beach, Kerala
INDIA

There it is, flagging in my mind's eye. *1993*. As though it bore more weight than the years that came before or after, as if all time weren't equally fleeting and its passage — already twenty-five years — impartial. *1993*. The year of my mother's death, four short years after my father was taken from us. And yet the year 1989 does not appear to me similarly marked, disfigured by his loss. I was perhaps too young, but it is more than this. Just as it was more than my mother's death that marks *1993*.

I am thirty-three years old, an age that should feel young, except I am older now than my birth mother ever became. You'll want to hear about the day she died. People always do. But I can't tell you about that without also telling you about the months that followed. My mother left a sister behind as well, her twin, my aunt Nayana. And in *1993* I should have gone to my aunt and her husband, Ramesh, my only surviving family, where they lived in London. Instead, with a few strokes of my pen, I rewrote our story without knowing it, changing our lives, and the lives of others, forever.

It turns out I was authoring original stories after all, even then. I know I've been responsible for unhappiness as a result, and not only for my aunt; there is always more than one life at stake. But it is also true that joy occasionally stems from the most fateful chain of events, and I suppose I have been responsible for that as well. Still, I've not always been immune to tracing the ghost of the life that might have been, not a better or worse one, but very different to be sure. Why is the fact that things are as they are never enough to help us to let go of what might have been?

I was eight years old, in grade 3, at a private school almost an hour by bus from our house in Varkala, the village just up the road from the place where I am now, returned a tourist after twenty-five years. I loved school back then, second only to my mother. If she was my galaxy, then school was my sun, and my life revolved around it. Though I wasn't able to articulate the idea at the time, I grasped from a young age the importance of success in school, what it would eventually mean for my mother and me. How it had already changed my aunt's life, bringing her to England on a scholarship. I believed my education had the power to reunite my mother with her sister. And because I knew my mother wanted this most of all, I wanted it, too.

My last class of the day was English. My mother told me often how much I was like her sister; we both delighted in memorizing new vocabulary and diagramming English sentences, reading English books. My teacher was Mr. Mon, and his English was exquisite to my eager ears. Naturally, I was pleased when he asked me — just me — to remain after the final bell rang that day. I stood at the sound, making sure the back of my shirt was tucked into my trousers. Painfully aware of the stain on my shirt from lunch, I approached Mr. Mon's desk cautiously. As the other students filed out of the room without a single glance in my direction, I grew worried that I'd somehow disappointed my teacher and that I was about to be punished. But I couldn't think of anything I might have done that day, and the week before, we had been on holiday to celebrate Diwali, the festival of lights, the most important holiday in India, which marks the triumph of good over evil, inner light over spiritual darkness.

At his metal desk, Mr. Mon was thumbing through the reports he'd assigned over the break: a family history. But he did not pick mine out from the pile. He pushed the reports aside and studied me over his glasses, which he then removed and cleaned with a handkerchief from his pocket.

"I won't keep you long, Birendra," he said. "I know you have a bus to catch."

I suddenly doubted my abilities despite how much I loved to speak in English, even in those years — it was at my insistence that my mother and I had begun using English almost exclusively at home. And yet I remained silent in front of Mr. Mon until he continued.

"I've been watching you these past months. I watch all the children, of course, and I've been impressed with your work. But that is not why I've asked you today. I'd like to commend you." He stopped and eyed me seriously. I began to sweat. "Do you know what that means?"

"No, sir," I said, though I felt certain it must mean "to punish," and I struggled not to look away with shame. I wrung my clammy hands together behind my back and anticipated a reprimand.

"It means to praise."

My hands sprang forward and almost clapped, so great was my relief. Then I thought better of it. "Oh, thank you, sir," I said.

"But I haven't said what I wish to commend you for," Mr. Mon continued, laughing a little at my relief.

I felt myself flush with embarrassment and wanted to be dismissed even more than I wanted to learn why I was being praised. I wasn't in trouble, and that was what mattered. That and keeping Mr. Mon's good opinion of me.

"Yes, I see in you a potential leader, Birendra," he said. Though I was filled with joy upon hearing this, he must have sensed my general discomfort and changed the subject. As much a question as a statement, he said, "You are eight years old."

"Yes, sir," I said.

"Well, you're off to a good start, Birendra. It so happens I've had an idea over the break and thought of you. How would you like to help me organize our very first English-language reading club?"

There was nothing I would have liked more. I nodded enthusiastically, but again I stood there mute, and again I was disappointed with myself. Mr. Mon rose to his feet and smiled down at me.

"I look forward to learning about your family," he added, taking the stack of reports in hand, and then he dismissed me.

I was so proud of that family report. As I ran to my bus, I couldn't help but smile at the thought of him reading it. I'd worked hard the week of Diwali, writing and rewriting each paragraph. I was already an inquisitive child, and the report was my chance to ask innumerable questions of my mother. *Kind* was the English word she used for my uncle Ramesh, and this, in turn, was how I described him in my report. My aunt Nayana, she said, was *clever.* And she'd specified that they lived in *West* London, which made it more real in my mind because I knew my geography and directions. I included a map of England with my report and placed a star just to the left of London. My uncle and aunt were also *generous;* it was thanks to them, my mother reminded me, that I attended a private school and was able to write that report for Mr. Mon at all.

The bus lurched forward, and I remembered I'd forgotten to return the library books I'd checked out before the holiday break. I determined to return them the following day, unaware that my world was already spiraling out of orbit. On the ride home, I imagined my mother detailing my triumph at school in her next letter to my aunt. This reminded me that I had to get off the bus at Varkala Junction to post the letter she'd written the night before.

Every year, on the last day of Diwali, instead of reading to my mother from a book at bedtime, as I usually did, my mother told me the story of Lord Yama and his twin sister, Yami. I was lying on her bed as I had every night that week. I remember the fading ocher design of the *mehndi* decorating her palms for the holiday. I traced them with my finger and listened to the familiar tale. I could see Yama arrive at Yami's door bearing gifts for his sister, who led his way with her lanterns and song. "That's why siblings exchange gifts on the last day of Diwali," she said, and then she told me about a time when she and her sister were small and my aunt Nayana asked my grandparents if she could give my mother a present because they were twins and she, Nayana, was older by thirteen minutes, a fact I also included in my report. She closed my hand in hers and gave it a little shake. It was time for bed, I knew, but I didn't want to go to my room, so I pretended to sleep. She took out her notepad, on which she would write her monthly letter to my aunt, resting it on her knees and leaning against the wall beside the lamp. Every month, I personalized the back of the envelope in some way, and whenever we went to the village kiosk to call my aunt, she told me how much she loved receiving my notes and drawings, which she called *special.* She said she'd saved every one. This month, I would send her Diwali greetings.

I opened my eyes to test the waters. My mother was smiling down at me the way I loved. She asked what news she should send on my behalf. In my excitement, I mixed Hindi and English and told her she should tell my aunt and uncle I'd written about them in my family report. "Good idea," she said. "Now off to bed. It's back to school tomorrow." I pleaded with her to let me sleep with her one more night. She ran her hands through my hair, and I knew she'd let me stay. I turned over quickly and closed my eyes again, breathing quietly so I could hear the sound of her pen brushing against the paper, a sound that has always brought me peace.

Sometimes you do the most mundane thing — mailing a letter, for instance — without knowing that your life has already come undone. I got off the bus at Varkala Junction and walked in the direction of the post office, my bag heavy behind me. I remember there was a lot of smoke in the air. In the days after Diwali, there were always men making small roadside piles to burn, remnants of the week's celebration. Some of the big white stars and strings of colorful lights were left to hang from houses and trees. The few Christian families in the village would soon add their decorations, and their children would dry grass for nativity scenes they built to hold their strangely ordinary gods and saints, who looked just like humans, even their little baby savior.

Our local post office was really only a window at the front of a one-room structure. It always seemed miraculous that a single envelope, passed through this modest window, should find its intended destination across oceans and continents, yet my aunt's letters arrived every month like clockwork, and this indicated that ours reached her as well. I could hear the postal worker's firm voice telling the old man in front of me that he would have to come back with the complete address. I wanted him to leave, so I crowded in, eager to pass my mother's letter, with news of my report, through the window, where it would begin its journey.

With my task complete, I began to walk home from the junction, a ten-minute trip that would have been easier if my bag weren't still heavy with library books. Our home was on a narrow dirt road where there were nearly a dozen houses, each within calling distance of the next. It's still there. In fact, many of the streets haven't changed much in Varkala Town, as they now call it to distinguish it from what has become, in my absence, Varkala Beach. My mother and I used to have to walk through coconut groves to get to Benji's shop once a month. The shop was really just a bit of tarp hanging from four posts along the cliff, which, at the time, had a few ramshackle places to stay. My mother made these little patchwork animals, and Benji, our neighbor's nephew, sold them to

the few tourists who'd found their way to Varkala. The trees
have mostly been razed to build resorts and restaurants, shops
with real walls. But when you retreat from the cliff, it's as
if time has left the village mostly alone. Our house has been
painted and feels disappointingly, though perhaps also mercifully, unfamiliar. It once belonged to my father's parents, but
they left Varkala to take my father and his brother to Delhi for
school. It was there he met my mother and they fell in love.
Every summer before they met, he returned to Varkala with
his family. During those visits my father continued to develop
his passion for Kathakali theater, a stylized classical dance
that incorporates Keralan martial arts. It features extravagant
costumes and makeup, and the stories are told largely through
gestures and expressions. I still have a photograph of my
father in Kathakali costume, his face painted green and white,
his eyes wild and framed by a golden headdress. My mother
surprised him one day, arranging for his friend to come from
the temple and prepare my father for this portrait, allowing
him to act out his childhood dream of becoming a Kathakali
performer, a dream that played a part in eventually leading
them back to Varkala. I once told my mother that I remembered the day the photograph was taken, but she said I was
too young. I was three. I can still feel the day, whether that's
a memory or not. I even forget what my father looked like out
of that costume.

After college, my parents left Delhi and returned to Kerala, where my father had secured a post as a PhD candidate
in history. My mother said it was his love of Kathakali more
than anything that brought them there. The year they met,
he claimed at the last minute to have forgotten about a final

exam and promised his parents and brother he would be along in a few days for their annual return to Varkala. The truth was that he had a date with my mother. That weekend, they met and ate mango ice cream, his favorite, while on a walk through Lodhi Garden. My father's parents and brother were killed in a wreck just outside Hyderabad the same weekend. My mother often told me that the gods saved him on that day so she and my father could eventually make me. But she said that no one could escape death forever. That was why, when I was four, they came to take him all the same.

The Nairs were our nearest neighbors, an older couple whose daughters had long since married and left the area. I believe they were already in their seventies back then. In any case, they're gone now, too. My mother thought it was nice to have them for neighbors, like grandparents for me, because I had none, even though the Nairs were older than my grandparents would have been. My mother's parents, too, had both died, while she was pregnant with me. First, my grandmother, after a stroke. Then, just days later, my grandfather, in his sleep. He died of missing her, my mother told me. She also often said we were unlucky to have such a small family — she used to call ours "the smallest family in India" — but she also assured me there was no shortage of love, that she was merely the keeper of all the love my father and grandparents would have had for me. I asked how she could hold it all, since she was just one person. She said love wasn't something like our flesh, with physical limitations. Love could take on any shape. The smallest amount, if pure, could fill us up, yet it would always make room for more.

Mrs. Nair was a garrulous woman with a hearty laugh and a broad smile and silver hair she always wore in a loose bun. I often came home from school to find her sitting in our living room, gossiping while my mother sewed her patchwork animals. Even though my mother had lived in Varkala for years, she never spoke the local language, Malayalam, very well. Still, Mrs. Nair provided endless updates about families who were moving to or from Varkala, land that was being divided near the cliff, and marriages that would unite various families. Sometimes my mother would have me translate a word or phrase for her, but mostly she would listen to Mrs. Nair, rarely asking questions, pretending to understand more than she did.

It was Mrs. Nair who found my mother that day. As I turned onto our road, I saw the strange white vehicle in front of our homes. And two men in uniforms standing in the road. Mrs. Nair was there, with one hand pressed to her head. She appeared to have lost something. I feared for Mr. Nair. When she noticed me approaching, her expression changed, not as though she'd found what was lost but rather as though she'd remembered something, something awful. She hurried to meet me, almost running the half dozen meters despite her age. Suddenly I was in her grasp, unable to move. My backpack slid easily to the ground under the weight of my books. I was stiff in her fleshy arms, my face consumed by the soap-scented fabric gathered at her chest.

Her embrace grew tighter as she prayed to Ram, repeating the name over and over again, pleadingly, in my ear. One of the uniformed men said something about "the son" to the other, and I was drawn away from Mrs. Nair and propelled in the direction of my home. There were other neighbors gathered on the street as well, and now it was Mr. Nair preparing to intercept me. At a slow pace, he approached until he was standing before me. Then he wouldn't let me pass by. I heard one neighbor say to another: *It was her heart,* but when I turned to see who had spoken, it could have been any one of a handful of people, all eyeing me solemnly. I understood what Mr. Nair was going to say and that nothing I did would stop him from uttering the words, from changing what was now true. Still, I wanted to delay his speech. I wanted to tell him that the neighbor had been mistaken. I wanted to ask why anyone would say such a thing about my mother. Didn't I know her heart better than anyone?

1993

I

In the darkness of that first, early morning, Birendra opened
his eyes to the surroundings of the Nairs' home once again.
Mr. Nair continued to snore loudly. The unfamiliar noise had
woken him up half a dozen times throughout the night. But
because he was lying on his own mattress, for just a moment
each time he forgot where he was, and why. Then he remembered: his mother was gone. And he heard that treacherous
refrain: *It was her heart.*

His neighbors' house might as well have been fifty miles
away from home, not fifty feet. Without his mother, it no
longer felt like he was next door to the house he'd grown
up in, the only home he'd ever known. And he was left with
so many questions and no one to ask. Was his mother going
to the same place as his father? Had his father known what
was going to happen? Would he be waiting for her somewhere, perhaps along with his brother and parents? And her
parents? Had his father asked her to come? And what if she
couldn't find him? And if she did, and they were reunited,
would they then send for Birendra as well? If his mother's
atma remained close by, it provided no answers. And now it

would fall to Birendra, Mr. Nair had said, as her only son, to set her soul free.

The night before, Mr. and Mrs. Nair had gone to his house. Mrs. Nair had taken his backpack and returned with it full of clothes, his toothbrush, pajamas. Mr. Nair came with Birendra's mattress and placed it in this unused room. Birendra declined dinner and lay on his mattress while they ate, arguing about him in hushed tones. Mr. Nair did not want Birendra there. He did not want to invite death into their home. Mrs. Nair said they had no choice. Where else would the boy go? "It's done now, anyway," said Mr. Nair. "He'll stay for his mourning, unless his family comes first, but not a day longer. Is that understood?" Birendra thought he heard Mrs. Nair crying, then Mr. Nair confirmed this by telling her to stop. Crying wasn't going to help, he said. "We'll have the priest come in the morning to instruct him. I suppose we'll have to pay for that as well." Birendra was ashamed and felt like a burden, but Mrs. Nair didn't seem to think so. She was upset and had spoken then as though she were scolding her husband. How could he count rupees at such a time, she wanted to know, and for the small amount it would cost them? The boy had lost his mother. And they were like family, she said. They'd watched the boy grow since he was hardly bigger than a cashew. "Yes," said Mr. Nair, "but he's not family." Birendra hadn't wanted to hear any more. He brought his backpack close to pull out his pajamas. The library books he'd forgotten to return earlier in the day were gone. Mrs. Nair must have left them next door to make room for his clothes. They still needed to be returned. Perhaps she put them on his bookshelf alongside the other books he'd acquired over the years, gifts from his mother or from his aunt and uncle, sent all the way from West London. He'd also forgotten to ask Mrs. Nair to pack a fresh shirt to complete his school uniform, for he had stained the one he'd worn that day at lunch. He could have explained these things to the Nairs, but he didn't. In fact, he'd not yet spoken a word since arriving home from school.

Now he looked out the window and sighed into the darkness. Without his mother, he feared every moment would pass this slowly. He put his fists to his eyes but couldn't keep the tears from escaping. He wanted to scream until his mother came to his side to comfort him. A snort, followed by a long nasally exhale, from the other room reminded him cruelly of all he'd lost. He needed his mother, but he could not have her. And surely Mr. Nair would not like to see him crying, either. He'd told Birendra he would have to be strong; there was much he would have to do now so that his mother could be at rest. But Mr. Nair had not said how Birendra was to accomplish this. His mother always taught him *how* to do something whenever he was faced with a new task.

He opened his eyes, blinking a few times to clear away the tears. There was just enough light outside now to distinguish between the shadows of the trees and the darkness of dawn. He would have to go back to the house for a fresh shirt. He could get the library books. It was a dreadful task, but there was no way around it. He moved quietly through the kitchen toward the door. He could barely make out the edges of his house through the trees, and the thought of entering it, alone now, was suddenly terrifying. Even as he wanted to be close again to his mother's room, her notepad, her sewing things, her scent — everything he'd woken up to only the day before — imagining those same things now without *her* scared him; everything had been tainted by whatever had happened to her. Their house was no longer a home.

The crows had never before sounded so angry. They seemed to be shouting at him as he made his way to his front door. The house was unlocked and eerily dark inside. He moved quickly to his bedroom, even averting his eyes when passing his mother's room. He hurried to his closet but closed his eyes once he was in front of it, trying to find the courage to reach inside. He held a deep breath and reached a timid hand out, feeling for the collar of the shirt he needed. Then he ran back down the hall and out the front door, stopping only once he'd reached the center of the yard. He turned and looked back at his house. Why had it been so terrifying? A creaking door in the distance made him spin again, and now he saw Mrs. Nair's figure begin to approach, like an apparition, glowing in the faint gray light. He held his shirt up to explain why he'd left the house without permission. As he did, he realized he'd forgotten the library books yet again. When he lowered the shirt, Mrs. Nair was standing before him, her hair long and silver and loose around her shoulders, over her nightdress, in a way he'd never seen it before. She shook her head and took the shirt from him. She spoke in a whisper.

"Come, you dear boy. You won't be needing that for now."

Birendra wanted to object, to tell Mrs. Nair that he *would* need his uniform. That he had to go to school; his mother would want him to. He longed for the bus that would, at least for a few hours, take him away from Varkala and the house that now made him feel so afraid. But he remained silent, overwhelmed and defeated by the upheaval of his life, school taken from him as well.

As he walked with Mrs. Nair back to her house, she reminded him that today the priest would come to guide Birendra, that his mother was waiting to be set free. Suddenly, he thought of the small portrait of his father, dressed up as a noble lord in Kathakali costume, on his mother's bedside table. If he closed his eyes he could feel the touch against his cheek of the dangling beads that hung from that headdress, just as he could smell the faint doughy scent of the makeup on his father's face. And beyond that the familiar smell of the sea his father used to swim in every morning, the same sea that one day swallowed him whole.

For the rest of the day, Birendra did what the Nairs and the priest told him he must do. He let Mrs. Nair fix his white dhoti with a red strip of fabric at his waist and fashion a ring made of grass to wear on his right hand. There was just one thing he couldn't bring himself to do. The priest said they must respect the departed by laying eyes on her body, but Birendra could not find the courage to lift his from the casket in which his mother had been laid to rest. He was too afraid to see her in death. He stared at the box and listened to the priest chanting, and the women singing, and the neighbors paying their respects, and then he accompanied the men who carried his mother's casket to the pyre they had built beside his old house. Holding the clay pot on his head as instructed, he counted as he made each tour around the pyre, allowing the priest to pierce the pot and free the holy water inside. He hoped he'd never get to three rotations, but he must have

BINDI

because he was then handed the fire, and he let the pot fall from his head and break behind him. He turned his gaze to the light of an oil lamp the priest had said was there to guide his mother's way, and he thrust the torch until it hit the pyre. The flame rose quickly, high above the casket, and he knew there was no risk of seeing her now. Still, he watched in the space above the flames, in the flickering sparks and smoke that danced there beneath the trees, hoping to see some sign of her there. He watched until he forgot where he was, and what was on fire, until time left him there, alone. Until the flame slowly fell into embers that folded into ash. He dreamed of a great fire that night, and he still felt the flame when early the following morning he awoke, once again on a familiar mattress in a strange home.

I I

The front door to their flat opened and closed. Ramesh had returned. Nayana threw her towel on the bed and quickly slipped into her underwear, then fastened her bra. If he walked into their bedroom right now, what would he choose to see? Would he allow the evidence — this underwear, that dress hanging there — to finally present itself? Would he at least acknowledge that she wasn't going to her teaching job? His voice from the hallway, though she could hear his good mood, reached her like a scolding.

"I've fed Felix, *jaanu*," he said.

Ramesh continually provided these updates on the neighbor's cat since Nayana had pawned its care off on him earlier in the week. Even when Beth had explained she would be away from London almost an entire month, working in Edinburgh, Nayana never hesitated to accept the task. She'd thought it would mean having a place to go, to be alone, to figure things out, maybe even get back on track. But having the keys to a flat downstairs had proved too tempting; she'd once picked up the phone while the cat was eating and begun to dial Daniel, intending to have him meet her there, in the same building. She'd come to her senses at the last moment and re-placed the receiver. She was so relieved to find she still had limits that she almost broke down in tears right then under the cat's scrutinizing gaze. It had come to this, to testing herself so she would know just how out of control she was. The following day, she claimed the lingering incense in Beth's flat gave her a headache, then she showed Ramesh where to find the cat food and handed him the keys. And now Felix and he were apparently best of friends.

I should stay home, she thought, seduce Ramesh instead. She thought of ways she might end her bad behavior. She could start by admitting to her husband that Tuesdays were no longer teaching days. She should have done that at the beginning of the semester. Instead she'd convinced herself that what she needed was more time alone. And where had that landed her? Not alone at all.

For years, when Nayana looked at her reflection she couldn't help thinking of Aditi. But her twin's likeness no longer appeared in the mirror, as if effaced by years of living in England, worn down by disappointment, failure, loss. Good Aditi. They'd promised never to miss a month's correspondence. And yet Nayana still owed her sister a letter for October. And here it was already mid-November. She'd told herself she was delaying to time her letter's arrival with Diwali, which had always been *their* holiday. Now it was her reflection scolding her in the mirror; she'd let Diwali pass without greetings at all. Aditi had always been a kind of enforcer of Nayana's conscience. No doubt the invisible shock waves of her recent infidelity had traveled all the way to Varkala. Why was it that she couldn't stay in tonight? Write her sister? Come clean to Ramesh? Why was she painting kohl under her eyes, running lavender oil the length of her hair? Why did she press the scent of gardenias along each forearm, along each thigh, down the back of her neck, and behind her ears?

On these Tuesday nights, she took her time getting ready. She dressed the part she assumed Daniel liked. Tonight, she was his mistress in a purple dress, cut tight. She covered the dress now with her coat and pulled her hair up into a low knot. In her pocket, she felt for the key to the hotel room she and Daniel had now used more times than she could remember with confidence. Six? Seven? The affair had a fast and furious start. After the first time, when she was getting dressed, already late to be returning home, Daniel told her he would stay in that room until she returned to him. She was almost annoyed by so romantic a proposition. She turned to him, considered the expression on his face. His desire for her. She said nothing, picked up her bag, and walked to the door, making no promise to return or even to repeat the occurrence. His desire became a panicked need to see her again, and it was this face that brought her back the following day, and in the weeks since, days in which the two of them silently explored each other's pleasure while Ramesh was at work or waiting for Nayana at home.

She threw a scarf around her neck and zipped the coat closed to conceal her dress from Ramesh. But was she hiding the truth from him or did he not allow himself to see her as she walked by? Did he not notice her painted eyes? Couldn't he smell the gardenias?

"I'm late for work," she said, rummaging for nothing in her

handbag, avoiding his gaze, though she was already facing the door.

"Always in such a hurry, woman."

His voice was slow and lilting, unexpected. She glanced at him over her shoulder. He had called her *woman,* as he used to. He was seated as always in his big brown chair, reading his newspaper by the light of his lamp. Maybe he does know, she thought. He'd always tried to give her freedom — he would give her anything — and this made the fact that it, that he, was not enough even harder to cope with. She scooped her house keys out of the bowl on the little table and reached for the door, frustrated by his unreproachful silence, then deeply moved by his ability to love her with such generosity. She paused in the doorway.

"Will you be all right for dinner?" she asked, with an old tenderness.

And then he did look at her, over the rim of his newly acquired reading glasses, and she believed he could see everything. She stood there, trying to make herself transparent. She wanted to be unburdened, to confess. She imagined him standing, finally fed up, and walking over to her, stripping her of her keys, pushing her into the landing, closing the door in her face. But he couldn't carry this for her. He remained in his chair and looked away again.

"I'll be just fine," he said, to his paper.

"Fine," she echoed. "See you after class."

"Oh, *jaanu,*" he said, chuckling to himself. "I think Felix prefers the kidney and liver. I might pick up some more. He was especially affectionate after his meal this evening. I could hear him purring his gratitude."

A new surge of affection for Ramesh was sufficiently sharp to feel like punishment for what she was about to do. She smiled — at her pain, and at the childlike wonder that occupied his face.

"I'm glad you two are getting on so well," she said.

"It's always a surprise, you know, when he hops onto your lap after he's eaten. Such interesting creatures, aren't they?"

Her smile fell. Beth's apartment never was the haven Nayana had hoped it would be. She hadn't sat down once. She'd merely paced behind the cat long enough to see that it was eating, then left.

"Just imagine what Mum would say if we got a cat."

"You want a cat?" She couldn't believe what she was hearing.

"No, of course not. I just thought . . ." He shook his head and returned to his paper. His voice grew quiet, unsure. "It's just nice taking care of something, isn't it?"

Nayana slipped out to the landing without a further word. That was their way now; they made allowances for each other's silences. Closing the door behind her, she felt a sense of relief, but it lasted only a moment. Shame and guilt always too close behind. The lift was in the lobby; she took the stairs, freeing her hair and letting it fall down her back. She imagined Ramesh sitting alone in their home. Her perfume might have made its way over to him. Perhaps he allowed his doubts to linger alongside its scent for a moment. But he would shake them off, fold his newspaper, and swat them both away. He might turn his thoughts to dinner instead, or find something on television. Would he check on the cat once more? Was he so lonely? Wasn't she?

I I I

Birendra was tired of sitting still in the Nairs' living room, tired of listening to the condolences offered by each visiting neighbor, tired of being reminded his mother was gone. He had to escape. Outside, it was mostly quiet. Other children were at school. The sounds he heard were familiar — squawking crows, the occasional moped in the distance — but their isolation, on a school day, in the wake of his mother's death, rendered them gloomy, haunting. He took a seat under the clean linens that Mrs. Nair had hanging on a clothesline strung between two coconut trees. They'd been there since the day before. He found a shard from a burst planter and began to scratch at the earth. The Nairs had stopped bickering about him, but he'd heard Mr. Nair remind Mrs. Nair that morning, "We honor the sixteen days of mourning, and then he must go." Birendra felt guilty for causing problems, but he'd not yet found the strength, or the words, to speak, and so he had no apology to offer.

Soon Mrs. Nair came to him, carrying with her one of the red plastic chairs from her kitchen. He was digging a hole in the dirt now. The legs and back of the chair bowed slightly under Mrs. Nair's weight as she sat down in front of him. He knew he should go to her, comfort her and be comforted, but he kept digging, finally pressing the shard firmly into the little hole he'd made.

"Birendra?" She dabbed at her eyes with a dish towel. Tears began to fall from his own eyes, though he hadn't known he was about to cry. "I'm going to need your help with something."

He wiped his eyes and prepared to stand, but she motioned for him to remain seated where he was.

"Your uncle and aunt are living in London, yes?"

"Yes," he said, and the word caught in his throat after so much silence.

West London, he thought, hearing the way his mother would say it. He looked down again and pressed the mound of dirt until it was flush beneath his palm. Did Mrs. Nair want to contact his aunt and uncle? To tell them about his mother? Or maybe, he thought, she was looking for a new home for him because Mr. Nair would not let him stay. Would he go to London after all, without his mother? He had so many questions, but he only wanted to pose them to his mother, and since he could not, he asked nothing at all.

"I'm sorry Mr. Nair is upset," he said. "I'll be good. I promise not to get in his way."

Mrs. Nair opened her arms wide now to receive him. He stood and dusted himself off, then climbed onto her lap, remembering how the chair had buckled under her weight, then forgetting as he was pulled tightly into her warmth.

"You don't have to worry about Mr. Nair, dear one. He

can't help himself. We will contact your uncle and aunt. And you will stay here until they can come for you."

These words made him feel sick. Sick with the fear of leaving home and sick with an overwhelming relief that he wasn't going to be alone after all. But London, *West London*, was so far from everything he'd ever known. He'd never imagined he would go there without his mother. He thought of the letter she had written to his aunt just the other day, the one he'd sent on his way home. He could write one now and impress his aunt and uncle with his English skills. It would be difficult, much more difficult than a brief greeting or a little drawing. Difficult because of the news he would have to share, but he would try his hardest. Surely they would come for him when they learned what had happened to his mother. They had invested in his education. The letter would show them how much he'd learned. And the Nairs could not write it, knowing neither Hindi nor English. They would have to ask someone else in any case.

"I could write them a letter," he said.

Mrs. Nair turned him in her arms and studied his face carefully.

"Do you think you could do that?"

"Yes," he said, trying to smile, preparing himself to stretch the truth. "Amma and I wrote them every month. Please, please, let me write it."

Mrs. Nair wiped his cheeks dry with her thumbs. She began rocking her head and he knew she would let him. A smile came more easily now.

"Perhaps that would be best," she said. "They will want to

know you are safe." She pulled him close once more. "And who could resist you, dear one?"

Back at the kitchen table, Mrs. Nair placed a notepad and a pen in front of Birendra. The blank page made him nervous because he wanted so much to impress his aunt and uncle but also because he didn't know how to tell them what had happened to his mother. He hated to cause such pain. He knew how close his mother was to his aunt, how much she loved her. He heard his mother's voice as they'd worked on his family report: *Your uncle is kind; your aunt is clever, just like you.* He was writing to family members who cared for him even though they were far away. He would try his best to write a good letter. And though he hadn't been able to tell his mother, perhaps he would one day tell his uncle and aunt that Mr. Mon had singled Birendra out to *commend* him, and they would be proud. He would continue his education in a school where they lived in England. He might even be able to join a reading club there, where every book would be in English.

He took the pen in hand. Mrs. Nair settled in beside him and began to dictate. He tried to translate her words from Malayalam into English, using his most careful penmanship. She asked if he shouldn't write in Hindi, as his mother had, but he insisted that his aunt always spoke English to him when they talked on the phone. Mrs. Nair suggested phrases he simply didn't know how to write in English. But he remembered Mr. Mon's "3-C" rules — clear, concise, correct — as he struggled to transcribe Mrs. Nair's meaning, if not her words. It took a fair bit of thinking and more than one false start for Birendra to complete the brief letter. He wrote:

Dear Mr. and Mrs. Bhatia,

I'm sorry to write with terrible news. Your blessed sister is with God. She died 16 November 1993. Please come for your Birendra. He is waiting for you.

This final sentence was his own. He read the letter silently, and he thought his teacher would be proud. He read it aloud to Mrs. Nair, and she nodded, but he knew she did not understand the words. He signed it from Mr. and Mrs. Nair, but he wanted his aunt and uncle to know the letter's true author, so he added a postscript: *Written by your loving nephew.*

Mrs. Nair appeared relieved when he set the pen down. She retrieved an envelope he recognized from his mother's room, one of his aunt's letters. Setting it down beside a blank envelope, she asked him to copy the address. They should post it right away, she said, so it would arrive as quickly as possible.

His aunt's return address was complicated, a combination of letters and numbers written in his aunt's cursive, which wasn't precise, like his mother's. But he did his best to copy each shape exactly as it was on his aunt's envelope, regardless of whether he knew its meaning. He tried to ignore Mrs. Nair's anxious pacing. She kept looking at the bedroom door. Was she afraid Mr. Nair would awaken from his nap and disapprove? But he couldn't worry about that right now. He had to focus and take his time. Was that a 1 or a 7? An S or a 5?

At last it was ready, and he lifted the letter into the air, as if it were an offering, then folded it carefully in thirds before placing it inside the envelope, licking the flap, and sealing it closed, as his mother had so often allowed him to do. He was eager for the letter to reach London. Mrs. Nair, he could see, was excited as well. Did she know, he wondered, that it took two weeks for a letter to arrive? Mrs. Nair now retrieved her wallet, took out one note, then another. She paused and looked at Birendra. He had forgotten he would need money and looked away, embarrassed.

"Do you know how much it costs?" He did know this. He could imagine the stamps his mother would let him lick and paste — there were two and they were different — but suddenly he couldn't remember their values. "It's okay," she said. "Don't worry."

She told him to wait there; she would be back any moment. It wasn't right for him to leave the house. He was in mourning. She would go to the neighbors and ask someone to post it on their behalf. From the window, he watched Mrs. Nair hurry down their narrow road. He wasn't accustomed to seeing her move so quickly. It made her look younger than she was, despite her silver hair. She disappeared around the bend and didn't return for several minutes. When he saw her again, her hands were empty. The letter was on its way. He remembered the price of the stamps just then and could imagine the man in the window placing the postage in one corner and then, with his square rubber block, imprinting the words *by air mail* below his aunt and uncle's address. It felt as if a part of him were sealed along with the letter in that envelope. They would both embark on the long journey away from home, away from Mr. and Mrs. Nair and the house next door that was no longer a home. The rest of him would follow before long, he thought. For now, he would have to wait.

I V

It was another Tuesday night, and Nayana was still pretending to have a class to teach. It had been two weeks since she'd last met Daniel at the hotel. They were slowing down. Nayana's dress more casual, her makeup subdued. In her pocket she once again carried a key to the hotel room, though she had yet to contact Daniel. She knew he would come as soon as she called. Ramesh was at the other end of the hallway, his hands resting on his hips. Nayana watched him from their bedroom door. He was stretching his back, looking up at the ceiling. He complained of stiffness in his neck and shoulders as well, and this had only gotten worse lately with the stress of work. Years of planning, and the tunnel's first test run was just over a week away. She didn't know how she felt about being in a train under water for so long, but to know that she would be leaving England for France might just make it worthwhile. Now he rubbed his knees, which he said creaked when he stood. She could see he was tired. He placed a hand on his belly, which he always said was slightly larger than the last time he was fitted for a suit. The aging process had begun to accelerate as he tumbled toward forty. Nayana assumed that he was making excuses for her, for the distance she kept; that he was afraid he was getting too old for a beautiful wife, seven years younger than he. He often told her she was *too* beautiful. And when he made this claim, she assured him he was being ridiculous and always replied, "You're as handsome as the day I met you." She had no trouble saying this. It was true, because he was a handsome man and because the most handsome part of Ramesh would never spoil with age. It was his goodness, his love for her. It was etched in every feature as though in marble. Ramesh had the remarkable ability to always remain himself. What she couldn't admit to him was that it was she who had changed so much that she was no longer certain she could remain.

She waited for him to leave the hallway and retreat to his reading chair, then she went to the little table in the entryway. Ramesh must have picked up the mail after caring for Felix, a responsibility that would not last much longer. Beth would be back over the weekend. Where would Ramesh steal away then, if not downstairs? She was convinced it was how he managed his doubts and fears, maybe even an anger he never let Nayana see. She seized her sister's letter from the bowl. He'd put it on top. As always, Nayana softened at the sight of her sister's handwriting, then softened further as she turned the envelope over to find whatever message or decoration awaited her from Birendra: this month, Diwali greetings from *your loving nephew.* She placed the letter in her purse, hating that she still hadn't responded to October's letter while Aditi remained, of course, right on schedule.

"We'll read it later. I have to get going now," she said, as much to herself as to Ramesh, and turned toward the door. She pressed the latch and opened the door.

"Oh, I'm sorry, but I won't be able to join you for that lunch after all. The dean has asked to meet."

"The dean?" he said, sounding impressed.

"We'll see," she said, attempting to project her concern. She knew what was coming; she just didn't know what she would tell Ramesh.

The air outside was the coldest it had been this year. She enjoyed the shock of it as she unzipped her coat and loosened her scarf. Winter nights in Delhi could be like this autumn evening in London. But in Varkala, where Aditi lived, it would be warm as always.

"Of course your letter would arrive today, sister," she said aloud, looking up at the brightest visible star — or was that Venus?

Star or planet didn't matter, as long as it carried Nayana's message of love and regret: a cosmic telegraph between twins, the way they so often communicated silently about their class-mates at school. Or at home, where they spent whole week-ends anticipating each other's thoughts and actions, hiding places. Two decades later, on a walk that ostensibly led her again to a lover and an act of adultery, Nayana felt Aditi was still seeing right through her. She could hear her sister's voice asking, *Who have you become?*

The hotel was dimly lit by a single lantern above the door. It looked drab and uglier than Nayana remembered, more so than it had even earlier that day when she'd stopped in to pay for the room, averting her eyes from those of the man at the reception desk, though he'd never shown much interest in whatever she and Daniel were up to. Her legs felt heavy as she climbed the stairs to the room where, until two weeks ago, Daniel would have already been waiting for her. She felt an irrational fear that he was inside the room, that she would turn the knob and the door would swing wide — the frequently borrowed space appearing again like a stage for her poor choices — and Daniel would be lying there, naked as before, under a single white sheet, boyishly smoking a cigarette. He was handsome, yes, more handsome than Ramesh in some respects, but impermanent, mere plaster to Ramesh's marble.

But there was no one inside this time, no lover stubbing out a cigarette and beckoning her to join him. She was relieved to be alone. The curtains were drawn, and she left the lights off. The room was dark except for the glow of a digital clock that faintly illuminated the familiar floral print of the quilt, which shamed Nayana now from the bed. Being with Daniel in that bed felt so different from being with Ramesh. It was more than the hotel room: physically, there was nothing to stand between them and their desire. They surrendered to each other's bodies with ease, their minds never getting in the way. When Daniel wanted her again, she simply knew it. And yet she felt no ties to the man inside. Not the thinking man, the colleague from school hallways and break room. She knew what she liked about being with him; they had no history, no shared loss. She didn't care what he thought about her, only that he wanted her. She had no fear of disappointing him. With Daniel, Nayana was finally not a failure.

She set her coat and scarf on the chair, unzipped her boots, and stepped onto the dense carpet, one foot at a time. The silence and solitude were perfect. She would not call Daniel tonight. It was the guilt she'd wanted to experience again, not the pleasure. Actually, she would never see him again, not here, though this wouldn't resolve anything, really. She set her arms free from the dress and slid it down to the floor. Unhooking her bra, she swayed under the sensitivity of lace brushing against her skin. She would miss lunch with Ramesh and her mother-in-law tomorrow, but it was not, as she'd claimed to Ramesh, because of the meeting with the dean, which would take place earlier in the morning. Her lunch conflict was an appointment with the gynecologist, though this was merely a formality. Nayana already knew that she was pregnant. And that the gynecologist would not be able to tell her, at least not tomorrow, what she truly wanted to know.

The sliding closet doors were covered with floor-to-ceiling mirrors. She stared at her feet and worked her eyes up from there. She studied her body, which had extinguished the life that had tried to grow there. Twice. She was afraid to ask if this pregnancy was the product of her affair. She looked back at the bed, as if it might provide the answer. With Ramesh, in the years since her last miscarriage, she had learned to be precise, to keep track. Eventually, though, she'd assumed herself incapable of getting pregnant again. And so with Daniel there had been no precision or precaution. This thought now made her nauseated. And yet she could not help but wonder, if the child were Daniel's, would that help or harm her chances of carrying to term? Who indeed has your sister become to even think such a thing?

She pulled back the covers and lay down, setting the alarm

for 9:00 p.m. Outside the window, she could see the flashing lights of a plane passing in the sky, and she apologized to it — as if to a star, to her sister, to herself, and to Ramesh. She would start there, with apologies, alone in no one's room. She remembered the letter from her sister in her bag and fished it out, then turned on the bedside lamp. As she opened the envelope, she studied her nephew's greeting again, noticing that his cursive had improved. He was growing older, and she was far away, missing out on that growth. She quickly skimmed her sister's words, feeling the need to take in the letter all at once. How she missed Aditi. How she needed her now. Then she read each word slowly, stopping only to wipe the tears from her eyes. And then she read it once more in order to fall asleep.

Dearest Nayana,

On this last day of Diwali, I miss my sister as always. Birendra is here beside me. Tonight I told him the story about when you asked Baba and Maa if you could bring me gifts on this day so long ago. I could sense his little mind at work, wondering what happens if you don't have a sister.

I can already tell that he will want to follow in your footsteps one day, and we will finally join you in London. He has grand ambitions and a mind like yours — so clever. And he's growing fast. He will want to go soon. And the truth is I'm lonely, Naya. But what will happen when I take him away from India altogether? I fear that his father's memory, of which he already has so little, will fade, as it will for me as well. Will I ever be ready for that? Sometimes I feel guilty for marrying a man with an even smaller family than ours. I maybe should have married into a big family, for Birendra's sake, but then he wouldn't have come from my Srikant and me. Please know I don't say any of this to make you feel responsible for being so far away. It is my own guilt I wrestle with. I try to comfort myself knowing that, when the day comes and we have to leave India, I'll have my sister close again. For now, you'll be happy to know I've finally done as you asked and put in a request for telephone service. Who knows how long it will take, but we will be able to talk more.

Birendra wants you both to know that he's written about you in his "family history," a report for his English class. This week alone, he's read three books in English. Sound like anyone you know? Please send more when you can.

I didn't want to press things when we last spoke, but you seemed a bit preoccupied. How is dear Ramesh? Please send my respects. With your work and Ramesh's family, I guess you wouldn't know loneliness there. Of course you can always visit. I won't push you, but you are welcome. I want Birendra to spend time with his brilliant aunt. To have a model of life beyond the small world I can offer him.

My diya *are always lit for you.*

Your loving sister,
Aditi

V

Though each day was much the same — frequent visits from the neighbors, Birendra helping Mrs. Nair prepare food for this period of mourning, for there was no one else to help and it occupied their time — the first week, mercifully, had finally come to an end. On the fifth day, they received a visit from the priest again, and with Mr. Nair's help, they gathered the ashes and remains from the pyre, placing some in an urn for the final ritual, in ten days' time. Those remaining went in a pot they buried at the site of the pyre, over which they planted a coconut tree, along with rice and wheat, holy basil and turmeric. Birendra no longer hoped to return to school, though there was nothing he would have liked more. The priest had made it clear that the activities of his former life had to stop during this time, when his duty was to his mother's atma; he alone was charged with delivering her peace. Birendra wanted to do this for his mother, but knowing that she, too, would not like him to be kept away from school, every day he missed it dreadfully. He listened carefully to the priest's instructions, which he explained were different from the ways of the north, where his mother was from. But because they were in Kerala, and because it was what they had done for Birendra's father, the southern customs would guide them.

And when the second week came, and the visitors disappeared, and Mrs. Nair's kitchen was stocked with the food they'd made together, Birendra found the time to worry about how much school he was missing and how he would fall behind. He wondered about Mr. Mon's plans for the reading club and about the library books he still needed to return. But he intuited that these concerns held no weight in the atmosphere of mourning, so he kept quiet and waited. He tried to focus on the fact that the letter he and Mrs. Nair had written was, each day, that much closer to its destination, but when days passed as slowly as this, it was small comfort. And while he felt certain that, upon learning the terrible news about his mother, his aunt and uncle would surely send a response immediately, he couldn't make his own letter go any faster. Mr. Nair must have known this. When the sixteenth day arrived, and his mourning period had come to an end, where would he go?

Birendra realized in time that, though Mr. Nair was a quiet and brooding man, he was not mean. Birendra was especially grateful to him on the fifth day of rituals, for he had not wanted to retrieve the pieces of bone from the ash, and Mr. Nair had seen his fear and helped him do this, then helped him prepare them for the urn. His kindness was just a little different from what Birendra was used to. It could be found in Mr. Nair's actions, not in his words.

On more than one morning the second week, Birendra awoke to damp earth, to droplets collected on the leaves of trees and plants from the night rains. He visited the site of his mother's cremation often, to see if the seeds they'd sown had sprouted. He wanted proof that time was moving forward, that each day he awoke was different from the one before, that the letter was on its way, and that his family would soon follow. But the mound of dirt showed no signs of life or of time passing.

And yet the fifteenth day finally arrived. Time had been carrying on after all. Mr. Nair had not forgotten his promise that Birendra would leave. He spoke to Mrs. Nair of his cousin in Trivandrum, who was "better suited" to take Birendra in. Mrs. Nair shushed her husband at the mention of sending Birendra away, using his mourning as her excuse. That evening, at the dinner table, Mr. Nair spoke, and, for once, he seemed to be addressing Birendra as much as Mrs. Nair.

"I have some good news," he said. Birendra's head went fuzzy with excitement, but then he remembered that not enough time had passed for a letter to return from London. "I've spoken with my cousin Mr. Channar, and he's agreed to take you in." Birendra turned to Mrs. Nair, who was shaking her head at her husband. This made Mr. Nair angry, and Birendra thought he might shout at her, but he did not. He spoke slowly, in a way that left no room for doubt. "He will go Friday, and he will wait for his family there."

Mrs. Nair sat back in her chair and stifled her tears. She seemed not to want to look at either of them. Birendra wanted to understand why she was opposed to the idea. Trivandrum was, after all, closer to his school, and he would be able to go back on the seventeenth day, wouldn't he? He so wanted to see his friends and his teachers; he wanted homework again and to be able to check out new library books. He wanted to have something to remind him how life was when his mother was still part of it, instead of, day after day, to have nothing except the reminder that she was gone.

"It's my cousin's business to deal with orphans," said Mr. Nair. "It's right the boy should go to him."

It took a moment for the full weight of the word to register. Birendra had never once considered that was what he was — an orphan — until he heard Mr. Nair say the word. Wasn't it different when you were waiting for someone to come for you?

After dinner, seated once again by the mound of dirt at his former home, he recalled the sad tales of orphans that he'd heard from his mother or read in books, the difficulties and dangers they almost always faced. It took two weeks for a letter to arrive from London. If they responded right away, it could be thirteen more days. And that meant at least thirteen more days before he could become an orphan.

He awoke the following morning to the hush of voices in the darkness. Then the faint glow of candlelight in the kitchen. The priest had returned and was drinking tea with the Nairs. They were ready for him. His mother's remains would now be taken out to sea. He carried her all the way from the village. Others joined them at the beach. For the first time since his mother died, Birendra wished that time would slow down. He wasn't ready to let go. He clung to the urn and watched Mrs. Nair prepare three rice balls, which she placed on a banana leaf before the priest, who chanted a repeated prayer over them. Then Birendra cast his eyes out to sea, hoping to find his father there waiting. The banana leaf was placed to one side, and Birendra was told to set the urn down and clap three times. A crow and two pigeons immediately descended on the rice. And the priest told him that the crow was the representative of Yama, the god of death, who would be pleased by the offering and grant passage to Birendra's mother. She had never told him that part of their story, and he was uncertain how he felt about its sudden revision. He chose instead to think of Yami, Yama's twin sister, and imagined her standing beside his father, with her *diya* lighting the path and her song guiding his mother. The tide was low, and he kept walking out to sea. Soon he could no longer hear the little waves lapping on the shore. Or the priest chanting. He felt like he'd arrived in the middle of the ocean, where there would be no shore in sight, alone with his mother. The water had reached the base of the urn. He closed his eyes and tried to see Yami's lanterns, to hear her song. The rhythm of the ocean guided him as he upended the urn.

The sun had yet to rise behind him, but the moon was nearly full and bright in the sky above. A faint lone star hovered close by. The shore was still there when he turned. Sometimes he and his mother had come to this beach to eat mango ice cream and walk along the shoreline, wade in its waters. Birendra knew it was because she had missed his father. He had missed him, too. He looked down at the water. There was still a film of ashes traveling across the ripples of its surface. There, it was done. His mother was free. Tomorrow he would go to Trivandrum.

VI

Nayana stepped off the bus and stood there on the sidewalk for a moment. Outside it was damp and gray, because when wasn't it in London? She was going to meet the dean. Just the year before, he had called her in for a meeting regarding changes that would occur as a result of the school's impending incorporated status. As a relatively recent hire, she'd been sure then, too, that she would be let go. Instead he told her she was his choice for the department's full-time evening lecturer. She'd been so surprised and relieved by the offer that she hadn't had the wherewithal in the moment to consider the repercussions of refusing the honor, which she did for fear that a larger class load would drain the creative life from her — she'd begun to think she might return to the book she abandoned in graduate school. She had no doubts about today's meeting. Whether it was irony or not, the part she'd played in arriving at this point today, about to be terminated, was not lost on her. And yet had Nayana been a man, a white, English man, there would undoubtedly have been no meeting at all.

Soon after she'd refused the promotion, Nayana realized her mistake, that she had offended the dean's sensibilities, that he regretted ever going to bat for her. He resented Nayana. It was not an unfamiliar position for her once she recognized it. She was a woman, foreign — an Indian in England — and she was expected to take whatever was offered, grateful to have been noticed and offered anything at all. Her preferences were inconsequential and her value diminished as soon as she forgot her place, that is, when she claimed to have one. It wasn't as though she were instructing the queen's greatest minds at Oxford; she was in West London teaching evening higher education courses. Her Tuesday night class was taken away in the new year, and now she was certain he would tell her the next semester would be her last.

The dean had Nayana sent in right away. He had taken to making her wait since she'd refused the full-time position, but he must have been eager today. He was unusually friendly in greeting her, inappropriately so, she thought, considering the task at hand. He asked her to sit and began to conduct the first part of their meeting with a faux-friendly formality that reeked of stale, colonial air. Would the British ever actually accept that the sun had set on the empire?

"It's jolly bad luck, Nayana," he said, eventually coming to his point, through an ugly grin. "We're still restructuring, you see, getting settled in our new setup, as it were, and, well, we just have no justification for two part-time appointments in addition to Jonathan."

Jonathan was the white man who'd received the position she'd been offered. The dean didn't even bother to subdue the pleasure he was taking in delivering the news of her dismissal, making it clear as well that she'd fallen from first to third place, become expendable. He kept using her name, overemphasizing the second syllable, as he always had done, as he danced around the subject of their meeting the previous year. It was as if he wanted to remind her that *she'd* had the audacity to refuse him while avoiding any acknowledgment that she was ever a candidate in the first place. After a while she stopped paying attention to his words, though she did follow his lips with a kind of disgusted glee, as the flabby expressions bounced about his pallid face. He'd probably expected her to weep or beg, or worse. That she'd been silent so far was, no doubt, another disappointment, so he kept repeating himself, perhaps hoping for a reaction.

"I see," she said, finally interrupting his redundancy. "Well, I guess it's good I don't have an office to pack up."

He didn't like her cheek, and she was pleased to see his complexion find a little color. It was something she'd taken pleasure in doing to her adviser in graduate school as well. These men and their prejudices, the way they pretend everything a woman does is extracurricular and therefore not a serious loss when taken away. They forgot she was actually qualified to be there. What did they see besides a pretty Indian girl? Did they congratulate themselves on finding a place for her in their ranks? The dean, unamused, closed the file on his desk and informed Nayana with a bland authority that she would finish out the autumn term, but in fact she would not be required to return in the new year. Her classes had been redistributed. This wasn't what she had expected to hear. If she was going to leave sooner than planned, she'd wanted to be the one to say so. But she was determined not to listen to this man gloat. She scooted to the edge of her seat and forced a cool countenance.

"So only a week to go?" she said, imitating his initial jolliness.

"That's right," he said, standing, with his arms immovable at his sides. He could no longer look at her, but she took pleasure in looking at his face for, she hoped, the last time. "Good luck, then."

He might as well have said "good riddance." Nayana left his office and felt herself flush as she walked, on instinct, to the break room down the hall.

What would Ramesh say about so sudden a change? What would she tell him? He would want her to rest anyhow once he knew she was pregnant. She could easily use it as an excuse not to return to work after the holidays. Again she could get away with lying to him. Why was it always so easy? Why did she continually take advantage? She knew the lies were adding up. Soon they would crush her — or, worse, they would crush Ramesh — completely. There would be the loss of income as well. It wasn't that they would suffer horribly without it, but it had enabled Nayana, for instance, to send money to her sister. Not a lot, but enough for her nephew's school and whatever else Aditi chose to spend it on. Nayana had been trying to get her to spend some of it on a phone installation for a year at least. If she had only not waited so long, Nayana might just call right now and tell Aditi the whole story — about Daniel, too — shocking her sister, yes, but ultimately Nayana would be relieved just to have heard Aditi's voice, even her dismay, perhaps especially that. The day she told Aditi she was going to stay on in London after university, to pursue a master's, she heard both Aditi's disappointment and her admiration. That now undeserved praise remained, however many failures later, haunting every letter Aditi wrote. When Nayana told Aditi of Ramesh's proposal of marriage, her sister had only asked if the wedding would interfere with Nayana's schooling. By *wedding*, she knew that Aditi had meant the whole of married life, just as she'd meant Nayana's career when she said *schooling*. Despite the very different path Aditi had chosen for herself, already married and starting a family of her own, in Varkala, of all places, her faith in Nayana to do more had never faltered. Even when Nayana had only managed to do less. It must be such a burden, she thought, for her sister to have to hide that much disappointment.

Nayana opened the break-room door with more strength than necessary, interrupting a colleague and his sad lunch, which he ate while reading and marking up student essays. She didn't know the daytime faculty well, and they weren't inclined to know her, either. She checked her mailbox and enjoyed the thought that soon her name would disappear, that she would one day never return to that break room — or the campus, for that matter. She didn't even enjoy teaching, not really. When the students took a real interest, it was easy to care about their progress, their learning, but mostly they were just ticking off boxes, uninterested in reading and writing, which were all Nayana wanted to do in life. Why wait? she thought, removing her name from under her mailbox and throwing it in the trash.

In the corridor, she smiled at the thought that there were only a few class meetings left before she would be set free. Few thoughts had made her so happy recently. And then there was Daniel, walking toward her. He'd clearly thought her smile was meant for him, for he returned it with a relish she suddenly found repulsive. She couldn't turn around, and there was no point in avoiding him.

"You're looking well," he said.

"Not too bad for someone who's just got the sack."

Her greeting proved the perfect detour from his awkward entreaties. He laughed at what he assumed to be a joke. And by the time he realized it wasn't, all threat of flirtation was gone. He reached for her shoulder to comfort her, but she retreated and smiled widely.

"It's a blessing in disguise, actually."

It was over now — seeing him again had just confirmed this — and she wished he could figure that out as well. Their meetings had been for one purpose only; she thought he'd known this. That he was still trying to get a read on her, perhaps hoping she was merely being coy, was now annoying her.

"I've just come to pick up some papers," he said. "Wait for me?"

She stepped into the courtyard outside. He looked different today, no longer as boyishly handsome. He appeared simply disheveled up close and smelled bitterly of cigarette smoke. She kept her distance when he rejoined her and relayed the highlights of her meeting with the dean. Daniel seemed genuinely upset, and Nayana softened to his sympathy, but she remained determined. He needed to get that it was over.

"I won't beat around the bush, Daniel. Perhaps you've gathered that our little interlude has reached its end as well. In any case, I wish you good luck. I do."

What could he say? It was all so neat, his dismissal following the tale of her own. She left him there, his raised hand frozen in a parting gesture. She would have felt something for him, some pang of regret at her own laconism, at least, if it weren't for the disarray of her life. Next up on this day of reckoning: her meeting with the gynecologist. She might as well know exactly where she stood in her life. Except, of course, she wouldn't; pregnant didn't mean pregnant by Ramesh.

The midday traffic seemed to attempt to drown out her thoughts like a kindness as she sat on a concrete wall behind her bus stop. She allowed herself now, as she sometimes did, to imagine her life in a more dramatic telling, a more desperate tale, in which she simply walked into the stream of cars, as those before her had walked, laden with rocks, into other currents. But that was not her story. She would never do that to Ramesh, who would somehow find a way to blame himself. Nothing was his fault, of course. And he would be thrilled to learn of her pregnancy. But what if she had reached her limit? If she couldn't tell another lie? What if she could only deliver that news along with everything else: the lost job, Tuesday nights, Daniel? What if she saw his face and confessed everything? That she had failed again, at work, in their marriage?

Her bus had arrived and was departing without her by the time its presence registered. She wouldn't wait for the next one. She stood and began to walk to her transfer point, running her fingers along the waxy leaves of the hedge bordering the sidewalk, trying to undo any damage to Ramesh that hadn't yet been done. She would make him something nice for dinner, his favorite. She would try to remember how, in the beginning, it had been a pleasure to do simple things, to want to make him happy with some small gesture every day.

When and why did it get so hard? And how could she find her way back?

Nayana passed a pay phone and thought of her sister again, of the two letters still waiting for replies. She passed through a noxious peroxide cloud that hovered in front of a beauty salon. It was time to trim her ends again. They now reached her tailbone when she let her hair down. If Aditi were only in London, she could do that for Nayana as well.

She was adding cream and tomato paste to the chicken when the door to the flat opened. Murgh makhani was a dish Ramesh loved and ordered often in restaurants. She rarely took the time to make it at home and hadn't done so once since she'd started teaching. She remained at the stove with her back to the hallway, stirring in the cream and hoping Ramesh would say hello and keep walking. He stopped at the entrance to the kitchen, and the muscles in her shoulders and neck contracted.

"That smells good. What are you making, *jaanu*?"

"Butter chicken and some spinach with rice." She didn't turn around. She fiddled with the knobs and lids, sensing that he wasn't leaving the doorway. Go on, she begged silently, and squeezed her eyes shut. She wanted him to carry on to the bedroom, change out of his work clothes, then sit in his study as he always did, decompressing. She needed their routine, the table and food between them on those nights when she was home and cooked. "It'll be ready soon," she added.

She heard the strain in her voice. Did he? He didn't leave. A chair slid a few inches gently, across the tile floor. He set something down. His briefcase?

"So how did it go with the dean?"

"What? Oh, yes, fine," she lied.

He approached from behind and rested a hand on Nayana's hip, sending a wave of sensations — guilt, pleasure, hope — that finished with goose flesh up her arms. And then he smoothed that over with the soft skin of his palms, parting her hair and breathing in the nape of her neck from behind. She set the spoon down and let her hands fall from the stove, limp at her sides. A tear fell as well. Her body began to fold into his. He kissed her neck now, and she was reminded how long she'd deprived herself of him, even on the occasions they'd been together, how she'd cut herself off from his affection.

"I've missed you, *jaanu*," he said.

His voice was soft and penetrating, her body once again permeable to his love. He pulled her even closer, as if she could pass right through his skin and into him, his body a place to hide, even from herself. This embrace unleashed the part of her that had forgotten to want him, to trust absolutely in him, in their love. Why hadn't she gone there first? Why had she ever left? And how did he know she was ready to come back to him now? She hadn't even known it for certain herself. She turned to face him. He was smiling with more affection than she felt she would ever deserve but as much as she might ever need. He turned the stove off and took her hand.

"The cat," she reminded him.

He guided her out of the kitchen and into the hall, toward their room.

"Felix," he said, "can wait."

VII

Birendra rode wedged between Mr. and Mrs. Nair in the rickshaw to the train station. Feeling entangled in so many conflicting emotions, he was returned to silence. There was his fear of leaving the only home he'd ever known, his eagerness to return to school, and his immense gratitude for all the Nairs had done for him. Each on its own could have succeeded in overwhelming him. On the platform, Mr. Nair handed Birendra his backpack and reminded him there would be someone to pick him up in Trivandrum. He was to wait beside the luggage storage office, on the platform closest to the entrance of the station. Mrs. Nair was doing her best to hold back tears. She told him to be careful and promised to visit and to bring any mail as soon as it arrived.

"And when your auntie and uncle arrive, of course I'll bring them to you myself."

Birendra had already stepped into the train by the time Mrs. Nair's words fully registered. It was possible that his family would arrive before a letter, or instead of one. It took much less time to fly to India than it did for mail to arrive. His aunt had told him all about her travels when she last visited Varkala. He was six, and it was the first time he'd ever thought about what it must be like to pilot a plane, to be floating up with the clouds. Any day now, they could arrive for him. And with this newfound hope, Birendra viewed the passing landscape from the train window with less trepidation than he'd felt in the rickshaw, even though he was now on his own. This was the beginning of his journey to a new home. The orphanage would only be a waiting place.

He and his mother had taken the same train two years earlier, to pick up his aunt Nayana from the airport. On the way home, he sat between his mother and aunt. He watched how they held each other's arms and hands as they spoke, then he closed his eyes and listened for the ways their voices were different. At one point he laid his head down in his mother's lap. He made a frame around his aunt's face with his hands. It was so like his mother's. She reached down and squeezed his nose and told him he was getting to be such a *big boy*. She spoke to him with many English words, which delighted him. He'd made so much progress since then, more than she would know from their brief conversations on the phone, and he hoped she would be proud of how much he'd learned since they'd last seen each other.

In Trivandrum, he stepped off the train and wondered which man might be Mr. Nair's cousin. He found a spot beside the luggage storage room and waited as he'd been told, watching the people come and go. A man was approaching, and he seemed to smile at Birendra, but he did not stop, and Birendra saw that he had been smiling at someone else. When he turned again, a tall and thin woman appeared. Even though she said his name, he was confused; he had expected a man to come for him. She said she was called Rani and told him she was there to take him to Mr. Channar.

"Is that Mr. Nair's cousin?" he asked, recalling the name.

"I believe so," she said. The way she smiled at him made him trust her. She had kind eyes, but he was suddenly reluctant to follow, to take up residence at an orphanage, even if it wouldn't be long now before his family came and even if *he* wasn't an orphan. "Are you ready to go?"

He had no choice but to accompany her. There was nowhere else he could go, and Mrs. Nair would bring his aunt and uncle to the orphanage as soon as they arrived. From the station, they took a rickshaw. Birendra searched the streets for a familiar landmark from his most recent visit, the year before with his mother. Then he looked for the busy restaurant they'd gone to, not far from the station on their way to the zoo. They'd eaten dosa for lunch. The coconut chutney was the best he'd ever had. His mother preferred the green chili and mint. But there were many restaurants in Trivandrum, and even more cars, so it was difficult to see anything at all. He asked Rani if they were getting close to the zoo. She pointed ahead in the distance and said it wasn't far from where they were going.

"And are there many children my age?" he asked.

"Not so very many. You will be the oldest. Mr. Channar prefers to take in babies and toddlers and children under four."

Did she think he was an orphan? Had she been told he was?

"I'm just waiting for my aunt and uncle to come for me." She smiled and made no indication that she didn't believe him. Perhaps she just didn't know. "They'll be here any day now."

"Then maybe they will take you to the zoo when they come."

He did not tell her that his mother had already taken him there or that he'd found the zoo to be a sad place in the end, the animals sitting alone in their cages, bored, scared, or angry while so many people gawked at them from the other side of the bars. He was growing more nervous by the moment, and now he imagined a cruel Mr. Channar locking the orphans in cages. They were filthy and hungry, screaming and crying, waiting to be thrown scraps of food, just like the sad animals at the zoo.

"Is Mr. Channar a nice man?" he asked, forcing himself to speak to escape the visions in his head.

"He is a good man." She touched his knee. "It will be okay, Birendra."

They rode the rest of the way in silence, the bustling city streets gradually giving way to quieter roads with tall trees, until finally they arrived. The orphanage wasn't the dark and scary building he'd imagined, but he followed closely behind Rani all the same as they entered through the large wooden door, ready to bury his head into her side if he got scared. He heard no children crying in the hallway. It was quiet and peaceful and clean as they walked along. On either side, there were a number of doors. Rani had picked up her pace and called to Birendra to keep up. She would introduce him to Dipika, who helped Rani take care of the children, and then she would show him to the room where he would sleep. She stopped in front of one of the last doors on the right.

"While you're here, you'll be helping us." He heard a child scream behind the door, then the laughter of children playing. There were also babies crying. He tried not to fret and to focus instead on the instructions Rani was giving him. "Mr. Channar has asked me to prepare a list of daily chores. Today Dipika and I will show you, and then you will do them on your own." He nodded after a moment, realizing she had been waiting for him to accept these terms. As she opened the door, the noise of the room at full volume gave him a start. Rani had to raise her voice to be heard. "This is the nursery."

Dipika had a plump-faced bundled baby in each arm and was speaking to another in a crib. She turned and appeared relieved to see Rani. She said something quickly, something that sounded like "Pasha is at it again," and Rani went straight to the children fighting in the corner. Three of them stood together. Two, a boy and a girl, were crying and pointing at the third, another little girl. Rani put out her hand, and the oldest girl reluctantly relinquished the wooden block she had been holding, which Rani gave back to the others, restoring order and stopping the flow of tears. She took the little girl by the hand and brought her to a chair alone in the corner. She seemed to be scolding the girl. With the noise in the room, he couldn't hear what Rani was saying, but he could see she was being gentle in her reprimand. There were babies crying in their cribs and toddlers crawling all around the room, occasionally stopping to shout at the top of their lungs for no apparent reason. He could hardly hear his own thoughts. But nothing seemed so terrible, and this, for the moment, was a relief despite the chaotic din of the room.

Now Rani retrieved the two babies Dipika had been holding so Dipika could change the diaper of another. Birendra set his bag by the door and approached, but he only got close enough to see a screaming purple face through the wooden slats of the crib. He thought again of the children in cages, but Dipika lifted the naked wailing baby from her crib, deftly swapped out the soiled diaper for a fresh one, then went about changing the child, unfazed by her continued screams. Dipika laid the child back in the crib, and her little arms reached and trembled as tiny fingers grasped at the air. Birendra came closer still. He put a finger out tentatively for the little girl, then jerked it back when a fresh wail departed those powerful lungs. Dipika had moved on to another crib, but she smiled at him and urged him on. She was younger than Rani, he thought, and she had a very long and pointy nose. The rest of her, unlike Rani, was not thin. She seemed friendly as well, and this put him more at ease. He tried again. He wanted the baby's trembling to stop, and it did when her fingers latched on, which surprised them both. The baby ceased her crying altogether for a moment as well, then let out a lesser cry and gradually fell silent.

He counted eight cribs in all. Some of the babies were sleeping, but others were reaching out and clasping at the air, as this little one had been, with their pudgy pink hands. He understood their need to hold on to something when everything around them was so uncertain. There were children crawling around him as well, and one went by him, brushing his leg. He would have to learn to look around him before he took a step in that room, which was as big as two rooms, really, and lined with windows high up on the wall, so he could only see the treetops and sky above. On the other side of the room, the little girl who'd been causing trouble was up from her chair now and talking to a boy Birendra hadn't yet seen, perhaps the oldest among them.

"You're very good with babies, Birendra," Rani said. "Did you have a brother or sister?" He shook his head. "Well, here you have many. That little girl over there," she said, pointing to the one she'd had to scold, "we need to keep an eye on her. She doesn't always play nicely with the others, but she will learn. Her name is Pasha. And the boy she's with is called Sanish. He doesn't talk much, but he is sweet and good for Pasha. The other two, with the block, they are Vidip and Sunita. Those are the four older children who will share a room with you. I'll show you now."

The hallway felt even quieter after his time in the nursery. Rani pointed out the kitchen, and she showed him where to find glasses if he wanted water and fruit if he was hungry in between meals. If he made a mess, though, he had to clean it up. Mr. Channar did not abide dirtiness, and he was old enough to care for himself, wasn't he? He promised he would clean up after himself. She showed him where they kept the broom and dustpan and said they'd be back for those after she showed him his room and the bathroom, for that would be his first duty. He followed her to the bathroom for guests, which was large and white and clean, and then to the bathrooms for the children — there were two, and they were smaller — each of which had a big bathing bucket inside. She asked if he had his own *thorthu* with which to dry himself, and he said he wasn't sure if Mrs. Nair had packed one or not. He would have to check. If not, she said, there were some on the shelf outside the bathroom, where he could also find soap and toothpaste and where he could keep his toothbrush.

"And this is your room through here," she said, stopping to take a sheet from a shelf beside the door.

The room was dark and green and small. There was no furniture besides the four mattresses that were laid out all in a row against one wall. She told him to open one of the mattresses that was still rolled up and place it in the corner. She set a crate on its side beside the bed and said he could use it to store his things. He looked around once more. There were an additional two rolled-up mattresses by the door. A lightbulb covered by a brown metal shade hung low in the center of the room. He wondered if the other children would snore, though certainly no one would snore as loudly as Mr. Nair. Rani had unfolded a sheet and was casting it out over his mattress. He kneeled to help her smooth it down. Then he put his backpack inside the crate and remembered something he'd left behind. His favorite figure of Ganesh, the best one his mother ever made. It was still in the hallway shrine of his house in Varkala, next to the mango offering they'd made on the last day of Diwali.

Birendra would be in charge of sweeping, first in the hall, then in front of the building and in the small courtyard at the back, where Mr. Channar smoked his cigarettes. When they had no visitors scheduled, or at the end of the day, he was tasked with mopping, which he did using a folded soapy rag Rani had given him. The hallway was so long that he wrapped the rag around the push broom and created a mop. Rani said it was clever of him when she saw him quickly moving up and down the length of the hallway. He should just be careful not to slip.

When he had finished his chores, he was invited to join the

others once again in the nursery. Birendra tried to make the toddlers laugh; he pulled faces and tickled their sides. Or he distracted the babies again with dangling fingers and stuffed animals that weren't as nice as the ones his mother used to make. He felt a tug from the side on his shirt. It was the little boy who Rani said didn't talk much. Birendra learned quickly enough that that didn't stop him from laughing. Everything was funny to him, even when Birendra wasn't trying to be. Contagiously so, and soon the other children had gathered, and they were all laughing together in the corner. It was then that Mr. Channar walked in. His entrance didn't seem to faze the children, who carried on with their senseless laughter until they collapsed on the floor and rolled around and on top of one another with even more laughter. Birendra alone stood at attention and moved away from the corner of the room, feeling the need to make a good impression. He'd promised Mr. Nair he would.

When Mr. Channar had finished speaking with Rani, he left the way he'd come, walking past Birendra and taking no apparent notice. Then he stopped and looked back, realizing who he was. Birendra tried to smile. He felt very nervous. He hoped to broach the subject of returning to school as soon as possible. But Mr. Channar merely nodded, then continued on out of the nursery.

That evening after dinner, Birendra told the children the first of many stories he chose from those he'd read so often with his mother, tales in English he translated into simpler stories in Malayalam so the children would understand. That first day, he told them about the boy who took up residence in a kangaroo's pouch. He wished he had the book so they could see what a kangaroo looked like. Since he didn't, he used his fingers and pretended to draw the kangaroo features around his body, the round ears and long tail, the big feet, and the pouch. He picked up a teddy bear and stuffed it into his trousers. Rani walked over, her hands full with a blanket-wrapped baby, to listen. He could tell she liked the story as well. The children paid close attention. And for the first time in weeks, Birendra felt close to his mother again, as if she were listening from wherever she'd gone.

In the days that followed, Birendra received the same brief nod but no further greetings from Mr. Channar. He decided it must be that Mr. Channar knew Birendra would soon be leaving. He was a busy man who didn't have time to get to know a boy who was only passing through. And yet if not Mr. Channar, whom could Birendra ask for news of his aunt and uncle or permission to return to school? And how could he ask if he'd not been granted the opportunity to speak to him?

He waited until his fifth day at the orphanage, after completing the last of his daily chores, to find Rani and ask for her help. Dipika was changing diapers as always, but Rani wasn't there. The nursery was strangely hushed compared to its usual chaos. Pasha and Sanish were there, watching Sunita quietly sob, slunk down against the wall. Pasha was being uncharacteristically quiet and well behaved, which, he thought, given the somber mood, meant she'd done something to poor Vidip that had upset Sunita. Perhaps Rani was already with him. Birendra checked the kitchen first. Then he passed by the bathroom and their bedroom, in case she had brought Vidip there to calm him, but both were empty. He checked the guest bathroom, not thinking he'd find Rani but wondering if little Vidip might have run off on his own. Still no one. And the courtyard, where they were occasionally allowed to play, was empty as well. In the hall again, he finally saw Rani. She was carrying a plastic bag and had just come in from outside. Had she gone to the market in the middle of the afternoon? He rushed to her.

"What is it?" she asked.

"I can't find Vidip," he said, forgetting momentarily that he'd wanted to talk to Rani about approaching Mr. Channar.

"Well, that's because he's been adopted, Birendra. He has a new home. I've just brought out his things and said good-bye." She lifted the bag she was holding. "He's left these behind for the others."

Birendra couldn't think what to say. Vidip was there, then gone, just like that. A new home. And yet Birendra remained at the orphanage, still waiting.

"How about I fetch you next time one of your friends is leaving?" Rani said. "Would that be good?"

He nodded, realizing they were no longer alone. He hadn't heard the office door open down the hall, and now Mr. Channar was standing beside them.

"They seemed very happy, didn't they, Rani?" said Mr. Channar. She said they did and told Mr. Channar that Vidip had donated his things. "Good, good. And you?" He was looking at Birendra now. "You're looking a bit glum. Everything okay?"

It was the first time Mr. Channar had actually spoken to Birendra. He was so nervous that he didn't know where to start. Did he ask about his aunt and uncle? Or get the matter of school settled first? He had to say something. Mr. Channar was waiting for a response. Without meaning to, he spoke in English.

"Yes, sir. Everything is okay."

"Ah, you can speak a little English, can you?"

He nodded, then forced himself to speak again. This was the chance he'd been waiting for.

"I can speak English. And Hindi. Like you, Mr. Channar."

"Well, well. Very impressive. I didn't know you were such a smart boy." Birendra was too nervous to smile at the compliment. "Perhaps you can help me with our guests. Making the tea. Even greeting them when they arrive. How would you like that?"

"Yes, sir. Very much."

He wanted to continue the sentence, to say, very much, *but what I really want is to return to school.* Mr. Channar, he suddenly felt certain, would approve of this. But Birendra hadn't been quick enough, and Mr. Channar's attention was lost. He was speaking to Rani again, telling her to show Birendra how to make the tea and to let him know if she thought Birendra might be up to the task.

"I'm sure he would," she said.

"Good. Well, we'll see about all that tomorrow when I get in. I have a meeting in town, so that won't be until after eleven. The answering machine is on already." He turned to Birendra, switching again to English. "Keep up the good work, young man. I'll see you tomorrow."

VIII

Nayana awoke to the still hush of their flat, to the endless chatter of her mind. The voices all reminding her in one way or another that she must admit to Ramesh she was pregnant. She could tell by the light that it was quite late, that she'd slept in again. She threw off the duvet and turned to the outline of Ramesh's body, still imprinted on the pale sheet beside her. She ran her fingers over his absence, then placed her whole body there. The cotton on his side was cool against her skin. Then she stretched her body long and felt warmth in the spot where a slant of rare late autumn sunlight had reached from across the room to the foot of their mattress. Ramesh would be home late again tonight. The test run for the channel tunnel was now just days away, and he was working more than ever. It felt as though they'd come back together only so she could be left alone with her unruly imagination to torment her, visions of another man's child exacerbating the general queasiness she felt. With another stretch, she forced herself to sit up and scoot to the edge of the mattress, touching both feet down on the wood flooring. She felt warm in the sunlight and closed her eyes, trying it on as a reason to get out of ɔed, to prepare for another endless day. Perhaps she would go out, take a walk if the weather didn't turn. Next to her sister, the thing Nayana missed most in London was the sun. And this reminded her that she had a task today. She would leave the house after all. She had to send Aditi and Birendra their Christmas gifts.

She stood to retrieve her robe where it hung alongside the standing mirror. She caught sight of the swollen skin that she knew indicated greater changes to come. She tried to push aside fears of loss and doubts of paternity to start the day differently. She wrapped herself in the robe and tied it closed, snug at her waist, a kind of safety belt for life. In the kitchen, Ramesh had left a note. He would make up for the endless hours at the office with dinner at her favorite restaurant the following week. They would celebrate properly. The idea of Ramesh having anything to make up was, of course, absurd. Much like the idea that Nayana could ever make up what she'd done to him. But it was also possible that her news would be a start. If she could wait that long, she would tell him over dinner. If not, they'd be celebrating twice over. The thought made her tired. She could easily crawl back into bed and wait for next week to come. But if she didn't get these gifts off to her sister and nephew, they weren't going to arrive in time for Christmas. If only she could bring them herself. That way she wouldn't have to decide whether to mention the pregnancy in her note. She didn't want to disappoint her sister if anything happened. Telling people she was pregnant felt like making a promise she wasn't sure she could keep.

And the last time she'd been pregnant and lost it was just before Srikant's funeral. Nayana couldn't bear to add to her sister's grief and so said nothing before she left for India. She had assumed with one look that her sister would know, just as she would surely understand that Nayana hadn't been able to announce her own loss in the face of Aditi's, which was undoubtedly greater. Aditi had looked awful, so tired, when Nayana arrived from the airport, already almost a week into her mourning. She looked like a widow and thus no longer like Nayana's twin. And yet she was still the one to scold Nayana, telling her, "You shouldn't have come in your condition." In her voice, Nayana heard none of Aditi's usual warmth and brightness. It was lacking, for the first time, in their bond. Nayana had never before felt anything but transparent in Aditi's presence, and this new sensation was terrifying and lonely. Nayana had counted on her sister's knowing with a mere glance and on being able to grieve both losses together, as they'd done when their parents died, but she kept silent when Aditi said nothing. Nayana had never thought it would be possible to keep something from Aditi until that day, and it would start a terrible trend. She could only hope she would be discovered during her stay. When she wasn't, she tried to blame grief, but she quietly feared it was something more — perhaps the distance and the years apart had, for Aditi, finally begun to wear away the connection that for Nayana had long since been more tenuous, always dependent on Aditi's strength of conviction.

She seized the card from the sack of gifts and took it with her to her study, recognizing as she held it again the cowardly act of buying a card so small, one that would allow for only the briefest note. *Dearest Aditi,* she wrote, standing behind the chair. She wrote as if hurried, as if she didn't have only that one task to achieve today. *Such small gifts for you and Birendra in the face of my immense regret for falling behind in our correspondence. What you must think of me!* She could have spent all morning, what was left of it, imagining what Aditi might think of her if she had only been in possession of the facts of Nayana's life, a life in total disarray. *I'll find a way to visit soon. For what it's still worth, dear sister, I promise. Please give my love to dear Birendra, and know I love you, as always.* — *N*

She remembered Birendra on the last day of that visit. They'd taken Nayana to the airport and were saying good-bye. He was so small, so young. It broke her heart that he would grow up without a father. She squeezed him until he squirmed, then she took his face in her hands. "You be good, sweet Birendra," she'd said. "And take care of your mother for me." She could see elements of her own face in his, and this forced her grief to leap to her throat. Grief at leaving India once again for a life in London that was growing more precarious by the day, grief at leaving behind her sister, widowed and more alone than ever, and grief for her own loss, which Aditi still hadn't acknowledged and Nayana still hadn't shared. For this, too, Nayana grieved. She didn't want to get on the plane. As they embraced, Aditi seemed to know Nayana's thoughts once again. Aditi, the stronger, calmer presence of the two, even in the anguish of mourning her husband. "Go back to your London. Become a famous scholar and buy us a mansion in Delhi where we can all live together one day."

Famous scholar. It was true that Nayana had once hoped to be a great voice in the literary arts, one whose opinions were important, revered. But the renown she'd coveted since arriving in London was just a substitute for the love she'd left behind in India. Then she'd met Ramesh, and his adoration was so abundant and so quickly became love; she never had the chance to reject it. And finally she hadn't wanted to. But she'd returned to London after Srikant's funeral out of step, losing hope finally that the dissertation would ever become the book she'd hoped for. It was still packed away in a box in the office closet. Gradually Nayana lost the aspiration to be great at all. She couldn't even use Ramesh as the excuse in her letters home: more often than not, she simply ignored her sister's praise and queries about Nayana's progress. The truth was that Ramesh never would have stopped her. But he'd never had to. Nayana had remained great in one regard, that of preventing her own success. By the time she visited her sister and nephew again, she wasn't even thinking about the book or her former dreams, and she'd all but stopped dreaming of children of her own. Aditi did her the kindness of not bringing up either subject, asking instead about the classes she taught, as though teaching, not writing, had always been Nayana's dream.

She sealed the card in its envelope and wrapped Birendra's books and the blouse and earrings she'd chosen for Aditi, hoping, as always, that her sister found occasion to wear them. And, as always, this hope made her feel sad for her sister, which gave Nayana occasion to feel sorry for herself as well. For they were both living away from home, with ghosts, and without each other.

IX

Mrs. Nair came as promised, visiting on Birendra's eighth day at the orphanage. She brought no letter with her from West London, and she came alone, carrying with her a basket lunch. Rani said they might like to sit in the courtyard at the back of the building. Mrs. Nair dished out the fish curry Birendra loved, then a pile of rice. It was the dish he always requested that she bring to him and his mother whenever she offered, and he had thought of it often during his recent stay with the Nairs, regretting that they could not eat it during his period of mourning.

"You're being a good boy and helping Mr. Channar, I'm sure," she said. She didn't look at him when she added, quietly, "Just until your auntie and uncle come."

Birendra only had one question: *When?* But he didn't ask because he was growing scared of the answer. Maybe to-morrow. Maybe not at all. The way Mrs. Nair had spoken just now, the way Mr. Channar said nothing at all, it seemed Birendra was not the only one losing hope. As it was, nearly enough time had passed for their letter to arrive. But this no longer held the promise it once had. He still hoped, if the letter came first, it would detail their impending arrival, but since that arrival had been possible for some time now, as Mrs. Nair had pointed out, he feared their letter would tell him something else.

He'd not yet worked up the nerve to ask Mr. Channar about school, but now that he was with Mrs. Nair, he hoped she might help him with that. He would have asked right then, but her food was more delicious than ever, and he couldn't stop eating. She was pleased to see him enjoying it so much and placed another piece of fish on his plate. She spoke of news from Varkala, but she appeared less interested in gossip than she had once been and soon fell silent as well. When he could stand to eat no more, he told her the food was wonderful and that he was really okay with Mr. Channar, who was nice to him, as were the women who worked there. And he explained that Mr. Channar had been impressed with his languages and asked Birendra to help with the guests who came to the orphanage. At first to pour tea but soon thereafter to greet the guests at the door and show them to Mr. Channar's office. And finally to lead them to Rani after their meeting with Mr. Channar so they could meet the child they were adopting.

"You do all that?" said Mrs. Nair, unable to hide her surprise.

He told her he did that and more, then detailed for her his daily chores. The days were sometimes long but always full. He did not volunteer that he preferred the little green room he shared with the older children at the orphanage to the Nairs' house, right next door to his real home, so empty now. Or that, at least in the beginning, he'd felt excited to be closer to where he was going, closer to West London, though lately he just felt far away. He thought he could ask now about school, but she had pulled something out of her bag and was removing the fabric with which it had been wrapped. There were two framed photographs from his house. She seemed not to want to let them go. Then she polished the glass of the first picture frame and handed it to him.

"Your beautiful mother," she said. "This must have been her graduation picture."

Birendra studied the photograph, trying first to remember where it had lived in the old house. It hadn't been in his mother's room. He thought it might have lived in the kitchen, high on the spice shelf, but maybe not. He wasn't even sure if it was a photograph of his mother or his aunt. The longer he stared at it the less sure he felt. If it was his mother, she was very young, and this made her look different. He brought it closer, holding it a few inches away from his face in both hands. Something opened up a little, lightening his mood, making it easier to breathe. It must be his mother, he thought, because of the way he felt, both happy and sad to see her again.

"And here is your father looking so impressive in his costume."

He studied his father's image now, holding the pictures side by side. He was so relieved to have them, for he would no longer have to rely entirely on his memory, and he would no longer feel entirely alone when he went to sleep. They would watch over him. And suddenly he wished he was going back to Varkala with Mrs. Nair. There were other things he'd left behind. He would have asked her to bring the library books if he could have, and his figure of Ganesh. Just then Mrs. Nair reached in her bag and pulled out an animal his mother had sewn. It was a monkey he'd never seen, but he would have recognized his mother's work anywhere. He seized it from Mrs. Nair and pulled it close. It was as if he could feel his mother's touch still lingering. He brought the monkey to his nose and tried to find the scent of home, of her. When he opened his eyes, she was holding his Ganesh. She'd brought it as well. He gushed with gratitude, thanking her three times in English before he finally said *Nandi.*

Mrs. Nair stroked his face, content to see him so happy. She asked him if he ate well at the orphanage. If he had time to play. If there were children his age. He told her that, when he was done with chores, he would eat with the other children and tell them stories or help Rani and Dipika with the babies. He didn't tell her that the babies came and went while he and the other, slightly older children remained since Vidip left, waiting and wondering why. He embellished the joyfulness of his time there, because he thought it was what Mrs. Nair needed to hear. The one thing he did still wish for, he said at last, was to return to school.

"You *want* to go back to school?"

"So much," he said. At last someone heard him say the words.

"And have you asked Mr. Channar? Maybe he would let you. It's not so far, and it is paid for, is it not?"

"Yes! And it's so close. Much closer than to Varkala." What he wouldn't give to walk back into Mr. Mon's classroom. To go into the lending library. To flip through the big reference books, the dictionary, with so many words. The encyclopedia, with so much knowledge. "I haven't asked him yet. Do you really think he would let me?"

She seemed to be considering the possibility, or maybe what she might do to help him. He could hardly keep still in his seat. And then a little yellow bird swooped down and stole a grain of rice. It scared them both, and this made them laugh. Then the door opened and Mr. Channar stepped into the courtyard, lighting a cigarette. He seemed surprised not to be alone and set his cigarette down at once to approach Mrs. Nair.

"Oh, Auntie," he said. "You are so kind to visit. I'm sorry I was out so long. How are you?"

"I'm fine, just busy getting old."

He laughed at Mrs. Nair's joke. She reached her hand out to Birendra now and said she would find him after she'd had a chat with Mr. Channar. The adults wanted to talk about him, and he hoped this would mean he could return to school. He placed a patchwork animal in each pocket and retrieved the two pictures she'd brought him, wrapping them in the fabric, then he left the adults alone. In his room, he placed the photographs on top of the crate and wedged his new monkey in between them. He removed his Ganesh now from his other pocket and, in both hands, held it close to his heart as he lay down. With his eyes closed, he tried to recall the wall at the end of the hallway of his house in Varkala and the small statues and prints of gods that lined it, the candles and the fruit they used to offer. He saw his mother lighting the candles on that last day of Diwali, the last time they'd prayed together. He felt the candles' warmth. And his mother's presence beside him, glowing in their light. He tried to pray as he and his mother had then, though now he prayed to Ganesh and to both his parents, asking that they all watch over him just a little longer and save him from a terrible fate, the life of an orphan. He promised he would be good. And kind, and to always do his best.

"Please, please, please," he whispered. "Help me find a home."

Mr. Channar woke Birendra to say that Mrs. Nair had to leave. He hadn't meant to fall asleep and was sorry to have slept so long. Together with Mr. Channar, they walked Mrs. Nair a few blocks to a rickshaw stand. Birendra thanked her for visiting him, and for the food, and especially for the things she'd brought him. And then they said good-bye, and he and Mr. Channar were alone together, returning to the orphanage. He wanted so badly to know what Mrs. Nair and he had discussed and waited for Mr. Channar to tell him. But they reached the orphanage and still Mr. Channar said nothing, and he gave no indication there was something to discuss as he headed to his office. Was there something the adults knew and weren't telling him? Birendra lingered at the entrance to Mr. Channar's office, silently waiting to be acknowledged.

"Is there something else, Birendra?"

"Yes, sir," he said and swallowed the lump in his throat. "May I please return to school?"

Mr. Channar studied him a moment longer, then motioned for him to come closer, out of the hallway and into his office. The stack of papers on the desk was even higher from this new proximity.

"Tell me this, Birendra. If you spent your days at school, how would you manage to help me here? Should the good people who come to us arrange their schedules around you? Or should you be allowed to enjoy our charity without contribution?"

He knew the answer Mr. Channar wanted to hear. If he went to school, he could still clean, but it was true that he would not be there to greet people during the week, or to pour tea, or to show them to the hall and introduce them to the children.

"No, sir," he said, "but I could clean before and after." Mr. Channar made no response, but he wasn't pleased. It might be Birendra's only chance, he thought, and so he suffered this confrontation. If Mr. Channar only knew how important school was, maybe he'd let Birendra return. "I've missed almost a month of classes. I'm afraid I'll be very behind, sir."

"It's good that you care about your studies, Birendra. Very good."

"Thank you, sir."

"But you help here as payment for your room and board. Remember, I'm keeping you as a favor to my family. I'm sorry, but that's the way it is. You will have to wait to return to school."

"My aunt and uncle have money," he said, despite the fear he felt as he said it. His voice trembled, his gaze fell, but he continued. "They can pay you when they come."

"And if they come, you will greet them with your debt? Must they adopt it as well as you?" His expression and tone were even harsher than his words. "Would you not rather make them proud by caring for yourself in their absence, Birendra?"

He *did* want to make them proud, more than anything.

Maybe Mr. Channar didn't know that they already paid for his schooling, that it was important to them as well. But all he could think was that Mr. Channar had said *if they come.* Perhaps he knew something after all. In any case, Mr. Channar made it clear that there was no point in discussing the matter further. The mention of the debt had left Birendra ashamed. He would have to be sure to make himself even more useful as long as he was at the orphanage, he thought.

"Would you like me to help with your papers, sir?"

The phone rang.

"No, you go on with the others. I'll see you tomorrow, Birendra."

On his bed again, Birendra sobbed into his crumpled sheet, grateful to be alone. He couldn't push away the fear that he had been hoping in vain, that West London was just too far away, and that his aunt and uncle didn't want a boy his age, either. How could he continue his studies if he had to stay at the orphanage and work? And who would pay for school if not his aunt and uncle? Would he be turned out of the orphanage eventually? More than once, he'd heard Mr. Channar exclaim: *Everyone wants a baby.* Now Birendra wondered what those words meant for him. He thought again of the dreadful tales about orphans his mother had told him — at the time to remind him he was still one of the lucky ones even though his father had died — tales about children who were sold into slavery, turned into beggars, crippled, even, to increase the profit for their captors. Tales of evil. There must be something he could do, he thought, drying his eyes on his sleeve. Would Mr. Channar find him a home if he asked? Was he an orphan after all?

X

Ramesh was especially handsome in the candlelight. He refilled his wineglass, apparently not noticing that Nayana had
only been swirling hers. There was a lightness about him again,
here at their favorite restaurant. He hadn't stopped smiling
since they sat down. The test run of the new tunnel had been
a success, and she could see the relief in his face. The festive
mood as he ordered a bottle of their special-occasion red wine.
Even as he spoke about work, the fine-tuning his team would
still have to do, he was excited again, and his voice lacked
the urgency and anxiety she had noticed in it of late. And he
promised the long hours he'd been putting in were coming to
an end. Nayana felt a twinge at the thought of sharing her
evenings again. She'd grown used to having them to herself.
She was just being silly. A defense in case he took the news
of her pregnancy badly. Would knowing add to his joy this
evening? Or dampen it, giving him something to worry about
again? Though a child was what he wanted, what they both
wanted, they'd retreated from expressing that desire since the
second loss. And then there was Daniel, casting a shadow of
uncertainty on the already agonizing guilt she felt, not to men-

tion her shame for being so terribly reckless in the first place. Would the sudden announcement force Ramesh from ignorance to face the truth he'd been denying? Was she wrong to think he had some idea about her recent transgressions? He was on his third glass of wine by the time their pastas arrived. He would get drunk at this rate, which he so rarely did. And she didn't like to rein in his celebratory spirit. Maybe she'd tell him over dessert, if the meal had sobered him up. And if not, then later tonight or tomorrow morning. She liked when he drank too much. He was jolly, flirtatious.

"My poor brother will still be in the thick of it for a while," he said. "A minor issue with the cooling pipes. I told Raj it's only fair, though; after all, he started after me. A younger brother thing, I told him." She smiled at his joke and his sudden hunger. "It is a shame, though," he continued, taking a break from his pasta to have more wine. "Jasmeen must miss her dad."

"As must his wife."

"Of course. But at least Tahira has Mum."

For once, Nayana might have preferred thinking of her mother-in-law to the thoughts that were suddenly floating through her mind. Could she justify waiting until she made it through the first trimester before telling him? Until after she'd done a paternity test and at least knew where they stood? All the doubt felt like so much pressure to put on the thing that was struggling just to grow and find a way to life in this world. But she wasn't sure she could contain another secret from Ramesh physically. It was as if there weren't room enough in her body for both. As if the lies would not make space for life.

"Ram," she said, making an effort to smile up at him. She could feel the desire in his locked gaze, and she almost blushed. "What if we took a little holiday? Got away for Christmas and the New Year? Paris?"

He looked away, and she knew he was disappointed to have the mood interrupted with such an impossible request. He hated to say no to her, and she knew this, too. But even worse was that she could feel herself pulling his strings: if he said no to this, it would be harder to resist her plan to visit India when she finally revealed it to him.

"*Jaanu,*" he signed. "You know we can't suddenly leave for the holidays. Mum lives for the times when we're all together. She would make our lives miserable. Especially yours."

It was true. His mother had never forgiven Nayana for stealing her elder son from the family home, for disrupting all natural order in their family, for not being Punjabi, for working and wanting a career, for acting so English. But mostly for giving her no grandchildren. Before meeting her mother-in-law, Nayana had been given no indication that anyone in Ramesh's family expected her to be a traditional wife. And while he most certainly did not, he'd never prepared his poor mother for Nayana, either, perhaps knowing this would not be possible. He'd told Nayana he was taking a flat where they could live together alone, outside the family home, because that was what he wanted. In time, she realized it was to spare them both what he must have known would be inevitable. Soon enough, Nayana learned what it truly meant that Indian women married whole families and not just sons: marital conflict could stem from more than two sides. Regardless, when Nayana decided to tell Ramesh about this pregnancy, she would make him promise not to tell his mother. The last time they'd gotten the woman's hopes up — they kept the first pregnancy, along with the loss that had burdened their early days of marriage, to themselves — she took it harder than anyone. So hard in fact that Nayana had felt like her own ration of mourning had been used up by her mother-in-law's grief. She wasn't going through that again.

"You're right," she said, smiling at him. She reached for his hand, hoping to recover his good mood. "I just thought you could use a break. You've been working so hard."

The waiter took away their plates. Her favorite pasta had proved too rich for her tonight. Ramesh ordered a tiramisu to share. As he had with the wine, he would enjoy it mostly alone. He had drunk most of the bottle by the time they left, and he found his frisky self again in the taxi. Clearly he had ideas about how they were going to spend the rest of their evening. In the lift alone together, he pushed back Nayana's hair from her neck and kissed her while she searched for the keys. As she was unlocking the door, he kissed her cheek, then turned her face to him. His breath sweet with wine, his lips and teeth stained purple. She told him to stop, as though she were being coy. He said he would never stop and tried to kiss her again in the entryway. She left him there, eyes closed and mouth waiting, and laughed her way down the hallway. She peeked her head into the office to check the answering machine. There were no messages. It was Saturday. What was the date? She looked at the calendar on her desk. It was the eighteenth, which meant Christmas was a week away. If she had thought of it, she would have stayed in tonight. Her sister always took Birendra into town on the Saturday before Christmas, and they called from the kiosk. Perhaps because Christmas fell on a Saturday this year, she would wait to ring on the day itself. She wanted to believe there was some explanation other than Aditi's disappointment. Ramesh was filling the kettle in the kitchen. She stepped into the hall and called to him, "Ram, you've been wiring the money to Adi, right?"

He came out from the kitchen and clumsily propped himself in the doorway. His drunkenness made her smile.

"Of course, *jaanu*. I go to the Western Union by my office at the beginning of every month. Has she not received a transfer?"

"No, I'm sure she has. It's just that she didn't call."

She told him to go sit down; she'd bring the tea. What if Aditi wasn't waiting to call the following Saturday, either? If she was giving Nayana time and space? It would be just like Aditi not to confront Nayana with her neglect. Why was it that people in her life gave her a wide berth when what she needed was their presence, their pressure? It was the same with her girlfriends from university, too, all married, rarely in contact. Nayana pushed people away, of course; she had grown reckless with the affections of others, a symptom of her unhappiness, itself a product of the loneliness she felt in her life in London.

She joined Ramesh with the tea. He reached for her hand and tried to pull her onto his lap once she'd set it down. She smiled but released herself and sat across from him. This was his corner of their house, where he read his newspapers and drank his tea and the occasional whiskey. Where the lamplight dimly touched down on the brown leather chairs. This corner functioned as an anchor for their home, as Ramesh did for her when she let him.

She prepared their tea, adding plenty of milk in hers. He was waiting for her to make eye contact. She could sense it.

"Naya," he said. "What is it?"

She looked at him over her teacup. It was his adoring gaze, protective of her, the love there, that finally gave her the strength. She set the cup down and put her hand over his.

"I'm pregnant," she said, just like that, and she thought she felt his hand try to retreat.

He was speechless a moment. She strained to smile. With a shrug, she squeezed his hand, feeling it relax a little. When he spoke, his speech had sobered, and she was sorry for it.

"How far along?" he asked.

She hated that he wasn't allowed a joyous response, for that moment of shock to quickly blossom as it once had to dreams of a family. Miscarriages took away that privilege, made a couple wary, distrustful of their biology, of everything. For Nayana, they brought into question his paternity, their marriage, her home there, as though the failure of the product of a love brought into question the love itself.

"About two months, and I feel okay — I feel great. Dr. Shah says there's every reason to hope."

The word, she knew when he looked at her, tasted bad in his mouth, too.

"Of course, *jaanu*. Still, you must rest now and let me take care of you." She nodded, but it was mostly that she was relieved to have told him. "Do we tell the others? Perhaps on Christmas?"

She wouldn't bring up his mother tonight.

"No, I think not. Let's wait a while yet," she said. "Our little secret?"

Ramesh responded, as he rarely did anymore, his head bobbing along the coronal plane, that Indian gesture reserved now for moments when there were no right words, no answers.

"Okay," he said. "Our little secret."

XI

A second week at the orphanage passed, and still no one had come for Birendra. There had been no word from anyone, not even Mrs. Nair. So when Mr. Channar came himself to wake Birendra, early in the morning before it was light, naturally he took it to mean his prayers had finally been answered. And Mr. Channar was animated in a way Birendra had not before witnessed. He instructed Birendra to bathe and prepare his own breakfast, then come and find Mr. Channar in his office. He'd compiled a list of special tasks for Birendra to perform before his usual morning chores.

"And put on your English cap today, Birendra," he said. "Our client this morning is an American."

His heart sank. It had been like a dream that felt real for just a moment. The visitors were not his aunt and uncle after all.

Mr. Channar's desk had never been so clean. All the stacks of papers that had piled up were gone, and there were only the folders, each of which Birendra knew belonged to one of the children. He was handed his list of chores and told to hop to it; their guest would be arriving at half past nine.

As Birendra made his way through Mr. Channar's list, he

practiced all the phrases he could recall having used, either in English or in Hindi, since he'd begun helping Mr. Channar with the guests. He polished the tea tray and scoured the pot and creamer. He scrubbed the sidewalk in front of the building with a soapy push broom. He chased out lizards and insects. And he spoke the phrases aloud to them, too: *Please follow me, sir. Your tea, madam. Right this way to our nursery, sir. Congratulations on your adoption, madam.*

By nine o'clock, he'd done everything but mop, because Mr. Channar had changed his mind and told him not to; he didn't want to risk wet floors. Instead Birendra could go around with a wet rag and do a spot mop, then put on water for tea. Mr. Channar wanted it ready as soon as their guest arrived. Birendra was measuring the tea when he heard Mr. Channar's voice boom throughout the hallway. At first he thought something was wrong, then he realized Mr. Channar had answered the door himself and was greeting their guest. Birendra took a peek down the hall, but the front door was closed, and the woman and Mr. Channar were both in shadow in the dim light of the entry.

"You may call me Madeline," the woman said.

"We are very excited to have you, Mrs. Madeline. Please join me in my office."

As the woman entered, Mr. Channar remained in the doorway and issued a curt command to Birendra to bring the tea. It would need time to steep. He quickly poured the hot water into the pot and gave it a stir until the leaves swirled and tinted the water brown. He replaced the lid and filled the creamer with milk, taking care not to spill any on the tray, in which he could now almost make out his reflection clearly.

When he entered the office, Mr. Channar was seated behind his desk, and his hands were resting on the stack of folders. He was smiling widely at the woman across from him.

"And tell me, how are you enjoying Kerala?"

"Oh, it's lovely," she said. Birendra set the tray on the side of the desk and could feel her eyes on him now. "The sea is so beautiful and warm. And everyone is so friendly."

Birendra situated a cup in front of the woman and another in front of Mr. Channar. Again he admired the sparkle of the ceramic pot as he placed three cubes of sugar on each saucer along with a teaspoon. He looked up at the woman, who continued to watch him, and smiled.

"Fifteen children," exclaimed Mr. Channar, and the sudden announcement made them both turn to him. He was speaking especially loudly today, already opening the first file on his desk. "All ages, from zero to four." Birendra had been so busy that morning checking off his list that he hadn't thought what a foreign visitor would mean for one of the children, who would be taken farther away than any since he'd arrived. "We actually have a number of couples in India registered, and there is a waiting list, but we are very happy to make exceptions for our clients who have traveled so far, Mrs. Madeline."

As he poured her tea through the strainer, Birendra looked at the American woman, whose gaze shifted repeatedly between the cup and Mr. Channar. She was the first American guest he'd met and the first woman to come alone. He wondered if her husband was working in America. It seemed so far away, and he could see this in her face, which was different from any he'd ever seen up close before. She had tiny brown spots scattered around her nose and cheeks, but the rest of her skin was so light. Her eyelashes were long and painted black, but her eyes were bright and blue under a fringe of reddish-brown hair the color of a tamarind. Her lips shined like they were made of glass. She caught him looking at her now and he blushed, but she smiled at him, then winked. He almost laughed aloud, but he restrained himself and retreated to his designated spot by the door.

"Now, a little about our philosophy," Mr. Channar said, and laid out each of the documents from the first dossier onto his desk. "As you probably know, in this country there are more orphans than we can deal with. Poverty forces children of all ages from their homes, and just as many newborn girls are cast aside. We cannot help all of them. It is the job of men like me to protect the children I *am* able to help. I do this by remaining a relatively small operation. But I must also judge the men and women who come here looking to adopt a child. I must determine if they will provide good homes. We achieve this by catering to a certain level of clientele, many of whom come to us from wealthy families in Delhi, Bombay, Calcutta; men and women who struggle to conceive. Some are Indians coming from England, where they have relocated. Occasionally, they are, like you, from other parts of the world. Over time, we have built a reputation for quality and discretion, and I believe this is why you've been recommended to us."

Birendra had never heard Mr. Channar speak English at such length. The woman nodded silently, and Mr. Channar placed the first document before her, suggesting she might be interested in the baby boy who'd come to them just that week.

"He is seven months old."

The woman interjected.

"I was thinking older," she said.

Birendra noticed the look of surprise on Mr. Channar's face. His refrain, that everyone wanted a baby, always made Birendra sad for Pasha, Sanish, and Sunita. Didn't they deserve homes as well? Mr. Channar pulled three files from the bottom of his stack and pushed the others aside. Birendra couldn't help but smile, even though he knew this meant that one more mattress would be rolled up and set aside in their little green room.

"Yes, yes," said Mr. Channar. "We have one older boy. Let me see." He opened the files side by side. "Sanish is four years old, our oldest. A quiet and shy boy. Very good. Perhaps you'd like to meet him."

"And they're all in good health?"

"Oh, yes. All our children see the doctor for a full checkup. Look here." He handed her another file and pointed toward the bottom. "There, you see? Completely healthy and approved for adoption."

"I see," she said. "And what about a girl?"

"Yes, of course. Let me see here." Mr. Channar opened the second folder. "Pasha is also four years old. You'll see she is a charming girl, very playful. And Sunita is just three, a sweet and intelligent little girl who comes to us from neighboring Karnataka."

He raised a hand, which was Birendra's cue to take the guests into the nursery.

"Are they sisters? Would I be separating them? I can't take two children."

"No, these two are not sisters. Each is alone here."

Birendra could see the woman's face again now. She was carefully studying the information she'd been given. She seemed very concerned, serious. Birendra thought that was a good sign; it meant she cared. Then she handed the file back to Mr. Channar and sat back in her chair.

"You've given me so much to think about, Mr. Channar. I wanted to come and meet you today to better know my options. I will, of course, need some time to consider what I've learned."

"Yes, I understand," said Mr. Channar. "Shall I take you in to meet the children, then?"

"Not today, Mr. Channar. I'm sorry, but I'm not ready to meet them today. I hope you understand." Birendra could see that Mr. Channar did not understand. "May I come again tomorrow?"

"Of course, yes, tomorrow is also fine, Mrs. Madeline."

Then the American woman stood and reached out her hand. Mr. Channar knocked over a stack of papers behind his desk when he stood. Birendra didn't know if he should go to them or not, but Mr. Channar acted as though nothing had happened.

"Birendra will see you out, Mrs. Madeline. Thank you so much for coming."

He walked alongside the American woman in silence down the hall to the front door. It wasn't at all how things usually went, and Mr. Channar's behavior had shown he felt the same. Birendra opened the door for the woman but wasn't sure what to say. None of his rehearsed phrases from earlier that morning felt appropriate. There was a taxi waiting for her. Before she got in, she turned and thanked him, as though she suddenly remembered he was there. He told her she was welcome, then watched as the car pulled away, wondering if the American woman really would be back tomorrow, ready to choose one of his friends.

XII

Madeline could breathe again, out of the taxi and returned to the comfort and mostly thoughtful design of her little seaside resort. After working herself up for days, and after the stress of actually visiting the orphanage, she would not have liked returning to the cold and sterile environment of the Ayurveda clinic where she'd originally planned to stay, the one Dr. Wright had suggested. In the end, she had been right to recognize and respect her needs and boundaries, to ask her assistant to seek out something pampering, something relatively luxurious. She'd earned it, after all. Despite the debacle in Barcelona, maybe she *was* getting a little wiser with age. It was this transformation, one indicating greater personal awareness, maybe even acceptance, that put a smile on Madeline's face as she sank into a chaise longue beside the tiled pool at the courtyard's center.

It wasn't that she didn't trust her nutritionist's recommendation. Dr. Wright had called the clinic *a place of transformation*, which sounded perfect when they first spoke of it, when Madeline was desperate to be anywhere but where she was, far away from her home in Los Angeles and her romantic calamity in Barcelona. A stay at the clinic would have far exceeded the requirements for the lifestyle Dr. Wright was always pushing on Madeline: whole foods, yoga three times a week, daily meditation, infrequent alcohol, all of which seemed impossible to sustain in Los Angeles. But this time, Madeline had focused on the part of Dr. Wright's pitch that recommended "tropical southern India." And here she sat, seaside, in India, despite forsaking all Dr. Wright's intended rigor. The orphanage had been her own idea. And now that she'd seen for herself that it was not the horror show of poverty and neglect she'd feared in the days leading up to her visit, she felt she could begin to sort through her feelings and make a decision.

Her eyes lazily wandered over the space, not even seeing anything she'd change if given the opportunity. Her lids grew heavy as she observed the peaceful, open plan of the courtyard, the clean lines and symmetry created by the purposeful placement of potted sago palms. In the covered areas, she appreciated the artful absence of inessential furniture, too, which allowed the intricate detail so prevalent in Indian design to embellish each piece of furniture and art, to stand in brilliant, if rustic, contrast to the innocuous taupe backdrop of the walls. And at the resort's center, beside her, the electric blue water of the pool seemed to glow in the sunlight within its tile-framed edge. She thought of her current project, the house in Los Feliz she was running out of excuses not to get back to, its pool and the elaborate tile work she might imagine for it. Every inch inside the pool, not merely the perimeter, would be tiled and smooth to the skin's touch. She saw it clearly in her mind's eye under the dry heat of a Los Angeles sun. Beside the pool, a veranda, its latticework disappearing beneath the creeping vines of wisteria, purple and heavy, framing a covered area for outdoor eating. Beneath the surface of the pool's water, she began to see more elaborate tiling, something abstract. Perhaps an om symbol. Her client, a yoga enthusiast, like Madeline's nutritionist, would eat it up, impressed with how far Madeline had gone for her — first to Barcelona for the tiles, then all the way to India for inspiration.

She opened her eyes. Beyond the courtyard's edge was the beach; beyond that, the sea. Antonio was probably splashing around with his children and wife at some other seaside resort, by some other sea, far away. She'd had to learn it all from the secretary, no less, completing the cliché and causing Madeline to flee from the humiliation. She had a perverse urge to get up from her chair and walk out onto the beach, to test the water and see how it felt with Antonio in mind. Whether it offered explanations as to why he'd lied to her about being married or why Madeline had never bothered to consider the truth. But she didn't move. She didn't actually care.

Mostly she felt relief. Even with so little hindsight, she knew it had been one of her most absurd plans. To time a last fling with Antonio so it coincided with her ovulation. She'd taken her vitamins, charted her temperature, and consulted fertility specialists. She'd known, even then, it was a ridiculous long shot, but she convinced herself it would work anyway. And why Antonio? He was no leading man. She'd fallen for his work first, big and bold furniture in black walnut, which obliterated the postmodern trinkets that seemed to dominate the market. She had used Antonio's pieces top to bottom when outfitting Hollywood's most infamously ruthless divorce-law firm. She liked to imagine it would inspire absolute confidence or fear, depending on which side of the table one sat on. The man behind the furniture was admittedly less imposing, but she'd liked his accent and the fact that he liked her. And perhaps the fact that he lived so far away most of all. It was that winning combination that later qualified him for the job for which neither of them had known she was hiring, not at first.

"A Spaniard?" her mother had exclaimed, either nonplussed or animated by gin or both, when Madeline first told her. "I hope you're not taking him seriously, Madeline. He's probably married with eight children." Madeline had called her mother under the guise of needing a phone number, but there was a part of her that had wanted her mother to be happy for her, to acknowledge that she was not only successful in her work but also capable of finding someone, having it all, even if that wasn't exactly the case. It was as if everything would always be a competition between them, one that Madeline was destined to lose. Thirty-nine and still desperate for her mother's approval.

She closed her eyes and let Antonio's image fill her mindscape. His crooked smile, those dark eyes in which she felt beautiful, even sexy sometimes. She'd really believed he was the key to her next great adventure, that he would open the door to motherhood, even if she passed through it without him. She wanted to believe it because it would mean she didn't have to buy random sperm or resort to adoption. She'd never felt desperate about her single status or the "ticking clock" behind her growing desire for a family. She preferred to believe it was possible to be a successful woman in a man's world, to not have to choose between a loving family and a satisfying career. Antonio clearly hadn't had to choose! How many children *did* he already have? What did it matter? She looked down to see her ankles, still swollen from the long flights. The massage she'd booked would help. As would, she hoped, being this far away, farther than she'd ever ventured from home. She'd just close her eyes until it was time for her massage.

Intermittent beams of light flickered across her face, rousing Madeline to consciousness. She had drifted off without even realizing it. The sunlight passed through the narrow gaps of a vibrant green palm leaf that hovered a bit more than a foot above her face. She yawned and stretched and felt the heat of the sun on her forearms. The leaf, offering her face and torso shade, was held by a young boy. She thought she might still be dreaming. Wasn't he the boy from the orphanage? Then the shadow on his face lightened, and she saw he was not the same at all. She remembered him from the day before. Younger and smaller than the boy at the orphanage.

She fished in her coin purse for a one-hundred-rupee note and handed it to him. The boy smiled a flash of white as he accepted the money, then ran off, letting the leaf fall from his grip when he hit the sandy beach just beyond the resort's edge. Madeline noticed that another guest had arrived or returned to the courtyard while she was dozing. The woman was seated at a table nearby, staring pensively out to sea. Elegant, if leathery brown, she looked like an older Sophia Loren. She had propped her feet on a second chair and appeared as comfortable as she would if she were in her own backyard. Now she accepted a coffee from the waiter and caught Madeline's gaze as she took her first sip. She nodded with a smile in greeting. Madeline said hello and introduced herself. The woman said her name was Simonetta. They were just close enough to speak to each other from their respective seats without awkwardness. Madeline asked if Simonetta was there alone as well. She wasn't. Her husband had gone fishing. The words, in her thick accent, bounced and rolled from her lips with an Italian flair that sounded wonderful to Madeline.

"I think it's an Indian girl he hopes to catch," said Simonetta.

Madeline wasn't sure if her allusion to adultery was a serious issue or the woman's sense of humor. In either case, she'd wait a little longer to find out.

"This is my first time in India," Madeline said. "Have you come before?"

"Your first time in India? And you found your way here?"

"Well, I flew into Delhi, but then came straight here."

"*Ha fatto bene.* Kerala is the most beautiful part of India. It's not so common for people to visit here first." She sipped her coffee, searching her memory. "I don't think I've ever met an American here, and we come most years."

Madeline felt a sense of pride hearing this. As if she could tell this worldly, effusive Italian woman anything — everything — without fear of judgment.

"I came here to adopt," she said, testing the words in her mouth.

"Ha!" The outburst was friendly, as if Madeline had told a joke. "You Americans are so creative."

She tried to read the woman's expression behind her over-size sunglasses and decided there was no condescension.

"That scarf is gorgeous, by the way," Madeline said, nodding toward the sumptuous silk fabric. "You wouldn't let a girl in on your source, would you? I'm in love with the patterns here."

"Darling, I know every good place to shop in India," Simonetta said warmly. "If you have time, you can join me today."

With the invitation still floating before a delighted Madeline, Simonetta's attention returned to the sea. Suddenly Madeline saw in Simonetta the woman she might like to become someday — a little eccentric, yes, but confident and wise. Alone and not alone. She wondered if Simonetta was a mother. Perhaps Madeline would make a friend in India, one who had nothing to do with work or LA connections. How long had it been since that happened?

Two hours later, refreshed after a massage and a long shower, Madeline met Simonetta near the entrance to their hotel. Simonetta pronounced that she never took taxis in India. They would have a car service for the afternoon. Their driver opened the door for them, and Madeline felt like she was on a date. With an easy smile, she resolved to follow Simonetta's lead, to embrace her love of life, her easy acceptance of whatever was to come.

And Simonetta moved unfazed through the crowds and bustle of the streets in town. Madeline had expected to be taken somewhere posh, but the car dropped them off on a street full of storefronts that looked identical to a dozen places they'd passed getting there. She beelined through a passageway that led to another level of shops, and Madeline tried to keep up, but she was easily distracted by all the hanging fabrics in the windows and the people noticing them. Finally Simonetta stopped before the largest boutique, with a long wall of windows that framed numerous mannequins wrapped in exquisite silks of a quality and variety she'd not seen elsewhere. When they walked through the doors, a man seated in a far corner jumped up and rushed over, obviously thrilled to see Simonetta.

"My friend from Los Angeles wants to buy some saree, Signor Premji. Naturally, I brought her to you."

"It will be our pleasure, madam." Then, turning to Madeline, he asked if she had a particular style of saree in mind. When she stared at him blankly, he politely assisted her. "A special occasion, perhaps?"

"Not exactly. At least not yet. I guess I just think they're beautiful," she said, feeling embarrassed and childish.

"Poornima, show madam some items from our designer collection."

Madeline was ushered behind a pair of plush plum curtains by a beautiful young woman. She admired the gold and copper threadwork of the elaborate embroidery, then the peacock print of the saree the woman was wearing. She had to stop herself from touching it. A second woman joined them, carrying a small, vibrant stack of silk that gave Madeline a thrill. The women were waiting for her. They wanted to help Madeline undress. She didn't usually think of herself as a modest person. There was something about her disdain for certain parts of her otherwise slim body that eradicated modesty, as if an obstinate display of belly bulge or the spread and sway of inner thigh to another human were her way of punishing the undisciplined flesh. But these women were delicate in their handling of Madeline. If theirs had been the hands of a man, Madeline would have demanded something less intimate. As it was, she merely surrendered to them. They worked swiftly, and Madeline let them guide her arms and legs and waited for the contact of silk against skin. First she stepped her naked feet into a kind of low-rise corset, holding her breath and belly in as the women pulled the elastic tube into place. The flash of fuchsia on top was unfolded once, then again to reveal a waterfall of teal. It kept changing as the women opened it further. One woman brought an end to Madeline's waist and tucked it into the front of the corset, while the other woman, like a magician, unraveled the fabric in her hands and let it fall to the floor. It must have been twelve feet long, and it finished with a black strip and then a shock of white, a stripe at the end, which was pleated and slung over Madeline's shoulder to rest like the sash of a beauty queen. Four hands worked together to wrap Madeline in the fuchsia section, creating a floor-length skirt, which was then tucked and pinned into place, forming a V shape just below her navel. Then the fuchsia section was pleated and secured with another tuck and pin at the front. Two hands perfected the pleats from floor to waist, while two more gently pulled everything into place at the top. And finally the length of black fabric was allowed to drape down one shoulder and arm, creating the illusion of a stunning hourglass figure Madeline had never before seen in her own reflection. When they opened the curtain, Mr. Premji was there waiting. Simonetta, too, flipping through a catalog. Mr. Premji turned Madeline to face him, then made two adjustments so slight she could not feel his force, though she felt its effect as he stepped away. Her image rebounded in triplicate from the ornate mirrors that sectioned off the dressing area like a screen.

"Bellissima," said Simonetta, looking up from her magazine.

Madeline smiled at her reflection, flashing back to the disaster of her prom night, more than twenty years earlier. Her mother had forgotten to bring home a dress as promised, so Madeline went to Macy's the day of the prom and, with the help of a woman on the selling floor, found something and charged it to her mother's account. That dress, a mauve monstrosity with a deep V back and tulle at the chest and shoulders, was far from what one would expect the daughter of a leading Hollywood costume designer to wear. Her brother, Eddie, was eight years old. He looked up from his coloring book, without hesitation, and said: *You look pretty*. It was the only compliment she received that night.

Now, with little Eddie's voice still echoing, she blushed at her image in the mirror. Yes, she was *bellissima*. One of the women approached with a raised hand.

"Excuse me, madam," she said and reached toward Madeline's face.

Madeline expected the woman to adjust her hair, but instead she felt a cool and gentle pressure at the space between her eyebrows. She closed her eyes. The sensation both calmed and invigorated her, as if a button had been found and pressed. When she opened her eyes to take in her reflection again, the small, sparkling jewel thrilled her, and Simonetta laughed kindly. She looked glorious, and she felt like a little girl dressing up as an Indian princess.

"There, madam," said Mr. Premji. "With the bindi, you are now complete."

They spent another hour selecting fabrics to take home. Madeline found two scarves and three other sarees she loved. On their way to a restaurant Simonetta knew, she spotted a stall selling ornate slippers and less expensive sarees as well as long embroidered men's shirts. An idea for a party was brewing. By the time they arrived at the restaurant, Madeline was weighed down with bags and famished. They ordered white wine, which was refreshingly ice cold, and they quickly found a pleasant groove of intoxication. Madeline couldn't remember a nicer day out shopping with a girlfriend.

"A bottle is a single serving," she said, pouring the last of the wine into Simonetta's glass and motioning to the server that they'd like another. When Simonetta excused herself to find the ladies' room, Madeline took the opportunity to select a bindi from one of the sheets of bindis she'd purchased at Mr. Premji's boutique. When Simonetta returned, Madeline reached over with it.

"*Pazza,*" Simonetta said, retreating and feigning embarrassed protest, but then she settled and let Madeline place the bindi on her forehead.

"This has been such a great day," she said. "Thank you so much, Simonetta."

Simonetta raised her glass silently; she wasn't going to get sentimental, but she also wouldn't hold it against Madeline.

"Do you have children, Simonetta?"

"*Sì.* Three boys. Grown now and making grandchildren," she said and smiled.

"What do they do? For work?"

The oldest, she explained, ran the family business: fine silks. The younger two were both lawyers. The second bottle of wine arrived and was poured. Madeline was trying to imagine Simonetta as a grandmother, full of love and joy. She had a lot in common with Madeline's once glamorous mother, a certain eccentricity and charisma. But it was the love Madeline had known from her grandmother that she granted Simonetta in her imaginings. Without Grandma June, Madeline would perhaps have no concept of the meaning of unconditional love, her mother having always focused on herself, her career, her men. Madeline could not let herself do the same, whatever she decided to do about adoption.

"Madeline," Simonetta said, her voice tinged with compassion, as though she were being forced to gently disabuse a younger woman of some untruth. "You have a big day tomorrow, I know. We're not just shopping today, eh? We are also taking your mind off a choice you must make. The thing you want but can't be sure of. The thing you are afraid of. But allow me to tell you something. Being a mother is like anything else you do. It's one part of you. You just have to give a damn."

Madeline used Simonetta's driver when she returned to the orphanage the following morning. She told him he could come back for her in two hours, leaving herself no chance of a quick escape. Now she was pacing before the entrance like a nervous building inspector ensuring that the lime-green walls were sound. There was a moment in the car when she'd felt close to certainty, but it was fleeting. She'd thought: Perhaps not being my biological child might give the boy a leg up, free him from the Almquist family hex. And this thought had turned out to provide an unexpected second reason for adoption, because she'd imagined a *boy*, and this reminded her that adoption meant she could choose. The door opened despite Madeline not yet having summoned the courage to knock. It was the same gentle boy from the day before, and the familiar face did wonders to calm her.

"Good morning, madam. Welcome back," he said, opening the door wide. "Mr. Channar is on the phone. You may wait inside."

She followed him into the dark hallway, then stopped, resting a hand against the rough wall, cool to the touch, until her eyes adjusted to the lack of light.

"May I use your restroom first?" Madeline couldn't make out his expression, which remained in shadow, but she guessed at his confusion from his silent stare. "The bathroom? A toilet?"

"It's down the hall," he said and led the way.

It was spacious, and the floors were lined with thousands of tiny hexagonal tiles that climbed halfway up the walls. She ran her fingers over them and was soothed. She splashed water over her face, then asked her blurred reflection, "Do you or do you not want to adopt a child?"

She did. She really did. This plan for motherhood wasn't perfect, but it was the best choice for her. And she was *here*. In India, at the orphanage, prepared to give a damn! It was time to find the nerve to act. She dried her face on the edge of a hanging towel. As she pressed it against her eyes she saw an image of her brother as a young boy. He turned out all right, and hadn't she essentially raised him while their mother was off living her life? Didn't that prove something? Besides, she reminded herself, she was under no obligation. She would go to the nursery and spend as much time as was necessary. If she felt a strong connection with one of the children, that she, in particular and not just anyone, was truly needed by another, she would know she was doing the right thing. If not, she would leave as she had come, alone.

The boy was waiting in the hallway under a framed print of a purple deity. His eyes were cast down in thought, beautiful lashes framing them. He had a cowlick that appeared to have been standing in perpetuity. And there was something about the awkward tuck of his shirt into his pants that made Madeline smile.

"What was your name again?" she asked.

He told her, but she still didn't catch it.

"Say that again. Slowly." She moved closer, bending to hear.

"Birendra, madam," he repeated softly, shyly.

"Birendra," she said, garnering a smile from the boy. "My name is Maddy. Are you Mr. Channar's son?" He shook his head. She looked down the hall toward Mr. Channar's office. Despite her pep talk moments ago, she wasn't quite ready to return to Mr. Channar and his folders. She much preferred this quiet boy's company. Perhaps it wouldn't be inappropriate to ask him to take her to the nursery. She pressed two fingers against his unruly sprout of hair and tried unsuccessfully to persuade it down. "Would it be possible to see the children before I went to Mr. Channar? It seems he's still on the phone."

He, too, looked in the direction of Mr. Channar's office, as though for permission. Then to another door, slightly closer, which opened as he pointed it out. A woman appeared and was obviously surprised to find Madeline and the boy standing where they were. She spoke to the boy in another language. Madeline could sense her affection for him, and this came as a relief. As the woman left them, she smiled at Madeline politely, shyly.

"Is that your mother?" She'd already forgotten how to say his name.

"No. Her name is Rani. She's working here."

Madeline stopped him from opening the door, which had a lite at eye level she could peer through and locate the three children Mr. Channar had mentioned before entering the room. She could see another woman attending to a baby, who was wrapped in a sheet and nestled in the woman's arm. Though the woman looked tired, Madeline could imagine the profound sense of peace that came from holding a tiny baby tightly in her arms, wet eyes staring back at her with absolute trust, unconditional love. But bottles, bibs, diapers, and toilet training? Sleepless nights? Is that why she abruptly suggested an older child to Mr. Channar the day before? She still had a business to run in Los Angeles. Of course she would rely on her unflappable assistant, Paige, for help at first. She relied on Paige for everything. But she didn't want to have nannies. She didn't want to be one of *those* moms. And she didn't want her child's life to be anything like hers had been.

One of the little girls Mr. Channar had mentioned came into view. She might have been the four-year-old. She wore a simple dress, and her hair was flat against her head, her bangs carelessly cut. Madeline imagined her in a white dress with pink embroidered flowers, something from her own childhood, a gift from Grandma June. The girl's hair hanging in delicate curls above her shoulders, pulled back at the sides in barrettes, two rows of tiny teeth smiling back. A swift movement shattered Madeline's fantasy. The girl snatched away a toy that a younger girl, the three-year-old, had been playing with and was now teasing the crying child, who was clearly terrified of her. Suddenly the dress and curls were gone, and Madeline saw a smoking, cursing teenager wearing too much eyeliner and an ugly snarl despising a haggard Madeline at fifty.

"It's okay," said the boy beside her. "You can go inside. Everyone does."

She shook her head and was about to retreat from the door when she remembered the boy, the four-year-old she'd wanted to locate. Was he the one Mr. Channar had described as shy and quiet? Of course it would be a boy, since she could choose.

"Thank you, Burenda — did I say it right?" He rocked his head and flashed a crooked smile. Perhaps not quite. Who was *this* adorable boy? And what was he doing here at all? He wasn't in one of Mr. Channar's files. "Are you related to Mr. Channar?"

He shook his head and dropped his chin, but his eyes remained on Madeline. He seemed to be studying her, perhaps determining if she were a worthy confidante. She tried to show that she was, waiting patiently for his response with a sympathetic smile. He looked away before he spoke.

"My parents are gone," he said. "I'm working here."

She felt her heart constrict and ache. His parents were gone. And he was alone. Her first instinct was to hate Mr. Channar for employing a boy so young, but she'd now seen enough to know it could have been worse. There were children wandering the streets of the city like feral cats. It was so devastating that she had to look away. But this sweet boy, clearly educated, so helpful and considerate, alone and working in an orphanage when he couldn't have been more than nine years old. When he'd so obviously known love. Why hadn't *his* name been on one of those folders in Mr. Channar's office? Was it only a matter of time? Or had that time come and gone?

"Do you know where California is?" He nodded, either with interest or relief at having the subject changed. "You do? Well, aren't you a clever boy?" This made him smile wide. "That's where I live. In Los Angeles."

"Is there a good school there?"

"The very best schools," she said, utterly charmed.

But the boy sighed heavily at this news. "I miss school very much."

Madeline had to blink away the gathering tears. The depths of his dismay had taken her breath away.

"I bet you do, you sweet boy."

Her certainty rushed in and consumed her completely. It expressed itself in her uncontainable smile, in the overwhelming sense of, yes, joy. It was undeniably joy. She had to laugh just to let some of it escape. The poor boy looked at her, perplexed, and this made her laugh even more, until they were both laughing, neither one sure of the reason. Except that Madeline did know the reason. She couldn't say why or how it had happened, only that she had arrived right where she was supposed to be. From Los Angeles to Barcelona and on to tropical southern India and to this particular orphanage — right here, in front of this beautiful boy. This boy who just wanted to go to school. This boy whose parents were gone. This boy who already felt familiar to her. That thoughtful gaze, perhaps, a gentleness not unlike Eddie's. The light entering from a high window at the end of the hall became brighter: the sun had shifted and was now in view. She placed a hand on the boy's head, where the light was brightest, reflecting off his black hair. Whether it was hormonal, biological, cerebral, or cosmic, she didn't care. Here, in front of her, was the small soul whose fate she would align with her own. This was what it felt like to start to be a mother.

XIII

Birendra pressed his ear close to Mr. Channar's office door, but the voices within were muffled, impossible to decipher. If he peered through the keyhole he caught glimpses — the back of the blue chair and the American woman's head, Mr. Channar's folded hands, his look of astonishment. Birendra placed his ear close to the keyhole. She'd made up her mind. It was that boy, she said, or she was leaving by herself. His heart beat faster.

"But Birendra is working here, Mrs. Madeline."

"I'm sorry, Mr. Channar. My mind is made up," she repeated.

Had his prayers finally been answered? Did Ganesh and his parents send this lady because they knew his aunt and uncle could not come?

"It would be most irregular," said Mr. Channar. "I don't have paperwork for Birendra. He was supposed to be here only temporarily, as a favor to a family member."

"Is it a matter of money? What do you mean 'temporarily'? He said his parents are gone. Is he an orphan or isn't he?"

Birendra had asked this very question so often he no longer

expected an answer to present itself, but here, with the American lady asking for him, he awaited Mr. Channar's response, breathless.

"Please, madam," said Mr. Channar. "There is someone I can call in Varkala, and he will go to collect my cousin or his wife, as they have no phone. Let me consult them."

The room was quiet a moment. Birendra turned to peer once again through the keyhole. Mr. Channar was holding the receiver and dialing. Then Birendra heard his name spoken loudly, behind him, and swung around with a terrible shame at being caught spying. It was Rani, and she wore the expression of baffled disappointment he'd only ever seen when she was dealing with Pasha.

"What do you think you're doing?" He made no response and hung his head. "Birendra?"

"Listening," he said. She raised an eyebrow and folded her arms, awaiting a confession that went beyond the obvious. "The American lady," he ventured, "she chooses me. Mr. Channar wants her to take Sanish or Sunita, but she wants *me*."

Rani approached, equally astonished by his claim. He thought she might pull him away so she could eavesdrop herself, but she simply rested a hand on his shoulder and smiled widely.

"Of course she wants you. You're a wonderful boy, Birendra." She took his ear between two fingers and gently tugged. "Now, do you want her to think you're a boy who enjoys spying on conversations not meant for his ears?"

Rani was right. He shouldn't be listening, but he desperately needed to know what was happening. Rani must have agreed because she continued silently down the hall, allowing Birendra to put his ear to the keyhole once more.

A silence followed, then Mr. Channar was speaking Malayalam, thanking someone for calling him back. He asked when Mr. Nair would be available. It must have been Mrs. Nair on the phone. Mr. Channar explained about the American woman who was interested in adopting the boy, "your neighbor's son," he added for clarification. The announcement to a third party sent a thrill through him.

"Auntie, Auntie, please," Mr. Channar said after an uncomfortably long pause. "Much time has passed and still no contact. How long will we wait? How long must we offer charity to the boy?"

Birendra wished he could know what Mrs. Nair was saying. Perhaps she was reminding Mr. Channar that Birendra worked hard for him, that he had earned his stay. If she was resisting him, did it mean she knew something, had heard from his uncle and aunt? If so, why did Birendra struggle to believe they would still come? Then Mr. Channar gutted him by speaking those very thoughts, leaving no chance for hope.

"It has been too long. They would have sent word. They would have come for him. No one is coming, and now there is a nice woman, a rich woman, from America. Who are we to deny the boy such a life? What can we give him in exchange? Will *you* take him to England to find these relatives? And what if they won't have him even then? Let's be reasonable. The boy is an orphan. We can help him find a home."

A moment later Mr. Channar was consoling Mrs. Nair, assuring her she'd done everything she could when Birendra's mother died. But Mr. Channar was also firm. She must now let the boy go. Birendra only hoped he would see her again. For weeks, he'd told himself that being with his aunt would make the great distance between Varkala and West London less frightening. But California! America was another world entirely, and with a woman he didn't know — he couldn't help it; he was scared. He looked again for Rani, but he was alone in the hall. Mr. Channar was off the phone and speaking in English again.

"No, no. Nothing like that," Mr. Channar was explaining. "The people who brought the boy here were his neighbors, a cousin of my father and his wife. We all hoped someone would come for the boy. My cousin and his wife cannot take in an orphan at their age."

Birendra could hear a concern for his welfare in Mr. Channar's voice he had not known was there. He would thank him. He would not admit that he had listened to their conversation, but he would thank Mr. Channar without saying what it was for and it would be especially for this.

"So he has other family?" the woman asked. She sounded distraught.

"It has been five weeks since the boy's mother died, and no one has come or made any attempt to contact us. If he had people to take him, they would have let us know by now."

"So he can't be adopted legally? What precisely is the issue?"

"No, this is just paperwork. And we are, fortunately, well respected and connected. Besides, Mrs. Madeline, you are an American. Your passport is your most important document. I can assure you there will be no issues."

"And the boy, does he want to be adopted?"

"I do want it," Birendra whispered from his side of the door.

He closed his eyes and repeated his nightly prayer: *Please, please, please help me find a home.*

"Birendra is a quiet boy," said Mr. Channar, "a very good boy. I may not be able to tell you what he thinks he wants. But every child needs a home and a mother. This I can say with great confidence."

On the day of his departure, Birendra was in his little green room, carefully wrapping the pictures of his mother and father in the fabric Mrs. Nair had left on her visit. She had not been able to come again before he left, but she had gone to town so she could call and wish him safe journeys. She promised he would remain in their thoughts and prayers. He thanked her for everything and he asked her to thank Mr. Nair as well. He would miss them, even grumpy old Mr. Nair. There were many people he would miss, and that's why he opted to spend his last day and night at the orphanage when given the choice the day before. The American lady, who was called Maddy, had said he could spend his last night with her at the hotel if he wanted. There was a pool he could swim in, and he might be able to play with a little boy who occasionally came around. But Birendra thought he should stay and tell the children one last story, and she gave him permission to spend the night in the orphanage, where he was also able to thank his parents and Ganesh for watching over him, for finding him a home. Now he put his Ganesh in the pocket of his trousers, where it often lived during the day, then he took the monkey in his hand. He poked his head into the hall to look at the hanging clock. There was still a little time.

Mr. Channar's office was empty. Birendra knew where to find the paper and tape. He could help himself, or he could go and find Mr. Channar to ask permission. He looked again at the clock. He might not have time to do both. He took a sheet of paper out of the drawer and, with one eye on the door, retrieved the Scotch tape dispenser from the desk. He tried wrapping the monkey according to its shape, but the paper wouldn't allow it, so he rolled it up with the monkey at its center, folded the ends in, and placed two pieces of tape at each side and one along the seam. He closed the drawer, replaced the dispenser, and he still had three minutes to get his bag and meet Mr. Channar at the front of the building as he'd been advised. He could hardly believe he was on his way.

When he opened the main door, this time to leave and not to welcome families in search of a son or daughter, he saw the car Mr. Channar had said would be coming just for Birendra. It would take him to the American woman's hotel, and from there they would go together to the airport, to take a plane to America. Mr. Channar and the driver were at the car's front end, talking and smoking cigarettes. They watched as Birendra approached, then they nodded at him, as though he were a man. He felt older than he ever had. Mr. Channar put out his cigarette and reached out his hand. Birendra set his bag down and took Mr. Channar's hand in his, remembering to thank him, while the other man took Birendra's bag and put it in the back of the car, squinting against the smoke that rose from his cigarette.

"My advice for you, Birendra," said Mr. Channar when they were alone, "is to go and never look back. You are fortunate to have a new life ahead of you. It will be different, but try to leave this one behind. Don't talk about your life here when you get to America. Behave and do as you're told. You don't want to upset anyone." Birendra nodded. He wanted to take any advice Mr. Channar offered, although he didn't understand why it would upset people if he talked about his life here. Did that include talking about Rani and the children he'd known? The Nairs? Mr. Mon and his praise? Mr. Channar must have seen his confusion. "You don't want to appear ungrateful and end up back here, do you?"

Birendra said nothing. That such a return was even possible terrified him. Clearly he would only be given this one chance. Mr. Channar opened the car door, and Birendra got in the front seat. Through the open window Mr. Channar wished him good luck, then disappeared through the entry of the orphanage.

Birendra's heart was racing as they drove away. Sure he'd forgotten something, he felt his pocket. Ganesh was there. He looked in the seat behind him, but then he remembered the man had put his bag in the trunk. They were farther from the orphanage than he'd been since the day of his arrival. Suddenly he realized he had forgotten to say thank you and a final good-bye to Rani and Dipika. And to the children. He imagined Sunita and Sanish and Pasha asking Rani, as he had once done, where their playmate had gone. She would tell them that he had found a new home and that they would make other friends until they, too, found homes. But who would tell them stories now?

"Why are you crying?" the man asked. "You're a rich boy now. Going off to America."

He raised his feet to the seat and dried his eyes against the knees of his trousers. He hadn't remembered Rani, when she had been so good to him. Now he would never see her again. Sometimes it felt like all Birendra did was never get to say good-bye.

XIV

This time Madeline was sure she heard a car coming down the dirt path to the resort. She wished Simonetta were there with her. She wanted someone else to witness his arrival, to ensure she acted appropriately. What did she say to the boy who would soon stand before her, depending on her absolutely? These days of phone calls and preparations, even securing an immigration lawyer — it was all, as Mr. Channar had said, paperwork; none of it prepared Madeline for this moment. How could she ever catch up on eight years of life? What was his favorite color? What foods did he like? What was his favorite subject at school? Did he like music? Movies? Television? Sports? Was he allergic to anything? What would he call Madeline? This was a question she'd been struggling with for days. She wanted to respect the mother he'd had, his relationship with her, which could obviously never be replaced; at the same time, it was important to establish intimacy. She didn't know what he'd called his own mother, and she wasn't about to ask, but she kept coming back to *Mama Maddy*, thinking he could one day decide whether or not to drop the second half. God forbid he would decide to drop the first half. And there was his name to discuss as well. She'd spent two days trying to get it right and had only just managed. She hated to think of him enduring a lifetime of people getting it wrong. It was his choice, but she had an idea. And her own mother? What would she say? More important, though, was her brother, Eddie. She hoped he would embrace the role of uncle. Madeline could certainly use the support.

The most terrifying realization was that her own nervousness would be nothing in the face of this boy's. And it would be up to Madeline to assuage his fears about what was to come. She needed to find a sense of calm for his sake. It took her back to the day she left home for college. A part of her couldn't wait to leave, but there had been Eddie to consider. He was still so young — he must have been about nine then — and she knew what she was abandoning him to. He'd hardly spoken a word since the week before, when Madeline told him she would be leaving. She'd received her acceptance letter months earlier but hadn't said anything to anyone about it. She warned him not to tell a soul, not even their mother, and wondered if it would take the tuition bill coming for her mother to notice Madeline had even left. Eddie never said the words, but they were emanating from his small soul, clenched in his quivering throat, spilling like tears from his puffy eyes; he was begging her with every silent fiber: *Don't leave me.*

But what choice did she have? She'd cared for him since she realized she had to. Since the days when their mother started disappearing and Madeline came to understand that waiting for her, or even learning where she was going, would do nothing to help her brother eat, get ready for school, do his homework, feel looked after. She'd sacrificed much of her own childhood — gladly, most of the time — but she never should have had to. She knew it was time to start a life of her own. And she needed to show Eddie that it was possible to leave, to eventually break free. Of course, she first had to prove it to herself.

She'd called him to come and say good-bye. He had slunk into the hall, not looking up at her, as she handed him her backpack to take down the stairs. Her suitcase was so heavy, but she hadn't wanted to leave anything behind. She let it thud down the stairs, one at a time. In the entryway, she'd turned for a final glimpse into their house. She hadn't actually expected their mother to be present for this send-off, even though Madeline had told her in the end that she was going and when. She'd done this for Eddie's sake, so he wouldn't be left alone. Her mother would have been sleeping off the night before if she was home at all. But then Madeline had heard something in the kitchen, and she went to look, as if her mother might have been there waiting with a batch of send-off cookies. Of course it was Ana, the housekeeper who occasionally helped care for Eddie, but Madeline hated getting her hopes up in that moment, which would haunt her for years. She was leaving her brother to endure their mother alone. She'd tried to stay strong for him as well. "Cheer up," she'd said. "Maybe you can visit me in New York." He was resisting the urge to cry. She tousled his hair and pulled his forehead to her lips, as Grandma June had done so many times, comforting Madeline when she was a little girl. "It's not forever, Eddie. It's just for now." Then she lifted her pinkie. He'd just stared at it. "Take my pinkie in yours," she said, and he gripped it with his whole hand, making her laugh, despite his tears. She wiggled it free and hooked her finger around his. "Pinkie promise?" she asked. "You have to say it, too." And he did.

How she'd cried for him in the taxi. Out of that house, that life, she finally had air to breathe. She heaved and sobbed all the way to the airport. And now she was tearing up again, her vision cloudy but her gaze locked on the entrance to the resort. The gate opened, and she was abruptly pulled to standing, as though the boy, entering with his cowlick and his little backpack, had thrown an invisible lasso around her. And now she was being pulled to him, into an embrace. She didn't have to say anything, she realized, and what a relief.

X V

The airplane was smaller than Birendra had thought it would be, though it did seem quite long. Mama Maddy — that's what they decided he would call her — got him situated first. She let him sit by the window and told him that he could have whatever he wanted to eat or drink on the next flight, from Delhi, which would be a much longer flight, across the ocean to America.

"As a special Christmas treat, we're going to be flying first class," she said. She cast a nervous glance around them and farther down the aisle. "I get claustrophobic with so many people on these little planes." She paused. "Do you know what *claustrophobic* means?"

He shook his head, worrying that his lack of vocabulary would disappoint her, but she didn't seem to mind.

"It's like you can't breathe because you don't have any space or air around you. Does that make sense?" He was considering his answer while at the same time trying to recall the word. "But you've never been on a plane before, have you?"

He shook his head again and was about to say he'd always wanted to go on one, that his aunt in West London had told him about flying. But he remembered Mr. Channar's warning and thought he shouldn't mention that.

"Oh, sweetheart, you must be a little scared, then. But there's nothing to worry about; it's the safest way to travel. I take planes all the time. All the time."

She tightened his seat belt across his lap and began explaining about how noisy it was for takeoff and landing and about the pulling sensation in the pit of your stomach when taking off. And the bumpiness when the wheels touched down. About the dinging noises that meant passengers could or could not get out of their seats. About the whooshing sound in the bathroom when flushing. He hadn't been scared before, but now he was getting concerned. It didn't sound as fun as he'd hoped. Then she began describing what she called the wonderful things about flying, such as looking out the window and seeing the world in miniature below. Houses and cars like ants, and you floating above the clouds like magic. He lifted the shade and looked out the window. There were two men leaning against a truck, all still ordinary in size. She showed him the button to push if you wanted someone to bring you Champagne, or juice in his case. The food wasn't even terrible, she said, certainly not in first class. Best of all, when you were on a plane, that was it: anything left undone back home was just too bad and would have to wait. No point even worrying about it. Not once you were up in the air. He tried hard to follow her words. He'd always thought English was English, but now he was beginning to fear it wasn't quite the same in America.

"How long?" he said, finally able to get a question in.

"How long what, sweetie?"

"How long will it have to wait?"

"Ah, well, in your case," she said, "you're leaving home, but you're also *going* home. And when you get there, everything will be ready and waiting for you. I've tried to cover all bases, but you'll let me know if I forgot something, won't you?"

She began speaking aloud to herself about rooms and furniture.

"A desk beneath the window would work; the blue dresser opposite the bed; only primary colors, don't you think?"

There was something about the way she talked to him, almost as if he were an adult and not a child, that he liked very much.

"I'm not scared," he said. Once he had her attention, he added, "I always wanted to fly in a plane."

"Of course you're not scared, you brave little man."

She fastened her own seat belt now, then she suddenly seized the arms of her chair.

"My God, Christmas is only two days away," she said. "I don't even have decorations!" She turned to him. "You want a tree, right?" But again she didn't wait for his answer. "And I'll have to call everyone so they can meet you. Do we host a Christmas dinner? Would that be too weird?"

He wondered who "everyone" was. Maybe Mama Maddy had a big family. That would make his mother happy, he thought. He unhooked his seat belt and reached for his backpack, which he had stowed below. He placed it on his lap and admired the face of his new watch, which she'd given him after breakfast; his early Christmas present, she'd called it. He'd never had a watch before, but he knew how to tell time. It was 2:34, and the plane would be leaving in just eleven minutes.

"At school," he said, "we learned about the twelve days of Christmas."

"Did you celebrate Christmas?"

"I think so," he said. "Not twelve days. Just one."

Again, he almost told her that his aunt and uncle always sent him books, and that he wrote special thank-you notes on the backs of his mother's letters, and that he and his mother always called them from town on the Saturday before Christmas. But again, he remembered Mr. Channar's warning. He reached in his backpack and pulled out her present.

"For you," he said, and she covered her mouth in surprise. He would make her something else for Christmas Day, maybe write down one of the stories he knew, with a drawing. He remembered what she'd called his watch, and he said, "Your early Christmas present."

She pulled at the taped ends, then stopped because she'd begun to cry. He worried he'd upset her somehow, but then she reached her hand to his leg and squeezed it, thanking him. She unrolled the paper to reveal the patchwork monkey that had watched him fall asleep from its spot on the crate near his bed in the little green room.

"Oh! It's just wonderful. I love it," she said, pulling it to her heart, and he was so glad she did.

"My mother made it," he said, feeling proud of the monkey.

She covered her mouth again and began to cry even more. He'd gone and upset her in the end, even though he was trying so hard to follow Mr. Channar's advice.

"I'm sorry," she said, wiping her tears away and smiling down at him. He felt confused. Maybe she wasn't upset. "Don't mind me."

But the tears kept coming, and he didn't know what to do or how to comfort her. Finally she lifted the arm that separated their seats and she reached for the back of his head and pulled him close, kissing his forehead and comforting him instead. She smelled nice, and she was warm. He felt better there at her side, but also tired. He stifled a yawn.

"It's perfect," she said, still holding him close. He could fall asleep like this, he thought. "I'll cherish it always."

XVI

Edward hung up the phone and sank into the sofa. The quiet house had a message for him: he was alone. Though Jane was asleep in the other room, in the bed they shared, Edward remained alone. Pieces from the latest puzzle Jane had started stared up at him, small clusters of green, black, and brown pieces, which together formed corners and borders but no recognizable shapes. Maddy had blamed jet lag for her early call. She was back in Los Angeles. She would have called last night, she explained, but they'd come home late and, by the time she'd gotten the boy settled, she collapsed, exhausted. He repeated her news to himself, imagining that he was relaying it to Jane: *My sister has adopted a boy from India.* Jane's imaginary reaction was unpleasant. His own reaction had already disappointed his sister, he knew. First with the shock and silence, then with his questions, concerns, doubts. As she'd said, it was done already. Didn't he know she'd posed those and a hundred other questions to herself countless times before making the decision? Couldn't he just be happy for her? He wanted to believe she'd thought it through, but something had made him doubt it. Still, he said he was happy for her, that she'd just caught him off guard, half asleep. He would love to see his sister happy, for her to have a life outside her work. But a boy from India, he feared, would further complicate what was, in the best of circumstances and with the best intentions, an already challenging situation. Would Maddy even have time to raise a child? Adoption held so many variables. And she said the boy was already eight years old. Had she called him Bindi? Wasn't that the dot Hindus wore between their eyebrows? Maybe he heard her wrong.

He pulled his encyclopedia from the shelf and opened it to the *B*s, then flipped to the entry for *Bindi*:

A bindi, from the Sanskrit bindu, *meaning "a drop, small particle, or dot," is a forehead decoration worn in South Asia and Southeast Asia. Traditionally, the area where the bindi is placed is said to be the sixth chakra, the seat of concealed wisdom.*

The final phrase gave Edward pause. He set the book down and returned his gaze to Jane's puzzle. What would she do, he wondered, if he connected a few of the pieces without her? Puzzle building used to be a joint activity, a way they passed time together. Now it would feel like an invasion of her privacy. And Jane already had so little patience for Edward's sister and what she called "that world," which basically meant anything to do with celebrity and Hollywood. She would no doubt say Maddy was trying to keep up with Cruise and Kidman. Never mind that Eddie and Jane also lived and worked in Hollywood, in the industry, along with almost everyone else they knew. He forced a smile and said the words aloud.

"My sister's adopted a boy from India."

He laughed at his own false tone, but then again, he wasn't an actor. The truth was he really was warming to the idea of a nephew. Jane was an only child and still wanted no children. He'd always assumed this would change in time. He'd also thought they'd be married by now. So there was that. Maddy had invited them to come over that afternoon to meet the boy. In fact, she needed a couple of hours to do some last-minute shopping. He should have asked where she planned to shop on Christmas Eve. Something must be open. And now he would need to get a present for the boy as well. What on earth would he get him? He imagined himself asking for help at the toy store. So my sister's just come home from India with an eight-year-old boy. What do you have for him?

Toys"R"Us was indeed open, and apparently eight-year-old boys were a no-brainer. The pimply kid working there had simply walked Edward over to a display at the center of the room and handed him a video-game console. Something called a Sega Genesis. Apparently Atari was no longer a thing. Jane was awake when he got home, working on her puzzle. She stared at the large bag for a moment, then at Edward quizzically.

"Are you trying to make some comment about my immaturity?"

Silly, witty, lighthearted Jane. Edward was relieved.

"So my sister called this morning."

"Ah. I wondered who was calling so early." Her attention was back on the puzzle. The piece in her hand resumed its tapping, twice on her chin, once at her cheek, and so on. "She's still in Spain?"

"No, actually. It turns out she went to India."

"Madeline went to India?" She looked up, flummoxed. Snarky, cynical, mean Jane. Damn. "Why?"

"Ostensibly for research for a current client who cannot be named." Jane rolled her eyes and returned to her puzzle. He ignored her, almost pleased the announcement would shock her. "But while she was there, she actually adopted an eight-year-old boy."

Jane let out a bark of a laugh, which was precisely the response he should have expected, yet it was no less irksome. Of course she wouldn't believe it. He waved the Toys"R"Us bag in front of her.

"See this? There's a Sega something or other in here, because that's apparently what eight-year-olds like. I'm an uncle, it turns out. So I guess that makes you — "

"Nothing," she interrupted. "That makes me nothing. How old did you say he was?"

"Eight."

"Uff."

"Come on, Jane. Don't."

"Sorry. It's just that you hear crazy stories."

"We're invited for Christmas, but I told her we're going to your folks', of course. So I'm going later today to meet him. I told her I wasn't sure you'd be able to make it. It's up to you."

"Wow, okay. Yeah, you go, do your thing. Have some family time? You know me and kids." She made an X with her fingers and grimaced. She was trying to make him laugh, but he suddenly had to resist the urge to sweep her puzzle from the table and send it flying against the wall.

"You know it's not a crime to want to be a mother, Jane."

He regretted it as soon as he'd said it. She liked to play the woman who had no interest in children and no compassion or understanding for those who chose to have them. He'd also believed she would change her mind, with time. Ten years later, he was still waiting, though he no longer knew what for.

Edward pulled alongside the van that was parked in Madeline's driveway behind her car, which was new to him — and to her, apparently. The "1994" sticker was still on the rear window, red like the car itself: a convertible BMW. She hadn't mentioned the purchase, but he hadn't been over in a while. The front door to the house was open. There were two adults inside he didn't recognize. They were setting up a Christmas tree. Maddy hadn't mentioned she was having other people over, but this was, he realized now, because they weren't friends who'd come by for eggnog and garland hanging. She'd hired some kind of service. Edward hadn't known such a thing existed, and he watched, mesmerized, as one man mechanically removed the ornaments from their boxes and the other found a place to hang them. He heard his name and turned to face his sister. She looked different but also somehow more like the sister he liked to remember, the one preceding the famous interior designer.

"You look great," he said, hugging her.

"I look awful," she said. "I'm running around like a chicken with its head cut off, and I'm completely jet-lagged." She released him. "Thanks for coming."

"Of course," he said, and he turned once again toward the tree and, now, two eyes that peeked over the top of the sofa. He couldn't help but smile. "Well, hello, there."

"Bindi," she said, "come meet your uncle Eddie."

Edward hadn't even seen that the boy was sitting on the sofa, watching the two men work. Now he walked over, and Edward sensed his sister watching him. He was still unsure how to greet his new nephew. He opted for a soft handshake and a tousle of the hair. The boy's hand in his own was small and smooth and allowed itself to be guided.

"Nice to meet you." He stopped himself just shy of saying the boy's name, though Maddy had confirmed what he thought he'd understood on the phone. "So are you enjoying your time in America so far?"

Maddy raised an eyebrow. He felt silly for asking.

"Yes, sir, very much," said the boy.

"Bindi, honey, remember what I told you," said Maddy. There was in her voice a similar tone of affection she'd had with Edward when he was a boy, but she'd grown into it with age. "'Sir' is only for special occasions here, just like 'madam.' He's Uncle Eddie."

Edward was distracted again by the men decorating the tree. They moved swiftly, efficiently, as though on fast-forward.

"So much for sitting around the tree, one ornament at a time," he said. She shot him an exasperated look. "Do they come and water, too?"

"Bindi, your smart-aleck uncle is going to take care of you while I go out for a bit. I need to get a few things still. Is that okay?"

The boy nodded, but his head remained tilted in thought.

"What is aleck?" he said.

"A smart aleck is someone who thinks he's being funny but he's not."

"Well, actually — " said Edward, but she made a sign for

him to zip it. He turned to the boy, pretending to be scared of his sister. "Rule number one," he said. "Don't talk back."

He realized he didn't know what to call Maddy in relation to the boy. Was it *Don't talk back to your mother? Madeline? Maddy?*

"Walk me out?" she asked, then turned to the boy. "I'll be back as soon as I can. Have fun with Uncle Eddie."

He suddenly felt like he should ask for rules or instructions. What were they supposed to do?

"Thank you for doing this. You can't imagine what it's like coming home the day before Christmas with an eight-year-old." He shook his head. She was right: he had no idea. "I just want him to feel comfortable."

"Of course. I understand. Whatever I can do to help."

"Just hang out with him. Get to know him."

When Edward returned to the living room, he put a hand on the boy's shoulder, and they watched the men at work. He was so small and such a mystery; Edward knew almost nothing about him or his life. He felt small talk was all they had, but it felt entirely inappropriate at the same time. He wanted to really get to know the boy, to catch up on his life so far. But he didn't even know if it had been a terribly traumatic life. He was an orphan, so it must have been. And yet he seemed oddly at ease, or at least curious about the new world around him in a healthy way.

"Hey, Bindi. Would you like to help me finish decorating that tree?" He turned to the man unwrapping the ornaments. "Hey, any chance my nephew and I can finish up?"

The man looked at the nearly empty box, then at Edward, annoyed.

"The ornaments are only covered if we hang them."

"Oh, sure. Of course we'd pay for any damages." He stepped around the sofa and lowered his voice. "Look, I'm just trying to let the kid have some Christmas fun."

"All the packaging has to be replaced in the same boxes, and then they're stored at the warehouse until the breakdown date."

This guy was a real modern-day Scrooge, thought Edward. Clearly he had missed his calling.

"How about this," said Edward, forcing a smile. "There's a star, right?" He looked back at Bindi. "There's always a star."

"You have a choice of a gold star, a silver star, or an angel."

"What do you say, Bindi? A star or an angel on top?"

The boy weighed his options seriously.

"Do you want to see them?" Edward suggested. The man now released an audible sigh behind him, and Edward felt himself flush with anger.

"I think a star," said Bindi. "A gold star."

"Excellent choice," said Edward, relieved to be able to conclude the frustrating exchange. "Would you and your friend mind leaving one gold star for the boy to put on top?"

"It won't be covered."

"Got it," said Edward, already walking away.

He returned to Bindi's side, and they soon watched each of the men carry a box out the door. He thought about making some sort of joke at the man's expense, but it didn't seem fair to his nephew. In fact, looking at him, alone now, he didn't know what to say at all, so he suggested they get something to drink first, then hang the star. They walked in tandem to the kitchen island, where the boy took a seat on one of Maddy's futuristic stools. There was tonic, which tempted him to look for the gin, but he'd be good. There was also 7Up, and there were maraschino cherries among the condiments that lined the inside of the door. Edward was about to ask if Bindi liked maraschino cherries, but then considered the likelihood that he had never heard of a maraschino cherry. Edward felt the boy's eyes on him as he filled their glasses with ice and soda, then a drizzle of juice from the cherry jar. He found the straws and gave the ice in each glass a spin, and now they were both following the red swirl. When the soda had gone pink, he dropped two bright cherries on top of the ice and slid the pint glass across the island. The way Bindi received it in both small hands made it look ridiculously huge. Welcome to America, he thought.

"That there's a Shirley Temple. With Coke, it's called a Roy Rogers." The boy had no idea what he was going on about. "So how do you spell your name, by the way?"

He set his drink aside and quickly began to spell his name, as though a contestant in a spelling bee.

"B-i-r. No, sorry." He was adorably embarrassed by his mistake and puffed himself up to try again, slowly this time. "B-i-n-d-i."

"That's just how I thought it was spelled. Now, is that a nickname or your full name?"

The boy leaned back in his chair. He had a curious look on his face, as if he wasn't sure how to respond. Edward thought he might not know the word and was about to explain what a nickname was, but the boy spoke again.

"Not a nickname. It's my name for America."

"I'm not sure I understand. What was your name before?"

"Birendra," he said quietly, almost a question.

"So Bindi was not your name before coming to America?"

he said, repeating what they'd already established. "And you wanted to change your old name for a new one when you came here?"

Bindi thought for a second, then nodded, a little more at ease.

"Mama Maddy said it was better on the plane," he added and returned to his straw.

Mama Maddy? Name for America?

"And is it better? I mean, do you prefer this name?"

The boy shrugged and took another sip of his soda. Then, clearly parroting Maddy's words, he said: "My other name is too challenging for Americans. They won't be able to say it."

"Let's go see about that star," said Edward. "Can you get down by yourself?"

He slid easily from the stool and waited for Edward to come around the island. As they walked to the tree, he grasped Edward's palm with his hand, and it took Edward completely by surprise. He really was an uncle, and here was the boy to prove it. Edward wondered what it all looked like to him. The tree. The house. A different country. Even Edward himself. In front of the tree, he went down on one knee to be level with the boy. He adjusted the collar of his nephew's sweater and returned his smile.

"How would you like it if I called you Birendra?" he asked. The boy just stared, wide-eyed, at Edward. His answer, half nodding, half shrugging, was a confused silence. "Only if you'd like."

Now he nodded with more conviction, and Edward leaned in close.

"It's so nice to meet you, Birendra. Now, if I'm not mistaken, we've got a gold star to hang."

XVII

Christmas with the Bhatias, despite her prickly relationship with her mother-in-law, was something Nayana looked forward to — usually. It was naturally a pleasure to watch her niece open presents, especially as Jasmeen grew older — she was six now — and knew the gifts were for her. She was overjoyed by each toy, every dress. And watching Ramesh enjoy his niece was itself a treat, even if Nayana knew how badly he wished they were watching a child of their own. Today he smiled freely, even if Nayana found herself out of sorts. In the end, Ramesh was delighted by her pregnancy, and she tried to accept this. Her betrayal was her cross to bear alone, at least for now. Christmas Day was always an easy time for Nayana to imagine a future in which her sister and nephew were part of the festivities, together with Nayana and Ramesh in London, and maybe one more. She'd so hoped her sister would call that morning, before she and Ramesh had to leave the flat. It wasn't that she would have confessed anything to Aditi, but she would have felt a little less alone now with Ramesh's family. Without their holiday phone call, she was incomplete and found it hard to daydream.

And so she smiled at her niece, but she thought of India. One way or another, she needed to go home, sooner rather than later. In her most recent letter, Aditi hadn't sounded ready for a move, but maybe it *was* time to discuss bringing them over. Selling their parents' flat in Delhi, if necessary. Maybe she was just waiting for Nayana to say so. To persuade her. To come in person and help her find the strength to say good-bye to the home she'd shared with Srikant, to give her permission to suggest selling their childhood home.

Her sister-in-law and Mrs. Bhatia retreated to the kitchen, taking Jasmeen with them. Ramesh and Raj went to watch the football match on television. Nayana remained with her book in the den. Years ago, she would have followed the women, trying to contribute, if only on holidays. But that was over now. She no longer cared to be told she couldn't chop an onion right or keep a sauce from separating. And it distressed Nayana to watch Tahira have to bite her tongue upon hearing the aspersions their mother-in-law cast in a tongue only they shared. Nayana may not have always understood what was being said, but she knew it was a criticism of her childlessness as much as her cooking skills. It helped, wielding a secret today, like a shield against her mother-in-law's disapproving gaze. Tahira, on the other hand, could do no wrong in Mrs. Bhatia's eyes. And Jasmeen was perfect, of course. Raj, too, except for the fact that he was the second son, and his ideal little family was eclipsing that of her firstborn. The words on the page fell under a shadow. Ramesh was leaning over her, kissing the top of her head. She closed her eyes and leaned into his kiss.

"Are you sure we can't tell them?" he whispered.

She smiled up at him, relieved to see him genuinely in such good spirits. Still, she shook her head gently. Jasmeen had joined them now.

"Will you tell me a story, Auntie?"

Like Nayana, Jasmeen preferred stories to helping in the kitchen. This felt like a small victory won against her mother-in-law.

"Come sit on my lap. I'll tell you a story about two little girls, not much older than you, living far, far away in a place called Delhi."

"The capital of India!" Jasmeen said, proud to know it.

Ramesh chuckled. She reached for his hand. He took hers, kissed it, and left the room. Jasmeen set to work on Nayana's hair as she often did — she loved how long it was — her delicate fingers strumming it like so many harp strings.

"Yes, in India, a place where two sisters were once blessed with amazing powers."

"Powers?" repeated Jasmeen, as much an expression of awe as a question.

"Yes, and these two little girls were twins. Many said that was bad luck, especially their evil stepmother, but the two girls thought differently. With one look, they knew each other's thoughts. This allowed them to communicate without speaking, using only their minds, and to make awful jokes about the wicked woman. One day, their stepmother grew tired of their sudden bursts of laughter and locked them up, each in a different part of the castle where they lived."

"Were they princesses?"

"Yes, they were, but the evil queen had charmed their father so he didn't know how awfully she treated his daughters. As she locked each girl away, she promised to keep them apart forever, hidden from the rest of the world, and especially from their father, the king."

"What did they do?"

"Oh, they were scared, and lonely, and they cried and cried, but no one heard them. The queen had been cunning and found parts of the castle where others didn't go. One day, Princess Aditi got an idea. Maybe she and her sister could still use their powers to talk to each other, she thought. She was always the first to have a good idea. Her sister thought it was because Aditi was thirteen minutes younger and had learned something important in that brief time alone in their mother's womb, something her thirteen-minute-older sister might never understand. It was Aditi who had discovered their powers and shown her sister how to use them in the first place. But once they were separated, her sister could not hear Aditi. She could only hear herself crying, alone in the abandoned broom closet where she'd been locked away. Finally she cried herself to sleep, and, in dreaming, was reunited with Aditi, who told her if she concentrated very hard, they could still use their powers to communicate. When they awoke the next morning, each in her faraway corner of the castle, they tested their powers until they could easily hear each other once again. They were so happy not to be alone, but soon enough they remembered they were still hidden from the rest of the world."

"Forever?" asked Jasmeen, apparently horrified at the thought. Nayana suddenly wasn't sure. Where was her story leading? How was she going to turn things around? Jasmeen stopped playing with Nayana's hair and stared wide-eyed up at her aunt, desperate, it seemed, to learn the fate of the girls. Nayana caressed her face and smiled.

"No, not forever, my dear." Jasmeen's relief was palpable. "You see, once again Princess Aditi had an idea. The sisters had a cousin whose name was Jasmeen, and she was the most beautiful princess in all of India. She lived in a faraway place in southern India called Kerala."

"I'm a princess, too?"

Nayana told her she was, and a brave one, who, while sleeping, dreamed of her cousins in Delhi. The cousins told her what their stepmother had done, that she'd locked them away from their father. They begged Princess Jasmeen to make the long journey north to their palace, where she could save them and expose the wicked queen. "'But,' they warned their cousin, 'you must be very careful with our stepmother, for she is dangerous and truly evil.'"

"I'm a princess, too!" Jasmeen announced to Ramesh, who had reentered the room, now carrying two beers on his way to rejoin Raj in the TV room.

"Yes, you are," he said.

"Did I save the princesses?" asked Jasmeen, eager to return to the tale.

"That's right. You traveled many, many miles, and you visited your uncle, the king of Delhi, King Ramesh," she said, looking back the way Ramesh had gone and hearing him chuckle.

"What did the king do?"

"Well, he found his daughters, and he banished the wicked queen far away to a place called London, where she's rumored to still be alive, torturing everyone around her because she's a miserable old witch."

Tahira called for Jasmeen from the kitchen. Jasmeen looked at Nayana, her eyes wide once again with fear. She whispered, "The evil queen lives in London, Auntie?"

"Yes, darling, but I will protect you. Now go and do what your mother tells you."

Nayana got up from the chair as well, leaving her book behind, and followed after Ramesh. He and Raj were seated on the floor, in front of the sofa, shouting at the football players on the screen. She wanted to be alone with Ramesh. She needed to be in his arms, right now.

"Ram, can you help me a minute?" she asked.

He turned from the television, then back just as quickly, as if he'd miss something in that instant. "What is it, *jaanu?*"

"I just need your help for a moment." He looked at her again. *In the bathroom,* she mouthed and pointed, then turned, leaving him perplexed.

She left the door cracked and hoisted herself onto the bathroom counter. The door opened, and Ramesh looked panicked. He went to her, his hands searching her body for the problem, passing from her shoulders to her waist and finally resting at her knees.

"What is it?" he said. "Is something the matter?"

She'd scared him without meaning to.

"Kiss me," she whispered.

"What? *Jaanu?*"

"Kiss me," she repeated.

His head fell against her chest, and he sighed. She ran her fingers through his hair, inhaled his scent.

"My God, woman, you scared me half to death." He looked back at the door, pushed it closed. "What's gotten into you?"

She pulled him close, sliding his hands to her waist again. She kissed him, and his fingers traced the length of her torso. Her head released to the mirror behind her, and Ramesh buried his face in her neck. There was love between them, and a future, and this seemed to demand at least a little hope.

"Happy Christmas, Ram," she said, and then she kissed him again.

XVIII

Their first Christmas. Madeline had stayed up late chatting with Eddie the night before, telling him all about her trip to India and as little about Spain as she could get away with. He even stayed and helped her wrap presents, then he surprised them both, it seemed, by saying he would stay the night and the next day as well. He left the room to call Jane and tell her he wouldn't be joining her and her family. Clearly there was something going on between him and Jane. Madeline had always thought Jane was simply the wrong choice for Eddie. As a person, she was fine, but she wasn't good for Eddie, who needed, in Madeline's opinion, someone less abrasive. She didn't know how they'd lasted so long.

She'd set her alarm for seven and was only able to force herself out of bed because she knew there was a café au lait in her immediate future. But downstairs it was so quiet, and the lights on the tree were blinking away, flashing against the gold star Bindi told her he had chosen himself and put on top with his uncle's help. Maybe there *were* too many presents under the tree for one child — her brother seemed to think so — but so be it. She wanted to spoil Bindi, to make up for whatever had landed him in that orphanage, but such bounty didn't have to turn him rotten. She would teach him to be generous as well. She had a sense he already was. And she wasn't going to change who she was or pretend that he wouldn't benefit from his new circumstances. She'd worked her entire adult life to build her career, and she'd been truly fortunate to succeed. Plenty of deserving, talented women didn't. It was a privilege she and Bindi would now share, but it would be her duty to teach him what privilege meant as much as what it didn't mean. It was the cumulative weight of all the big lessons she would have to teach him — the immense responsibility she felt for molding the mind of a future man in this world — that struck her so often and so completely with momentary fears and doubts. What would she learn about herself in the process? What if she didn't like what she saw? What if *he* didn't?

She shook her head and took a step back, as if to rebuff the questions. Not today. Today she wanted to be like one of those families on an after-school special, just enjoying the holiday together. Being enough for each other. Playing Christmas music and opening presents. Feasting on too much food and just enough holiday cheer. And Eddie would be there with them today as well. She had left his present in her room, where she'd wrapped it before going to bed. The stockings were also upstairs. She wanted nothing more than to sit down and close her eyes, but she forced herself up the stairs. Maybe they could have pancakes for breakfast. Eddie liked bananas in his. Bindi was allergic to bananas, she'd discovered on the plane. It was the only allergy he knew of. She might have some frozen strawberries, or they could decorate the pancakes with raisins, if he liked those. She crept past his room quietly, resisting the urge to peek in. And just moments after she'd placed Eddie's gift among the rest and hung the stockings, Bindi was coming down the stairs, sleepy-eyed and barefoot. She wondered if he felt cold and turned up the heat on her way to him.

"Merry Christmas," she said, holding her coffee to one side while she squeezed him close with her free arm.

"Merry Christmas," he said, and his eyes grew wide upon seeing all the gifts under the tree. He looked at Madeline, asking without words if they were for him. She gave him an encouraging smile and said he could open one before breakfast.

"Pick one that's from me and come to the kitchen. I thought we'd have pancakes."

"With coconut?"

"Coconut?" She recalled a whole coconut out of which she'd once drunk a piña colada in Mexico. "Do you mean dried, shredded coconut? Little pieces?"

"Not dry," he said, seeking the right description. "Like sticky and sweet and rolled up inside."

Rolled up? Apparently they were not talking about the same kinds of pancakes. Eddie walked in, stretching his arms overhead. He was more adventurous in the kitchen. Perhaps he could figure out the pancakes.

"How's everyone this morning?" he asked. "Merry Christmas."

It was odd, all of them there together. She could hear it in her brother's voice, too, and see it in his expression, a smile that said it was all a bit surreal. But who cared, if it felt this good? Surprisingly, Bindi had chosen one of the flat boxes, which any other kid would have cast aside, knowing they contained clothes. She almost told him to pick a different one, but he'd already torn the wrapping open and was removing the lid from the box. He slowed down now, gently unfolding the tissue paper to reveal a sweater inside. She nodded to indicate he could pull it out. Eddie walked over and felt the sweater with one hand, then put the other on Bindi's shoulder.

"That's a good-looking sweater," he said. "Oh, I think there's something else in there."

Bindi set the sweater on his lap and pulled out the Levi's below as if they were some great hidden treasure and not a pair of blue jeans. "Thank you, Mama Maddy."

"You're welcome, sweetie. Now, how about you tell Uncle Eddie just how you like those pancakes? He's a real whiz in the kitchen. I'll make some orange juice and put on some Christmas music. Sound good? Oh, Eddie, there's coffee in the pot and some hot milk on the stove."

She pulled a can of concentrate from the freezer and set it on the counter. Then she called Bindi over to help her. Her grandmother always let her make the juice. Madeline was happy to have these small lessons in life to balance the big ones they had ahead. Everything was new and exciting for Bindi. That made it so for her, as well. What a gift this was. He stirred and stirred until the frozen block grew smaller and finally became something he could break apart. Eddie, meanwhile, was at work on those mystery pancakes. She left her boys in the kitchen and went to put on some Christmas music, shocked to find that she wouldn't actually mind hearing it. For once she wasn't sick of it, and this, she realized, was because she'd been out of the country for most of December.

Eddie had managed to concoct a pancake-crepe hybrid, which he then filled with strawberries he'd cooked down with sugar and rolled up per Bindi's directions. Bindi seemed to love every bite. And Madeline couldn't get over the day. She rested a hand on her brother's shoulder and thanked him. He smiled at her seriousness. It wasn't merely a thank you for breakfast. She didn't know what it was for, exactly, except being there with them.

"Who's ready for more presents?" she asked.

Bindi looked at his uncle, then at Madeline, then slowly raised his hand. She had to laugh in order not to cry. He had a systematic way of choosing the gifts he opened, by similar size and shape, and he soon must have thought he was only getting clothes. Even so, each outfit thrilled him. Eddie intervened, finally, and handed Madeline a gift from Bindi. She recognized his wrapping handiwork from the monkey. And he'd written *Mama Maddy* on top of the wrapping paper in black marker. It looked like an oversize square envelope, and inside there was a piece of construction paper that had been folded in half twice. A drawing of three lions perched on the edge of an island, looking out. It was remarkable how he'd captured their anxiety and how they seemed to be looking at Madeline across the water, bidding her to come.

"There's a story that goes with it. I didn't have time to finish it."

"This is wonderful, Bindi," she said and passed it to her brother. "Isn't that good?"

"It's very good," he said. "Well done. Can I open mine?"

Bindi nodded enthusiastically. He took as much pleasure, it seemed, in watching others open the gifts he had given them as he did in tearing through the mountain of gifts he received.

"This is really cool. Look, Maddy." She took the drawing Eddie handed her and saw that Bindi once again made the viewer an active participant in the picture, which this time depicted a brown bear seated on a bench and staring out at a rooster in the foreground and thus at the beholder as well. They were technically uncomplicated, but there was beauty in that, too. "Pretty good, don't you think, sis? Looks like we've got another artist in the family." She said it was excellent and handed the drawing back. "Why don't you open that one just there?" she prompted Bindi.

Eddie moved closer to Madeline on the sofa, not quite whispering as he inquired after their mother and Jack. Had she at least invited them? She shook her head.

"Do they know?"

"Not yet. I'm not sure what to do."

"Well, you have to tell her," he said.

"Have you spoken to her recently? I called before my trip and something wasn't right. She sounded off."

"Drunk?" he suggested.

"Maybe, but not only. It's that man, I'm sure of it. I've never trusted him, and now they're so far away."

"Palm Desert? It's not so far," he said, as if Madeline were making excuses.

"So you've gone recently?"

"No. I haven't." He was guilty, too. She could hear it. The sad part is that Madeline knew their mother might love this, all of them sitting around together. Perhaps her mother had finally moved past whatever heartbreak had made it so impossible for her to show her love when they were young. Bindi was trying to determine what he was looking at, what the image on the big box represented. "Maybe we could all go over together."

"Maybe." She didn't want to think about it now. No one was going to spoil this day. In the same hushed tone, she said, "He doesn't know what it is. Tell him."

"That there is a Sega Genesis, which is a video-game console you can connect to your TV."

Bindi was now unwrapping the smaller gift that had been taped on top of the box. It was a video game to accompany the console: Sonic the Hedgehog.

"What's a . . ." He hesitated. "Hedgehog?"

"It's a small animal, about this big." Eddie held up his hands to show the size. "It's covered in — what?" He looked at Madeline, and she shrugged. "Like quills. Do you know what a porcupine is?"

"Yes!" Bindi answered, excited that he knew it.

"Well, it's like a miniature porcupine with little spiky things instead of hair." He turned to Madeline again. She could only think of comparing it to a mole or groundhog, which didn't seem particularly helpful. She shook her head and shrugged again.

"Does it look like this?" Bindi showed them both the video-game cover.

"No, nothing like that," Eddie said, then asked Madeline, "Where's your encyclopedia?"

"I don't have one," she said, almost defensively. "You're the nerd."

"I love encyclopedias," Bindi chimed in. "There was a set at my school. In the library. They didn't allow us to borrow them, but I could look at lunchtime or before school. Sometimes I went during recess if I thought of a question."

Eddie put his hand out and Bindi stared at it.

"Give me five."

Bindi tapped Eddie's hand with his fingers. Madeline laughed.

"Bindi, when your uncle graduated from high school, unlike the other kids, who wanted cars and who knows what else, he asked for — what was it?"

"The *World Book Encyclopedia* set, of course. I still use it all the time. I used it yesterday, in fact."

"Ah, yes. The *World Book Encyclopedia*. That's what your uncle wanted for his high school graduation!"

"And you got it for me."

"That I did."

"When's your birthday, Bindi?" asked Edward.

"January 29, 1985."

"Well, then, you might just be in luck."

Madeline looked around the living room, at the carefully arranged stacks of architecture and design books, the vases, and the small pieces of sculpture that decorated her bookcase. She'd designed it herself, knowing exactly what would go where. She couldn't imagine an unwieldy encyclopedia set lining one of the shelves. No, it would have to go in Bindi's room. And for the first time in weeks, since Barcelona, as a matter of fact, the thought of returning to work truly took hold. But she had the catalogs of Spanish tiles to inspire her and the patternwork of the fabrics she'd bought in India. She was already imagining turning select motifs into stencils she would use to decorate some of the walls and the yoga studio by the pool. Bindi pulled a Rubik's Cube from his stocking. He seemed intrigued, spinning it around in his hand. Work would be waiting for her tomorrow, and the next day, and the day after that. But so would he. She would figure it out and catch up on both somehow. She wasn't alone. Everything was about to be different, and different would be good.

1994

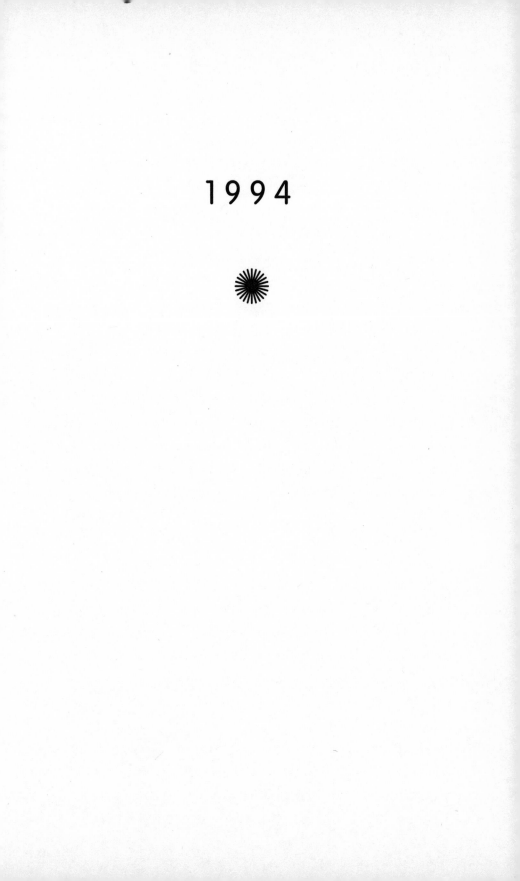

XIX

Carrying his brown-bag lunch into the cafeteria, Birendra looked for Eli, the boy he'd been paired with that morning and told to find again at lunchtime. Mama Maddy had prepared his lunch while he was getting ready for school. He was surprised when she handed him the bag, told him what it was, and explained that he would not be eating meals provided by his new school. Now he noticed that the other kids had similar brown bags or colorful boxes with handles, and they sat together at long tables, pulling out the contents of their lunches one item at a time, as if unveiling a great mystery. He was curious now what he'd find in his own brown bag but resisted the urge to stop and look right there in the middle of the room. Eli waved from a table where he was already seated with two other boys.

"That's Clark," said Eli, nodding across the table to indicate the biggest of the three. Clark had the lightest blue eyes Birendra had ever seen and a face full of freckles. "And this is Sammy." Sammy was the smallest of them, and he wore glasses. He said hello to both boys and sat across from Eli, next to Clark. "That's Bindi," concluded Eli, unwrapping his sandwich now that he'd made introductions. "Ah, man," he said, clearly disappointed.

The others also had their lunch items lined up and were busy inspecting them. Then they looked at one another's food, acknowledging with grumbles and taunts who had the "better" lunch. He listened closely, trying to determine which items might be favored. Meanwhile he emptied his own lunch bag one item at a time. Fruit roll-ups were good, he learned. Fruit was just okay. Celery sticks with no peanut butter were not good at all. Peanut butter and jelly sandwiches were the best. Sandwiches with meat and lettuce, and especially tomatoes, weren't good because the bread got mushy, a word he'd never heard before but immediately understood because it sounded like the thing it described. Cookies, unsurprisingly, trumped everything. Sammy and Eli made an audible sound of defeat when Clark unwrapped two chocolate chip cookies. Then Sammy drew everyone's attention to a boy at the next table who was proudly eating something called a Hostess cupcake. Even Clark, despite his cookies, looked on with envy. The last item from his own bag was a small box, which he cupped in his hand to inspect before revealing it to the others. He wanted to know what he was entering into the competition.

"What kind is it?" Eli asked.

"Oh, it's Hi-C," he said, hoping it was pronounced as it was written.

"Yeah, what flavor?"

"It's fruit punch," he said. He turned it so Eli could see.

"Ah, man. I got grape," Eli said, disappointed again. The others laughed, confirming Birendra had the better juice.

"Do you want to trade?" he asked Eli.

"You'd trade fruit punch for grape?"

Eli sounded suspicious, and Birendra was concerned there might be something he didn't know, but he also wanted the boys to like him, and he'd tried grape juice before and liked it just fine. It didn't seem like a big deal to trade.

"Sure. Here."

"All right," Eli said, sliding his juice to the middle of the table. As soon as he let go, Eli snatched the fruit punch quickly, as though he'd stolen it. "Sucker," he said, and the three of them laughed again.

He thought for a moment that *sucker* meant they would race to finish their juices, but Eli made no indication he was hurrying, so Birendra smiled and shrugged. He didn't think he was being teased. They all seemed to be having fun.

"Where are you from, Bindi?" asked Clark.

"From Kerala," he said, distracted still by the juice box and straw in his hands. Then he remembered that people didn't know where Kerala is. "India," he added.

"Cool," Sammy said.

"Are there really elephants there? Like, not in the zoo?" Eli asked.

He tried to remember if he'd ever seen an elephant outside the Trivandrum zoo. He was sure that someone had brought one through Varkala at some point when he was younger, that he'd touched its rough skin — he remembered the feel and look, like dry, cracked earth — but he couldn't place the memory in a particular time or place. That wouldn't make a very good story, he thought, considering the expectant faces around him.

"Yes, there are elephants," he said. "And an hour away from where I lived, there are lions, too."

"Lions?" Eli was skeptical again, squeezing the last of the juice from his Hi-C box.

But he could see they all wanted to be convinced. He felt a little like he had at the orphanage in Trivandrum, telling stories to the other kids waiting to be adopted; he had to tell a good story, so he told the one he'd always loved, the one he wrote down to accompany Mama Maddy's drawing. He'd first heard it from Mrs. Nair when he was younger, and he had made his mother repeat the story in Hindi and then in English over the years. As he began to tell it now, it once again felt as if she were guiding him, his voice an echo.

"There are two lions, and they live on an island in a mountain lake. Every morning they..." He searched for the English word. "They growl very loudly at the water around the island, and the sound echoes all through the mountains. Men and women from the village wake up and take turns throwing meat and fish to the lions from their boats. They have to be careful not to get too close, but they also have to throw the food far enough away from them so the lions won't come after them."

"No way! Those lions would eat them," said Eli.

"The lions never ate anyone, but a crocodile in the same lake once ate a tourist." This addition to the story he'd learned more recently from Rani at the orphanage.

"Whoa!" Sammy said. "India's crazy. I'm never going there."

Then Clark was telling them about all the things in Australia that might kill you: there were sharks, stingrays, spiders, crocodiles — even the kangaroos sometimes kicked people to death. It sounded like an awful place. Birendra thought of the story he told about the kangaroo named Joey who kept a little boy in his pouch. He wondered if Clark and his family had come to California to escape all the dangers of home. Eli crushed his Hi-C box flat with his fist. The straw went flying, and they all laughed. When Birendra finished, he did the same, but the box wasn't empty, so a stream of purple juice splashed to the floor as well, which made them laugh even harder. Then Sammy and Eli watched with envy as Clark finished his second cookie. Birendra wondered where the other boys came from. He asked Eli first.

"I was born in Beirut." He gave his flattened box a spin.

"Anything that'll kill you in Beirut?" asked Sammy.

"Nah, I don't think so," he said, gathering his garbage and placing it in his bag. "I don't really remember it."

Though he hadn't finished all his food, Birendra did the same.

"Time for *le français*," Clark said in an exaggerated accent, and the other boys thought this was hilarious.

Birendra had been nervous about French class all morning. He wouldn't know what anyone was saying, and he preferred, in any case, to focus on American English, which was already very different from what he was used to. In French class, what could he possibly understand?

He had been classified as a non-French-speaking second grader. He would be older than the students in his classes, but if he did well, the headmaster had said, he could catch up before long. He was so happy to be back in school that he didn't even mind the grade change. And he liked the boys he'd met so far. Sammy and Clark were in French class with him, but Eli spoke French already, so he was in a different class. But there was something strange about looking at a teacher who spoke a stream of words he couldn't understand no matter how hard he tried. The other students in the class responded to her on occasion, with short phrases in the same language, or repeated things she said. Soon he could distinguish between a time to repeat, which he could at least pretend to do, and a time to respond, which he could not do. The teacher seemed to accept this and refrained from calling on him, but she did not stop speaking to him or watching to see if he was repeating the phrases. He was happier when they moved on to copying phrases down in their notebooks, even though the words themselves meant nothing to him. Finally the class was over, but his teacher called his name. The way she pronounced it was something like "Bean-D." She said something else he took to mean she wanted to talk to him. He thought of his teacher Mr. Mon, but he was certain that this woman had no intention of praising him, since he spoke not a word of French.

As he walked up to her desk, his notebook tucked in the fold of his right arm, he hoped she could speak English, too. He was struck as he came closer by a longing for home — not Mama Maddy's home but India, home to Mr. Mon and his mother, where things had been going so well at school. He read the sign on her desk. MADAME LAPIERRE. She had introduced herself, too, as Madame Lapierre when he first entered the classroom. Mama Maddy had told him repeatedly not to call people sir and madam in America. Maybe it was different in France. He just wished it wasn't all so confusing. He couldn't understand why he had come to America just to learn French. Thankfully, his teacher spoke to him in English. She just wanted to ask him questions about where he was from. He spoke excitedly about Varkala and his old school. She nodded along as he spoke, then stood to erase the chalkboard. When she turned, dusting the chalk from her hands, he admired her smile again. Her brown hair was shiny and looked soft. She was pretty.

"It sounds like a wonderful place, Bindi," she said. She sat against the edge of her desk. "Am I right that you have never studied French before?"

"Yes, never, madam."

"*Madame*," she said, correcting him. "*Madame* Lapierre." She used the same tone she'd used in class to indicate that he should repeat her, which he did without hesitation. "And your parents?" She looked back at a paper on her desk before continuing. "Does your mother speak French?"

He was now used to the fact that people at school meant Mama Maddy when they asked about his mother, but he didn't know if she spoke French and said so.

"You will be fine, Bindi. I know this. And we are here to help you. The other students in your class also came to *le lycée* without French, so don't worry. You will work hard and learn, *n'est-ce pas*?" She was waiting for a response. "*Oui?*"

"*Oui*, Madame Lapierre."

"*Très bien*, Bindi."

He remained for a moment at her desk, though he knew their conversation had come to a close. She was smiling down at him, but not in a way that intimidated him. That his teachers took the time to speak to him after class was a good sign, he thought. It meant they cared about their students, that this was a good school. And this motivated him to prove he would eventually be worthy of their praise as well.

"Good-bye, Madame Lapierre."

"*À demain,* Bindi."

As he left the building, he checked the time on his watch. His book bag felt light on his shoulders. He hoped he would still be able to fill it up with books from the library, which he'd learned had more than fifteen thousand books in total. Maybe he could read them all by the time he graduated. There was a honk, and he could see Mama Maddy's assistant, Paige, in a taxi, just where Mama Maddy promised him she would be that morning. She was on her phone, the kind that Mama Maddy also carried with her everywhere. Mama Maddy was in Los Feliz, working. Paige was still on the phone when the taxi pulled into the driveway.

The inside phone was ringing when they entered the house. Paige got off the one phone so she could answer the other. She called for Birendra as he was climbing the stairs to drop his bag in his room. He left it at the top of the stairs and hurried back to the kitchen.

"We just got home," he said into the receiver, assuming he was speaking to Mama Maddy.

But it wasn't Mama Maddy. It was Uncle Eddie. At first he was sorry not to be able to tell Mama Maddy about his day, but then he realized he had two people to talk to about it, and this thrilled him.

"I thought this might be a good time. So? How was it? Did you have fun?"

He told his uncle about his new friends and about his

teachers. And all the library books and his plan to read them. Uncle Eddie seemed to think that was a worthy ambition. "Did you have a nice day, Uncle Eddie?"

"Hey, thanks for asking. Let's see. I was at home this morning, then I had to go check out a pound as a possible location for work."

"What's a pound?"

"It's a place where dogs go to get rescued."

Uncle Eddie was a scout — like a Boy Scout, except that he looked for places where people could make movies. And there was a movie out now starring a dog with a funny name that he'd worked on. He promised to take Birendra.

"Maybe we could visit the dogs one day. Who knows? We might be able to persuade my sister to get you a puppy."

It was strange to think of Mama Maddy as Uncle Eddie's sister. They didn't really look alike, and Mama Maddy told him she was nine years older than Uncle Eddie. His mother was only thirteen minutes younger than Aunt Nayana. Paige removed the apple he hadn't eaten from his lunch bag and handed it to him.

"My mother has a sister, too," he said.

"Sorry — what did you say?"

He took a bite of the apple and realized his mistake. Now he had to say it again, which he did quietly through a mouthful of apple.

"I didn't know that. Where is she?"

"West London."

Birendra knew now how far away he was from West London. Even farther than he'd been when he was in India. He'd looked at Uncle Eddie's atlas. California and India were on different pages, and England was close to the middle but on the India page. They both felt very far away from Los Angeles.

"You have an aunt in London?" He sounded upset, so Birendra didn't tell him he also had an uncle. "I had no idea. Is my — is Mama Maddy aware of this?"

"I don't know," he said. He tried to recall her conversation with Mr. Channar, but he could only think of what Mr. Channar had told him on the day he left; he'd said not to talk about his family after coming to America. Birendra needed to remember, but it had just slipped out.

"I see. I'm sorry. Are you with my sister now?"

He didn't understand why Uncle Eddie apologized, and he wished they could change the subject. He told him that only Paige was there, that she had picked him up from school in a taxi.

"Well, I bet you have a lot of homework."

"Not really. I get to write an introduction for my home-room."

"Then I'd better let you get to it. But it was nice chatting with you. I'll see you soon, okay?"

"Okay. Bye, Uncle Eddie."

He didn't sound upset anymore, but Birendra hoped Uncle Eddie wouldn't say anything to Mama Maddy. He'd been careless, not following Mr. Channar's warning. He would try harder to remember from now on.

X X

The new year had wrapped London in a blanket of freezing Scandinavian fog that had kept Nayana indoors for weeks with the radiators cranked up to combat the unusual cold. She boiled water at regular intervals to keep the air inside from getting too dry, and she used it to make herbal tea to address the persistent low-level nausea she felt. The new year had also put an end to Nayana's procrastinating. She would have nothing but time now that she would not be returning to teach. She no longer had an excuse and resolved to get back to work, to writing the book.

It wasn't the book she'd originally wanted to write in graduate school. The one for which she'd even chosen a title: *Parroting Madame Bovary: The Politics of Translation*. The book whose proposal her adviser had shut down; instead, he firmly encouraged Nayana to focus on "what she knew," which was the postcolonial experience, according to him. At first, she'd persisted with her ideas for *Bovary*, and her professors humored her for a while. "Yes, that idea is good, very good." But sooner or later, she was advised that her idea might more productively be applied to South Asian writing. They may as well have suggested the title: *Parroting the Queen's English: Contemporary Indian Literature*. Dismayed and dejected, but finally angry, Nayana yielded, if only to show them they were wrong. She'd wanted to outline Indian traditions in literature that defied colonization by the English language. She didn't have all the Indian languages required to truly do the research, so she read Hindi or English translations and fudged it, pitting them against classic literature in English. Her plan was then to do the same comparison against contemporary writing in English. But this, it turned out, had not been her main impediment. Writing from a place of anger and retaliation had. Eventually, her desire to prove the academy wrong fizzled, deadlines came and went, and she finally submitted a thesis of which she was not proud and for which she was certain she would not have received credit if her professors hadn't been eager to see the back of her.

It was this book she'd come back to. The truth was she'd never had the French required to write the other, and she certainly didn't have it now. But she was still convinced she could have made up for it with gumption if she'd had even a little support. This book, though it seemed to make an obvious point to her, felt just as important today as it had in graduate school. There was still no title, but she decided to start with a state-of-affairs introductory section — looking at the trajectory of writers from South Asia and the diaspora, from Sake Dean Mahomet to Saadat Hasan Manto to Raja Rao; from Naipaul and Rushdie to Ghosh and Mistry. She was debating whether to include a personal preface about her own experience as an Indian scholar of literature in England. She could compare the widespread presumption of inferiority she'd encountered so frequently as a woman in the academy to that of Indian writers writing in English, as though she'd been trying to access something that was not rightfully hers. As if so-called postcolonial literature, by definition, were inherently an adopted tradition and not something new entirely. Something that had long been produced by writers who were Irish, Scottish, American, Canadian, African, and, yes, Asian.

But how could she write a word of that introduction without first responding to her sister? December's letter never came from Aditi, and there was no message left on the answering machine Christmas Day. Nayana had started a dozen letters since, first as drafts in her journal, trying to weave words into a confession without hiding behind the happy news of her pregnancy. She read Aditi's letter from November so often she could recite it from memory. The first line: *On this last day of Diwali, I miss my sister as always.* But it had yet to lead to a promising first line of her own. She had tried writing how happy they were about the pregnancy, how she and Ramesh hadn't been this good together in years, and this was true. But nothing she wrote seemed true enough. She tried writing in no uncertain terms of her transgressions the year before, the way she had flirted with other men — not just Daniel — to feel better about herself, to *feel*, period. In one attempt, she admitted that the baby might not be Ramesh's at all. Seeing this written down, even though it was only intended for Aditi, had shocked and scared Nayana. She'd torn that sheet from her journal and burned it over the sink in the bathroom. Ramesh was kind, thoughtful, a good husband. This had never been in question, and her straying had not been motivated by that sort of logic. There was no reason she could pluck from her life to explain her discontent or her betrayal. *How can we be honest about the things we do when we don't understand them ourselves?* She took out a piece of stationery and wrote down this thought. It might be a start. She retraced the question mark, then addressed the letter to Aditi and wrote today's date. But her eyes soon strayed from the page. It had likely been her reluctance to write Aditi that led to her renewed commitment to the book. It had been three years since Aditi had asked about it but much longer since the project had been abandoned. Aditi always had too much faith in Nayana. Now she perused her bookshelf, but the great names there offered no osmotic support or inspiration. What would dear Proust say to Aditi? How would he confess? Would it take another four thousand pages to do it, or could he manage with just one? It didn't matter, she reasoned; there was no comparison. Besides, she wasn't seeking perfection. She wanted only to be free to write her sister again, as she always had, unselfconsciously. Now she only felt blocked; it seemed impossible to find the right words. Of course it was. But maybe, she thought, all the examples we hold up, waving them about, canonizing as so many books of gospel — maybe those authors, too, wouldn't claim to have found the right words. Perhaps they'd say they simply wrote long, and sometimes this helped the books come closer, as a whole. Maybe they'd consider the posthumous praise a disservice to their memories, to their own struggles to find the right words. Now she was just creating grand excuses for herself. Of those she had no shortage.

She had plenty of excuses for not telling Ramesh's family about the pregnancy, too. Raj would tell Tahira, or vice versa, and Jasmeen would overhear them and say something to her grandmother. Mrs. Bhatia would warm to the idea, but not to Nayana. She entertained a fantasy of flying Aditi over and sending her to Mrs. Bhatia in Nayana's stead. Aditi could pretend to be her. No one could resist Aditi's sweet charm. Not even Mrs. Bhatia. *I need to channel you, dear sister. You've always been the strong one, but I've never felt weaker than I do now.* She looked at a baby photo of Birendra she'd put back on her desk, next to his most recent photo, in his private school uniform. *I have your darling Birendra here with me, at my desk.* She wrote *It gives me hope in your absence,* but thought this might be taken as a criticism of the fact that Aditi had stopped writing in response to Nayana's own neglect. Still, it hurt not to have heard from Aditi at Christmas. She erased the sentence and tried again. *He gives me hope, as Ramesh and I expect a child of our own.*

The warm scent of peppers and tomatoes filled the room as the office door opened. She'd forgotten she wasn't home alone, that it was a weekend and Ramesh was cooking.

"Lunch is ready, Naya." She stared at him blankly, not registering his words. *"Jaanu?"*

"Do you think Aditi's upset with me?"

"No, my love. I don't," he said, moving toward her. He leaned against the desk and tried to take the pencil from her hand so he could hold it. But she jerked it away and, through her tears, admitted the extent to which their correspondence had ceased. He knelt beside her, favoring his bad knee. He said he understood, though he couldn't, not really.

"Is there someone we could call?" he asked. "A local business, perhaps? Should I call the police?"

The word scared Nayana. "I told her to get a phone installed with some of the money."

"Then perhaps she's waiting for the installation, *jaanu*. I'm sure it takes time down there."

"Yes, but she waited so long." Nayana knew she sounded ridiculous through her tears. But she couldn't stop herself. "I didn't respond to her letter, and now she doesn't want to talk to me at all."

Ramesh took her hands in his and kissed them. He was smiling, almost laughing at her, as though she were a child.

"Why would you say that? You're being silly, goose."

She wanted to believe this, to see with his clarity. To be the person he saw, the person he loved. He told her to come eat something and not to worry for now. He took a step toward the door, then stopped and attempted to lure her with details of the lunch he'd prepared for them: ratatouille, one of her favorites.

"I have to go to India," she blurted. At least, for his sake, she'd said *India* and not *home*. He joined her again at her desk.

"*Jaanu,*" he pleaded, but she ignored him this time.

"I could rest well there. You could visit when work calms down. I could write and come back in plenty of time to have the baby here."

Ramesh sighed deeply, and she allowed herself to hope in the momentary silence that followed.

"It's too big a risk, Naya."

"The doctor says I'm doing fine. She's my sister, Ram. I miss her. I need her." Admitting this made the feeling more desperate. "And now you've got me worried, talking about the police."

Ramesh lifted himself to standing. Despite his towering figure over her, he looked like a little boy, still holding her hands.

"I'm sorry, *jaanu*. It's just not possible."

"What if we went together?" she said. "I could wait a few weeks, until — "

But he cut her off, exasperated. "You know I can't go right now. Or anytime soon. There's still too much going on at work. And you're not going alone."

She turned away from him in the chair. She knew she would soften if she looked at him.

"If Dr. Shah gives the okay — " He tried to interrupt, but she spoke over him. "If she does, I'm going. With or without you."

He sighed, frustrated by her obstinacy but clearly also deeply concerned, regardless of what the doctor might or might not agree to. And yet it felt good for Nayana to be unwavering about at least one thing. When he embraced her, she knew she'd won. He would find a way to join her when he could. She didn't want to talk any more about it. She didn't want to go to the table or eat the ratatouille he'd made for her. She wanted to stay like this, with her arms around him, the side of her face pressed against his sternum, breathing him in, and feeling the vibration of his voice in her ear. She was already transporting herself to a desk by a window in Varkala, hearing the crows in the trees, enjoying the warm southern breeze, knowing her sister was close. She hadn't been listening to Ramesh, who was now pleading with her not to shut him out. He could forgive her for anything, he said, only she shouldn't shut him out. She held him tighter in response. Her letter to Aditi was staring up at them from her desk, and she suddenly worried he'd catch her out in a lie. But then she read the words — *as Ramesh and I expect a child of our own* — and prayed to all that was good that it wasn't a lie.

XXI

Edward had been enjoying regular after-school chats with
Birendra, but he thought it might be better if they could
spend some time alone together. For both of them. Questions
had come up in their conversations that seemed best to discuss in person. The boy's aunt, for one. As a kind of celebration for Birendra's completing his second week at his new
school, Edward suggested to Maddy that he pick his nephew
up and the two of them hang out at Edward's place. He said
he knew she was busy with work but was silently thinking it
would also be preferable to another taxi ride with her assistant. What kind of assistant didn't drive in LA, anyway? They
might finally catch that movie later as well. And dinner. Make
a Friday evening of it. Madeline could join them when she finished work, and Jane would be out late with her girlfriends
at a bachelorette party. But now that they were here at his
place, Edward realized there was another reason: he wanted
to know what it felt like to have a child around with no other
adults present. To see if it struck a paternal chord.

Birendra gravitated immediately toward the encyclopedia
set Madeline had bought Edward as his graduation present.

Watching him flip through the pages, Edward was tempted to give his nephew an early birthday gift. He'd found a beautiful set, and besides, it wasn't like he could put the whole thing in a box and wrap it. But he decided to wait. Birendra's birthday was only two weeks away. Perhaps he'd want to come over again before then.

"What are you looking up?"

"I wanted to see what a hedgehog looks like."

Edward moved closer and looked at the entry over his nephew's shoulder. Birendra was like a sponge. He loved to read and learn new things. He was always asking questions, probing questions. He didn't simply ask why something was the way it was and stop there; he always wanted to understand. Driving home today, they got stuck in traffic next to a nearly empty bus. Why was the bus so empty? Why did people prefer to drive? Why indeed? Edward didn't think he'd had the same curiosity at that age. He wondered where it came from. His mother's encouragement? Some biological imperative for those having suffered the incomprehensible? It seemed to Edward the boy had every right to be solemn, angry, and in pain, but he somehow managed to navigate his new life without ever manifesting such negative but understandable feelings. And at such a young age. It was remarkable. Edward hoped it wasn't a defense mechanism, that all the bad feelings weren't being bottled up to one day explode. Was Edward just projecting? He couldn't stop thinking about this aunt in London. He wanted to broach the subject again, but it made him feel guilty. For Birendra, it might be a difficult subject, certainly a reminder of all he'd lost. And yet it seemed important that he feel able to share whatever he wanted to about his life before he was adopted and that Maddy and Edward know as much as possible about his past. Why hadn't the aunt gone to him when her sister died? It didn't sound like they were estranged at all. But it was his own sister he felt most conflicted about. Was it even Edward's place to get involved? Did Maddy already know about the aunt? And if she didn't, and Edward admitted to trying to learn more about her, would Maddy feel betrayed? Would she take it to mean he didn't think she was ready for motherhood? *Is* that what was driving him? All he knew for certain was that he was compelled to learn more.

"Last week, on the phone, you mentioned your aunt in London." Birendra looked up from the encyclopedia and went rigid, staring at the wall in front of him. "I'm sorry. Do you mind talking about her?"

Now he looked at Edward, but he couldn't get a read. The young boy had never felt so beyond Edward's grasp.

"Have you been to London?" Birendra asked, either changing the subject or finding his way to it.

"I have, yes. Briefly, with Jane, a few years after we graduated from college. I had wanted to go to London for many years." He seemed to have his nephew's rapt attention. London was going to be Edward's big escape after high school. Maddy had New York; he would have London. What would that life have looked like? His mind flashed from one possibility to another, each version canceling out some memory he wanted to keep, and now those included his time with his nephew. Few involved Jane in recent years, if he was honest. If anything, he would have been relieved to efface the memory that came to mind, that very same trip to London.

"I...uh...met an English girl in high school and fell head over heels in love with her. Or so I thought." This made Birendra giggle. It had been ages since Edward had thought of his high school crush. "One day she told me her family was going back to London. I was heartbroken and promised I would visit her. I even thought I'd try to go to college there."

"But you didn't go?"

"No. Not then. Life has a way of surprising us. I met Jane the summer after I graduated from high school." He realized he sounded disappointed and tried to enliven his tone. "We ended up going to college together here in California."

Years later, on that trip to London, Jane had been mysterious and quiet on the morning they went sightseeing around the city center, across bridges, through parks. Big Ben. Finally Edward had begged her to tell him what was wrong. He was sure she was going to break up with him, that it had taken traveling together for her to realize they weren't right for each other after so many years. Then she collapsed into him, crying. "We fucked up," she said, and her tone scared him. "I'm pregnant." The words were so unexpected, so surprising and unbelievable — as though the connection between the sex they'd been having and the possibility of conception had never occurred to him — that she was already halfway across the street before Edward realized he was standing alone. What was he supposed to say or do? What did she want him to say and do? Every response felt wrong in its own way. He wasn't even twenty-five. Could he be a good father so young? But she wasn't interested in his questions. She'd decided what must be done and insisted on returning home alone to do it, to have the abortion. She was right then — they weren't ready. But he was ready now, or so he believed. He wanted a family. And spending time with his nephew had made that more clear than ever. He felt he truly understood Maddy's decision to adopt. You can't always wait around for what you want to happen. He might be waiting forever with Jane.

The phone was ringing. Birendra had turned back to the encyclopedia. It was Jack calling, otherwise known to Edward and Maddy as *that man*. He'd never called Edward before, and this strange fact alone would have been enough to catch Edward off guard. Combined with the lingering memories from his trip and Jane's abortion, he felt sick and sat down. As Jack spoke, Edward tried both to deflect the voice coming through the receiver and parse the terrible message that was being relayed. Who was gone? Why was Jack calling him?

"What?" It was all he could say.

Jack said it again. "She's gone. I'm sorry."

And all at once Edward understood that his mother had died. He didn't know how that could be. Was she so sick? Had they ignored some sign? And yet he didn't ask Jack how she had died. He only managed to ask when, a single-word question, whose answer — earlier that afternoon — was meaningless in the end, for it didn't matter when. It only mattered that now and forever after, the woman who'd brought Edward so much confusion, loneliness, and pain was gone. And when he remembered that Birendra was in the room, watching him, he instinctively wanted to protect his nephew from this news, from the event, but looking at him, Edward knew it was already too late for that. Maybe the boy even recognized and translated the look on Edward's face. Here he'd been contemplating his life without a family, without his own children, only to discover that he was now an adult without parents.

XXII

The rest of Friday and much of Saturday, Birendra kept close to Mama Maddy and waited for the day of the funeral to arrive. Uncle Eddie had brought him home Friday evening and told Mama Maddy about their mother. For a long time, they sat and said nothing. And then it was time for bed. On Saturday, Mama Maddy explained to him that nothing would happen for now, that the funeral for her mother would take place on one day only, the following Friday. And that she would be buried and not cremated. She didn't know what an atma was, and he couldn't really explain it to her. Nor was she sure why they waited so long in America to bury a person, except that everything took time, and that people who wanted to come needed to arrange their schedules. Even dying, he thought, was different in America.

On Sunday morning, at breakfast, she told him not to eat too much cereal and that he should get ready to go someplace special. Maybe he'd misunderstood. Maybe there was more than one day of ceremonies here as well. Either way, he was looking forward to a day with Mama Maddy. She'd been working a lot lately at the big house. He missed those days just after they arrived in California, when they spent all their time together. But he was also glad to have school again, even if learning French was difficult. Now he chose his favorite sweater and jeans and went to her bedroom. He was impatient to ask where they were going, but she was biting her lower lip when he reached her doorway, as she did sometimes. He didn't like to disturb her in these moments, so he waited until she caught his eye in the mirror.

"What do you think?" she asked.

"You look nice. Where are we going?"

She waved him over and began to pull at his cowlick, trying to smooth it down. She often did this, even though it always sprang back up.

"Come with me," she said and led him to her bathroom. She ran a comb under the tap, then passed it through his hair, straight back, not to the side as he always combed it. "There," she said.

His hair was standing straight up, but she was laughing, and he was glad to see she had been teasing but also happy she was not as sad as she had been. She combed his hair down again neatly and turned him toward the mirror in front of her. His cowlick was still there.

"We, my little Bindi, are going to the Huntington gardens for high tea."

"What's that?"

"The Huntington or high tea?"

"Um…both?" She squeezed a small mound of white mousse into the palm of her hands, then ran it through his hair until the foam disappeared.

"The Huntington gardens was once the home of a very

wealthy family that, I think, made its money in railroads at the turn of the century."

"You have trains in Los Angeles?" he asked.

"Of course we do. They've actually been trying to revive the whole system. There's even a subway now, an underground train. Next time we go to dinner in Chinatown, I'll take you to see the downtown station. It's a beautiful old building." She began to brush her hair now, then fixed her lipstick while he waited for her. "Oh, and high tea is just a fancy way of saying tea and sandwiches and little sweets. My grandmother liked to take me there when I was a little girl. It was my favorite place to go." He followed her back to her bed. She'd never mentioned her grandmother before. That's what her mother would have been for him. "There's a museum and beautiful gardens and forests, with a koi pond and giant cacti that make the desert garden look like another planet."

She pulled out a folded square of fabric and held it up to her chin.

"Is your grandmother with God, too?"

"What a nice way to think of it. Yes, she is, dear." She held up a different scarf. "I was not much older than you are when she died."

She'd told him that it wasn't just one thing that took her mother's life. She was on the wrong medication and she didn't care of herself. And the man she was with was a bad influence. It all caught up with her. She seemed sad but not as surprised as Uncle Eddie. He thought of his own father, who had drowned. And the shock of coming home to find his mother gone.

"How did your grandmother die?"

"Pneumonia killed her in the end, but her body had been struggling already."

"Was she nice?"

"She was perfect," she said, then she walked over to him and pulled his forehead to her lips. "The best grandmother ever."

"Was your mother like her?"

"No, sweetie."

She held up both scarves for him to choose. He would have liked to have a grandmother. "The green one," he said.

"My mother was not like Grandma June at all. I wish she had been, but that's life." She took his hand and they went downstairs. "You know how we were talking about my mother's funeral next week and what will happen there?" He nodded. "Well, I was thinking that going to tea today might be something special that you and I could do to remember my mother, something for — what was it you called it? Her atma?"

He didn't know if it worked that way, or if there was a priest they could ask, but he nodded. Maybe the priests here knew different ways of achieving the same results. And he was happy to do whatever Mama Maddy thought might help, like seeing the garden and eating little sweets and sandwiches so she could remember. He pulled her purse from where it hung on the hook below the mirror at the base of the stairs.

"Here you go."

"Thanks, sweetie," she said and followed him out of the house.

"Did your mother take you to high tea when you were a girl?" he asked.

"Actually," Mama Maddy said, waiting for him to buckle his seat belt, "the three of us went together once — my mother, Grandma June, and me. It's one of my favorite memories. I was obsessed with this little doll in a white dress, and I insisted that she come along. And that we dress identically."

She shook her head and laughed a little. Then she changed the radio to her grandmother's favorite station. He tried to think of more questions, but she'd gone quiet, listening to the music, as though she were far away. They turned in a new direction once they hit the main road, so he watched the unfamiliar landscape as it passed by. A woman began to sing. It was in a foreign language, but not French. At first the song sounded dark and scary, and then it was just very sad. It filled the car completely, and he felt even stranger than he had before listening to the music. So lonely. They passed over a bridge, and the sun was bright on his face for a moment, then it hid behind the hill. When the song was over, the announcer said the title translated as "You Are with Me," and this surprised Birendra, for he'd never heard a lonelier-sounding song.

The bridge led to a town called Pasadena. Mama Maddy said they were getting close now. The houses were enormous, much bigger than Mama Maddy's, more like the one she was working on in Los Feliz. They'd driven by it once, and she'd pointed it out and said a very famous singer was going to live there. He wondered if famous people lived in these houses as well. And then the houses were gone and they drove into a tree-shaded parking lot. The air outside was fresh, and there was a cool breeze. He could hear the tweeting sounds of excited birds, and he caught sight of a squirrel, staring back at him through a pair of scared black eyes. He listened for crows, remembering how they squawked constantly in India. In Los Angeles, he often saw them, but only one or two at a time, nothing like what he saw in Varkala, where they swarmed, sometimes so numerous they made the sky go black. Mama Maddy joined him and looked up into the trees as well. It was often the absence of crows, whenever he was somewhere like this, with a lot of trees around, that made him remember the crows in India. And he couldn't remember the crows without thinking a little of his mother as well. He wondered what it was that made Mama Maddy think of her mother. He would ask her. He took her hand and they walked toward the entrance. Maybe it *would* help to remember her mother in this special place.

XXIII

How long had Nayana been staring at the dust ball in the corner? She looked away only to find there were others. She'd been struggling all week to work, though what she wanted most was to pass the time before her appointment with Dr. Shah tomorrow. She might as well have spent it cleaning for all the progress she made on the book. She stood and collected the dust balls, then shook out the rug and fetched the broom and dustpan. She did the same in the hallway, in their bedroom, in Ramesh's nook. She moved the coffee table. The kitchen chairs. The waste bins. It had not been a particularly good morning. She was almost used to the nausea and heartburn, but she'd been faint as well. Now she was all energy. She shook and swept until she had gone through the whole house, and everywhere she looked the dancing motes slowly fell right back into place. She removed the mop from its bucket, then filled it with hot water and ammonia. She gagged on the harsh sting of steamy chemicals, then added dish soap to mask the scent. While the dust settled, she went into the bathroom and scrubbed the sink, the bathtub, and the toilet. Everywhere she looked, she saw dirt. She felt trapped. In her flat, in London, in her marriage. But mostly in her body.

She was always tired. And after all these years, she had discovered that even Ramesh's patience had limits. She'd worn him down, and he'd all but agreed to let her go to India. She'd called the airline and found a flight. She'd almost purchased the ticket. But her doctor had ordered an ultrasound, and, with India in the balance, the uncertainty was driving Nayana to distraction. She'd been taking it out on poor Ramesh, hot then cold, wanting his help, then biting his head off for coming too close. She was mopping the hallway when she heard the front door open. He was home early, and she couldn't even be sure if she was relieved or annoyed, if she wanted to be held or tell him to turn around and go.

"It's wet," she called, keeping her eyes on the tile. She cleaned one thing only to find grime and grit clinging to another. How had they stood it so long? "This place was filthy."

Ramesh didn't say a word. He was taking his socks off at the door with one hand when she looked up. In the other, he held a bottle of wine. He appeared hurt, as though she had been accusing him of dirtying the place by himself. Or maybe he was frightened by her appearance. She leaned the mop against the wall and collected her hair into a neater, tighter bun, then wiped the sheen of sweat from her face.

"It's from Beth," he said, holding the bottle up. "A thank you for watching Felix. There's a card."

"It's all yours," she said with a weak smile. "You earned every drop." Then, hoping to put him more at ease, she added, "Sorry I'm such a poor housekeeper."

He set the wine down and retrieved the mop.

"*Jaanu,* what are you doing? You should be resting."

"I can't just sit around all day."

He took the mop and bucket into the kitchen and left her standing in the hall. She must have looked like a madwoman. She was buzzing from her cleaning spree, as though she'd drunk a pot of coffee by herself. He didn't look at her as he passed by in the hallway again, pulling his tie loose on the way to their bedroom. If he was going to pout, she was going to close herself in her office. She stopped the door from slamming, then nearly collapsed in her seat. A few minutes passed, and he knocked and opened the door. She might have fallen asleep like that, with her head on her desk. He had once again set his frustration aside and was trying to care for her. Would she like a bath drawn? No. Maybe some tea? No. He was at a loss. What could he do to make her comfortable? Happy? Nothing. Wounded, he left the way he had come. There, she thought. Now everyone I love is disappointed in me.

She'd been making herself sick all week, trying to serve a twofold purpose with one visit: the purpose Ramesh knew about — the ultrasound, which her doctor assured her would have been routine regardless of her intended travels — and the one he didn't know about, the paternity test, for which Nayana planned to sequester a few strands of his hair from his side of the bed.

She was sick of herself, and now she got up to check on him. He had retreated to his chair, as she knew he would. She would do something nice for him. Rub his shoulders. Cook something extravagant. She had to keep in mind that he was just trying to care for her. He would find a way to blame himself if anything happened. She told him she'd invited her sister-in-law to accompany her to her doctor's appointment, thinking it would ease Ramesh's concern as well as ensure he would not insist upon coming. She knew Tahira would sit politely outside in the waiting room rather than join her in the examining room, as Ramesh surely would have.

"So we'll tell them?" he said.

"Of course, dear," she said, to appease him. Her preference was not to tell anyone in London for a while yet. She simply wanted to be on a plane, leaving. Ramesh could have the pleasure and pride in telling them after she'd gone. Or they could call and make the announcement together if he wouldn't wait. Anything to avoid feeling like a brood mare paraded around for her mother-in-law's benefit. She retrieved the bottle of wine and placed it on the table in front of him. Ramesh would be missing having the flat downstairs to escape to. Had he kept something to drink at Beth's for those visits?

"Why don't you open up Beth's wine and pour yourself a glass? I'll be back in a few minutes, and we'll have something nice for dinner."

Fifteen minutes later, smoked salmon, lemon, and parsley in hand, Nayana returned from the store to find Ramesh snoozing before an unopened bottle. She put it on the dining table, along with the candles, and went to the kitchen, resisting the urge to fall asleep beside him. She began cooking before she knew what she was making. She ended up with several sides and no main course: peppers seared black, steamed asparagus, smoked salmon with the lemon and parsley as a garnish. He awoke when she turned off the light and was impressed by the candles she'd lit. She poured him a glass of wine. The smell of the alcohol turned her stomach, and she suddenly wasn't sure she'd be able to eat the salmon at all. She was sweating again, and her back ached. She sat down and called him to join her. He leaned across the table to kiss her cheek before taking a seat. He lingered a moment, whispering his thanks in her ear. She told herself she was just tired. There was nothing to worry about and no need to worry Ramesh. He served himself, and they spoke about his work. He seemed not to remember when she repeated a question she'd asked just the day before, about Raj's progress. He was silent for a moment, then said he'd mentioned to his boss the need to schedule a trip to India. The hesitant way he spoke made her think he hadn't planned on telling her.

"Just in case you get the all-clear, I wanted to plant the seed. It's as I expected — mid-February at the earliest."

"That's wonderful. It's only a few weeks away, and I'll have Adi to care for me until you arrive."

"I wish you'd wait." He shook his head at the pepper dangling from his pinched fingers, then ate it in one bite. "Mum will think it's foolish, of course. And a waste of money."

"What she'll think is that I'm trying to steal her son and take him back to India without her." He smiled because he knew she was right. "She thinks I've sullied her golden first-born boy."

"Am I sullied, my love?" She was relieved to see him acting playful again. "I think I have the perfect solution, actually."

He raised a mischievous eyebrow. Nayana shot him a skeptical glance as she rose from the table to get some water. She was suddenly parched, but standing had made the room spin and go dark. She put a hand on Ramesh to steady herself, but he just thought she was being sweet and squeezed it.

"Let's ask Mum to organize a baby shower for when we're back. She will be so pleased to plan the party that she won't be thinking about your trip at all or about the fact that I'll be joining you."

Her balance was back, but she remained at his side. He was right: his mother would be thrilled to have Nayana out of the way while making all the arrangements. Ramesh was too generous, assuming his mother would relish the opportunity to plan this for him and Nayana. She would be planning it for *herself*. Her friends, her menu, her grandchild! Nayana reached for the chair now. Ramesh's voice came through as though under water. The room was spinning again.

"Naya? What's wrong? You've gone pale." She pulled the chair toward her.

"It's a brilliant idea, Ram," she said, and, trying to wave his concern away, she released her hold on him. Then he stood up, or maybe it was that she fell down.

Nayana felt she'd been reduced to a pair of eyes, eyes that rejected the light cast by the bedside lamp, light that failed to illuminate the familiar molding of her bedroom ceiling. How and when had she gotten there? And why couldn't she feel the collective entirety of her body? She tried to shift her head toward the light, but there was a disconnect between thinking the movement and the movement itself. Only her eyes were free to employ their limited range. There was a shadow just beyond her peripheral vision, someone walking there. She closed her eyes for a long second and felt her tear ducts at work, quenching the dryness. If only they could quench her terrible thirst. A steady buzz gave way to the muffled sounds of a voice. Ramesh. And then she remembered. When she opened her eyes again, her body had returned to her. And the room sounded louder than it had any right to. It was cold, too, but she was damp with perspiration. She wanted to know what Ramesh had been saying to her.

"What was that?" she asked.

But he hadn't been speaking to her. He was on the phone, repeating their address, with such urgency. She tried to push herself up, but she couldn't move through the pain, which sat on her midsection like a weight. She looked down and saw it in the dim light, a small, terrible stain, a black hole collapsing.

"Ram?"

"Nearly three months." He was still speaking on the phone. "I don't know. We were at dinner. She fainted. There's some blood."

His voice cracked. She closed her eyes again. He soon came to her with a damp towel, no longer on the phone. He pressed it against her forehead and whispered to her as the water trickled down to her temples.

"You're bleeding just a little, Naya. The ambulance is coming." He stroked her damp hair clumsily with his free hand. "It's going to be all right. You're going to be fine. We'll be fine, *jaanu*."

But his lips were pale, his eyes frightened, and his brow damp with fresh sweat. He began mumbling not to her but to himself, to the room, looking for some kind of answer there. Or just looking away from Nayana.

"Ram?" she said again, though there was no question.

She felt the tears falling. They were for him. She was awake, lucid. So this is my punishment, she thought. She seized his wrist and pulled him close.

"I'm sorry, *jaaneman.* I'm so sorry."

"It's going to be okay," he said. He held her face in his hands and repeated the promise, though neither of them believed it. At last she could no longer hide from him. She felt completely exposed, and what a weight lifted.

"I'm sorry," she said once again.

XXIV

It was an extravagance, perhaps, buying Bindi a suit when he would just grow out of it. But one never knew. After today's somber gathering, surely there was a gala on the horizon they might attend together, or a wedding — would Eddie and Jane ever get married? — or just a special occasion. There was always something to attend in this town, and now Madeline had a date to take with her. Bindi stood there patiently while she clipped his little paisley tie in place, glad to have had the foresight to realize she could not have properly knotted one herself. Besides, the suit just seemed right, a way of paying their respects to her mother, the Costumer. She twisted his cowlick and gave it a tug.

"You ready?"

He was. And so was Madeline, for the most part. Something about explaining the process to Bindi had grounded her. She was certainly less likely to have the emotional meltdown she'd been expecting. He'd been quiet all morning. She worried it was dredging up his own mother's death. And so she needed to be strong for him, which turned out to be a blessing. Wouldn't any freak-out she might have experienced be less about her mother's death and more about their shared past, or even just Madeline's harbored resentment? What good did it do to hold the dead hostage? In any case, a funeral wasn't the place for that. Therapy, perhaps, but today was about saying good-bye to the woman, good or bad, she'd called Mother.

It was a hazy and balmy winter morning in Los Angeles. Franklin Avenue was dark under the cover of tree shade. This was the route she took to Los Feliz as well, though that job, too, would soon come to an end. Just ahead, they would stop to pick up Eddie and Jane. Bindi had folded over the hem of his jacket and was making little circles on the silk lining with his thumb and forefinger.

"You doing okay?" He nodded. It was going to be a long day for all of them. She hated to put him through another funeral. Of course she'd given him the option not to come, but he said he wanted to be there. And thank goodness he was. "I'm glad you're with me."

He lifted his fingers from the coat and pointed. She'd nearly missed the turn to Eddie's place but was able to get over and make the light.

"Good save, Bindi. I don't know where my head is today."

Eddie came out alone, looking dapper in his suit and tie. His hair tidily brushed back so she could see his handsome face. Bindi moved to the back. Eddie told him he was looking sharp as he got in the passenger seat.

"Jane?" asked Madeline.

"She's not coming this morning, but she'll come this afternoon for the funeral. I'll tell you later." He fastened his seat belt and stared ahead. Madeline waited a moment, trying to gauge his mood. When he looked back at her, he softened at her concern. "She didn't want to come for the viewing anyway."

"I'm not sure *I* do. Does anyone?" She ran her fingers along the breast of his blazer. "How are you doing?"

He let out a sigh and gave a small shrug. He was distraught, of course, but did she really know how he was feeling? It seemed suddenly facile to think they were experiencing this day in the same way, despite having a mother in common, *their* mother in particular. She squeezed his hand.

"Next stop: Hollywood Forever," she said.

She scrunched her nose at her brother and her own inso-lence, and this, combined with the comment itself, made him smirk as he shook his head at her. She mouthed a silent apol-ogy, and hoped Bindi had remained oblivious to the whole exchange. It *was* a ridiculous name for a cemetery.

"Did you see our golden boy might be involved in a Real Estate scandal?"

"Clinton?" she asked. "He's not my golden boy. I voted for his wife."

"You and Jane both," he said and laughed. "Maybe me, too. She's certainly the sharp one. Actually, I think I wouldn't have cared who was running. I'm just so glad to have a Democrat in office again. It feels like an eternity since Carter." It did, she realized, but the greater relief was to have a First Lady in office who didn't just stand mute, *baking cookies*, behind her husband. "You doing all right back there?"

Bindi said he was fine again, but Madeline wondered. He kept saying so, but how could he be? Madeline checked out her brother's tie. It seemed to be in order and not a clip-on. They would have to ask him to teach them at some point.

The viewing room was empty, the lights respectfully dim. There were a half dozen chairs, presumably for those who wished to stay for a while. This was Madeline's first visit, and she had no desire to sit down. They had not even moved beyond the doorway.

"Is this your first time coming, too?"

"For the viewing, yes," he said.

Of course, he'd come to confirm the arrangements their mother had made long ago. Madeline could imagine her mother, perhaps at the height of her career, still too young to worry about dying but deciding anyway that she would be buried at the Hollywood Forever cemetery to guarantee good company in death. Like so much in this town, something commonplace — where else did we all have so much in common? — could garner endless cachet by attaching a glamorous name to it.

"Thanks for handling everything, Eddie. And the lawyers. I really appreciate it." She looked at Bindi, who was staring at the casket. "Bindi, sweetie, why don't you sit down for a minute? I need to talk to your uncle."

"Is he really doing okay with all this?" Eddie asked. "It must bring up so much for him."

"I know. I've been keeping a close eye on him. I'm just so sorry it's happening right before his party. I know how that sounds, but I've been planning it since I got back. I just don't want his day to fall in the shadow of this one and whatever else comes with it."

"No, I get it," he said. "The other day, after I got the call from Jack, you know what Bindi asked me?" Madeline shook her head. "If there was something wrong with her heart. It surprised me because it was so specific. Not simply, 'How did she die?' Or even, 'Did she have a heart attack?' But boy, did that question haunt me later. I thought, if that doesn't describe our mother better than any doctor or shrink ever could."

Madeline's first thought was malicious, but that just as quickly fell away. She had often wondered if their mother's heart had been broken before Eddie ever came along, before she was barely old enough to understand. Not exactly an excuse for a mother to abandon her children, emotionally if not physically, but it did explain a tiny piece of the mystery that had shrouded their icy, unfeeling, intoxicated mother.

"There wasn't so much money left," he said after a moment. "I assumed she'd leave it to Jack."

"Ugh, that man. I'm convinced he killed her." Eddie's eyes bulged, as though he'd just watched it happen. "I mean, by not getting her the care she needed."

"Well, the house was in her name, and he doesn't have access to her accounts now. She gave what was left to us." Madeline nodded, again not sure what to say. "You know, we didn't get her the care she needed, either."

There were so many ways to respond to this. Their mother had decided to move to Palm Desert with *that man*. She'd chosen *him* over them. When had she ever cared for them? She'd never lavished the care *a child* needed on her son or her daughter. But Madeline said none of this. What Eddie implied wasn't wrong, but it didn't mean this was their fault. It was complicated, as family often is.

"Is everything okay with Jane?"

"The short answer is no." He leaned in and whispered, "We broke up."

"Oh, my God, Eddie." Why was he smiling like that? Was he not devastated? "Are you okay?"

"It's definitely for the best."

They'd been together since so young an age. She had to admit she'd wished for this, but she had never considered that they might actually split up.

"When did it happen? Did she move out?" He shook his head. "Do you need a place to stay?"

"Thanks. We've actually been fine in the house together. Maybe we've both known this was coming for years. Anyway, this is just closure, I guess."

"I'm so sorry. It's terrible timing."

"Well, timing might have had something to do with it. You and Bindi, Mom's death. Life's too short and all that."

"Let me know if there's anything you need, anything I can do."

"You're busy, sis." He put a hand on her shoulder. "I know that."

"Hey, none of that. I'm not too busy for you."

"I appreciate that." He squeezed her shoulder, then hugged her close. "Actually, I'm planning a trip. Thanks to Mom."

Something about his embrace and their mother's body lying in the same room started to weird her out. She released herself and asked where he was going.

"London, as of now." He looked at Bindi, who had taken a seat close to the front of the room. "Hey, do you think anyone has come to see her?"

"Let's look at the guest book."

There were roughly a dozen names, most of them having come the first day. She knew her father's name wouldn't be there, but she looked all the same. She didn't even know if he was alive, though she assumed she would hear from his lawyer if he had died. This was the lawyer who had contacted Madeline when she was eighteen about a modest trust set up in her and her brother's name. Prior to that, she hadn't seen or heard from her father since Eddie was in utero. She'd used some of the money to relocate to New York for school. Even if she thought of her father, she saw the lawyer in her mind's eye. But Eddie had no image of their father at all to confuse him.

"Oh, no, Maddy, what's he doing?"

It hadn't immediately registered that her brother meant Bindi until she looked and found him standing before the open casket. She'd warned him it would be open, but she never thought he'd want to look inside. In fact, she'd told him it would be open on purpose, thinking he'd stay away. She only wanted to protect him from the sight of the dead body. She rushed to him but tried to appear calm when she reached his side.

"Bindi, sweetie, why didn't you wait for me? You didn't have to see this."

"I wanted to," he said. "The priest told me it's a sign of respect. I was too scared to look at my mother, even though I was supposed to."

Madeline looked down. Her mother's eyes were lined in the same smudgy black she'd been wearing since the sixties, her lips painted with a variation of the coral lipstick she so often used. But her face was utterly changed in death — quiet and restful, at peace. Seeing her mother like this, Madeline felt she finally had words to describe that same face in life: pained and hopeless, in misery. She wore an embroidered cloak, one of many she owned. It didn't matter if she was going to the grocery store or the Emmys, she never left the house without a damn cloak.

"It's not so scary," he said quietly. "I thought it would be."

He was right. It wasn't scary. It was something else, something she couldn't argue or find fault with, something final. A silent farewell, which — and now it seemed obvious — was the point of a viewing.

"No," she said. "You're right. Will you take my hand, sweetie? I'm ready to go now, if you are."

XXV

**bindi's birthday bash
bollywood goes hollywood**

The sign hung between the pair of jacarandas that flanked the lower part of his sister's driveway. Edward stopped his car in front of the valet service and studied its bright pastels, its Indian flourish. Maddy had clearly spared no expense for this party. She'd mentioned a theme but hadn't told him it would be an Indian theme. He reminded himself that she was a smart woman, an artistically talented woman, and she would exercise good judgment and taste. But then why was he suddenly so nervous? The couple ahead of him stepped out of their shiny black Mercedes, then locked arms under the sign, which clearly tickled them pink. They turned together to the next in line, Edward, in his aging, once silver, now gray Honda Civic, perhaps wanting to share in the sheer joy of it, the cleverness, but something about his car distracted them — or was that embarrassment for his sake? They looked away and carried on. He took a moment to consider the pulsing bass line he heard coming from the house. All this for a nine-year-old? It was already hopping and sounded more like a club on the Sunset Strip than a child's birthday party. Edward had arrived later than he'd wanted to. Jane and he were finally separating their lives on paper, and it had taken longer than expected. There was still more to do, but he didn't want to miss another minute of his nephew's birthday. She saw this and told him to go.

A week had passed since they'd all gathered for the funeral. Today they came together again to celebrate a young life, forging his way into the future, a life that had already known such hardship and loss. But Birendra was doing remarkably well, adjusting to his new life, and he brought so much to their own lives. They had a good deal to celebrate.

Edward reached for the present in the passenger seat. He had only wrapped volume 1 of the set. The rest, all twenty-one volumes, were in a box he could barely get to the car. He handed the valet five dollars and asked if he wouldn't mind carrying the box up the driveway and setting it next to the door. There Edward discovered a stunning young woman who greeted him from behind a kind of hostess stand with her hands together in prayer. He approached and said hello, feeling single, yes, for the first time ever. She was extraordinarily thin and very tall, wearing an intricately wrapped head scarf, black eyeliner thick and long, peacock-feather earrings, a purple glass-bead necklace wrapped around her neck in four loose loops, and a dazzling cluster of jewels that sparkled between her eyebrows. She looked like a younger, more exotic Barbara Eden, from *I Dream of Jeannie,* if she'd just stepped off a catwalk. She reached into the hostess stand to retrieve a slim stack of items.

"Your kurta and slippers," she said.

Edward was so distracted, first by this beautiful woman, then by the noise and movement down the hall, that he didn't immediately accept the items: a pair of pointy melon-colored slippers, intricately decorated with copper spirals and other beads, and a matching embroidered shirt, neatly folded to frame an ornate neckline. What an interesting party gift, he thought. On his way to the guest room, a flash of teal caught his eye as a man walked past him on his way to the bathroom. He was wearing the same long, collarless shirt in a different shade. It fell to mid-thigh on him, over his jeans, and his matching slippers made a light tapping sound on the blond wood floors, a kind of emphasis of joy and acceptance. There was a shoe rack he'd never seen in the hall. It was half full. Edward suppressed a groan, realizing he was going to have to put these things on. Hollywood, he reminded himself. Go with it. Make-believe. Jane would never have approved of any of this.

He followed the man down the hall, stopping at the guest room, where he'd slept on Christmas Eve. He closed the door and changed into the shirt and slippers, then stared at his colorful reflection. He looked ridiculous and almost forgot the present as he left the room. Tap. Tap. His footwear sang and sparkled below.

Maddy's living room, normally so precisely appointed, had been cleared of all furniture. The ceiling was draped with long, billowing sheets of satin in the same pastel shades as the men's kurtas. At the front of the room, a woman wearing a kind of half saree, half aerobics outfit that artfully exposed her midsection was counting down from five into a headset. She held one hand on her hip while the other twirled toward the ceiling. Several women guests, all white and all dressed in sarees, stood behind her and tried to follow but were mostly preoccupied with keeping their own wraps from unraveling. The music came from a DJ station that had been installed beside the sliding doors that led to the backyard, where he hoped to find his nephew.

A man in a turban passed with a tray of colorful cocktails. Edward chose the orange one and took a large gulp. It was sweet with the slight bite of vodka. He turned and almost fell over; there was a painted elephant walking his way. When he was certain he was not hallucinating — surely it was something mechanical — he moved closer. The elephant was flesh and blood and walking right in front of him on a path flanked by two parallel plastic rails that formed a guided track. The elephant was only slightly taller than Edward, and its rotund body was covered with floral motifs that had been drawn in pastel chalks. The chalk was wet and muted at the elephant's center, where the man riding it had spilled his drink. An elephant, no less! And Edward himself stood there in a kurta and pointy bejeweled slippers. He looked around at the other costumed men, like pastel eggs scattered about the yard at Easter. By the pool, he found a fair amount of glistening skin. Finally, in the water, he saw some children his nephew's age, but Birendra was not among them. There was a young man in a turban handing a drink to a woman who looked an awful lot like Pamela Anderson hiding behind a pair of oversize sunglasses. And a second woman, dressed in a saree, was seated at the other end of the busty blonde's lounge chair, applying a henna tattoo to the tops of her sun-kissed feet. Edward had to hand it to Maddy. She had created another world for anyone willing to enter. But where was *she* in all this? And the birthday boy? He spun in a circle but couldn't find either of them — or anyone he knew, actually. He took another turn, this time looking for anything that would indicate he was at a nine-year-old's birthday party: a cake, a stack of presents, other nine-year-olds. One of the men in a turban walked up to him with a tray of bite-size samosas. When he got closer, Edward saw he was not Indian and accepted the snack, much relieved that his sister hadn't felt the need to complete the aesthetic on that front. A second server appeared in his field of vision, carrying delicate wafers of papadum topped with a red mousse. Edward took two, suddenly aware of his hunger. As the server left him, Edward did a double take, then looked around the yard at the other men with trays, all of them in turbans, all of them Hispanic.

Behind the pool area, a decorative gazebo came into view. It was designed, it seemed, as an homage in miniature to the Taj Mahal. He'd noticed only the colorful sheer drapes before, but now he saw beyond them to the place where two ornate thrones were perched, along with Maddy and Birendra. At their feet were several floor pillows in vibrant pinks and blues, and there was a pile of presents to one side. From this distance his sister looked like a madam running a harem. Birendra was in a turban, though his was not white like those of the servers; it was purple and gold, with a peacock feather at its center. Edward finished his drink and grabbed another on his way over, passing an area on the grass to his right that had been sectioned off by a knee-high picket fence. A few babies and toddlers played inside under the supervision of yet another costumed woman, hired for the occasion. A second sign read:

baby bollywood

Edward froze on the first step of the gazebo. Maddy was silently communicating a greeting to someone on the other side, through the drapes, with her glass raised high in the air, a rock-and-roll curl of the lip, and the kick of a sequined platform shoe. Jane would have died at the sight. Edward was doing his best to reserve judgment. He caught Birendra's eye over Maddy's raised foot and searched the boy's face for an indication of how he might be reacting to his own party. He lit up when he saw Edward and slid off of his throne. Maddy caught him by the shoulder, pulled him close, and whispered into his ear. Over his nephew's head, Edward could only make out Maddy's eyes, which seemed to be glowering at him. Maybe it was just the makeup. When she released Birendra, Edward could see she was smiling at him, but it was not a smile that made him any more at ease. She was drunk. He stepped up and through the gap in the hanging fabrics, entering their chambers.

"Hi, Uncle Eddie!"

Edward got down on one knee to admire the fake sword attached to Birendra's side. Then he handed Birendra his present, the heavy book sinking nearly to the ground in his hands before he adjusted for its unexpected weight.

"Who are you supposed to be?" asked Edward.

"I'm a Sikh warrior," he said, ripping open the wrapping paper.

"It's twenty-two volumes. The rest are inside."

Birendra looked as though Edward had just handed him a puppy. He held the book up for Maddy to see, but she was still talking to her friend.

"This is so awesome, Uncle Eddie," he said, then set the book down so he could hug Edward.

Trying to ignore the Indian garb, Edward sensed how much Birendra had already changed from the boy he'd met just over a month ago. Hearing him say "awesome," with hardly a detectable accent, with mannerisms so sure and at ease — it was all evidence of a transformation. How quickly children adapt to their surroundings, he thought. He supposed this happened whether the surroundings were good or bad. But what did it mean to respect an adopted child's cultural heritage while at the same time ensuring that he was adjusting to his new environment, comfortable in his new life? It seemed somehow impossible to achieve both. The answer was certainly not an Indian Jane Fonda, an elephant, and *Bollywood goes Hollywood*. Surely Maddy knew that. But then this was not really his nephew's party in the end. As much as he loved her, Edward knew his sister well enough, her insecurity, her need for attention. Traits she'd fought against but that she'd learned at their mother's knee and that she'd never entirely eradicated. As he took in the "Taj Mahal" and its thrones, his nephew's costume, her own, he had to admit:

this was a party Maddy had thrown for herself. To show off the beautiful boy she'd "rescued."

"Are you having fun, B?" He was admiring his book again. "Careful — there's a little money in the front."

Maddy's cackle drew their attention in her direction. Her head was thrown back again, and the beads and jewels of her headdress flashed around her in the soft light that filtered through the sheer fabric walls of her palace. She said good-bye to her friend and turned her attention to Edward and Birendra.

"Hey, Maddy," he said.

Her eyes were outlined in thick kohl and swimming under the weight of her false lashes. An ornate composite of jewels, just like the ones her greeter wore, flickered between her eyebrows. She composed herself like a queen addressing her subject.

"Come to pay tribute, dear brother?" Then, animated with the wave of a silk-draped arm, but otherwise more or less herself again, she said, "Did you see my elephant?"

"I did. Amazing. Truly. You've outdone yourself." She nodded in agreement. He turned to his nephew. "Why don't you show me around, B?"

It was the second time he'd called Birendra B in a matter of minutes. It had not been intentional, but suddenly the nickname, a term of both familiarity and affection, felt just right, and it struck Edward that using it held the additional benefit of not contradicting his sister by calling him Birendra in front of her.

"Do you remember *your* ninth birthday, Eddie?"

Her excited tone and reference to his youth made him feel

like her kid brother again. He softened a little. This was his sister, even under all the garish makeup, the garish costume, the drunken gestures — the elephant! — and he tried to put aside his thoughts of the self-centeredness that lurked just beneath the surface of his sister's generosity. She might have meant to say his eighth birthday, the last they'd actually spent together. But now she'd brought his ninth birthday to mind.

"I do. You called to wish me a happy birthday from New York," he said. "Mom was off wherever she went those days. I was so happy to hear from you."

The look of confusion on her face stopped him from wanting to needle her further. She'd obviously meant his earlier birthday, which they celebrated together in his bedroom.

"Do you maybe mean my *eighth* birthday?" he asked. "When you brought me a tray of eight Hostess cupcakes you'd bought with your allowance, each with its own candle, and sang 'Happy Birthday' all the way from the kitchen?" He could tell by her smile they were now sharing the same memory. "That was really sweet of you, Maddy. In fact, on my ninth birthday, before I went to bed, I put a candle in a Hostess cupcake and wished that I could join you in New York."

Something cool pressed against his neck. Birendra had stepped forward from his throne and extended his sword. Edward had learned that the name Birendra in Sanskrit means "great warrior." Had this informed his costume? Had Birendra told Maddy the meaning of his real name? Edward just hoped that it didn't signify a lifetime of battles awaiting him.

"Yield," the boy gleefully commanded.

"I yield, great warrior. I yield."

The pride in his expression moved Edward.

"Do you want to see the elephant I painted?"

"Absolutely. Let's go."

Edward took his nephew's hand. Maddy looked sorry to see them leave. As if she didn't know what to do with herself. These past weeks, he'd felt close to her in a way he hadn't in years. He'd long since thought of his sister and himself as casualties of the same war. The battlefield: the home of an emotionally unpredictable mother. This had created its own Cold War between them as adults. Maddy went away to school, and by the time she returned Edward was already gone to college. And he was with Jane. They both had their own lives, perhaps maintaining a safe distance from each other to keep their shared past at bay. He'd watched her become the woman she was today, trying to judge her as little as possible. But he would have to talk to her. He wasn't sure exactly what needed to be said, but he had to warn her not to screw everything up, as their mother had. It was time to put the past behind them for the future who was right beside him.

X X V I

Birendra could hear they were still arguing when he finished brushing his teeth. He went to the top of the stairs, but he didn't want to be caught listening, so he went to his room and changed into his pajamas and set aside the book he was going to read to Uncle Eddie. Still no one had come up. He peeked his head out of his room, then returned to the top of the stairs and listened. Now he could hear Uncle Eddie talking. He was asking Mama Maddy to do something, or maybe to not do something. "It's his birthday," he said. They were arguing about him. But why? What had he done? Mama Maddy had already been acting strangely, and now she sounded angry. "Is it so much to ask? One night? I haven't seen anyone in months. They've offered to take me out." It sounded like they were in her office. It grew quiet. He slipped down to the next step. Mama Maddy was saying something, but she was no longer raising her voice. Birendra closed his eyes and listened harder. She said she'd be back tomorrow. He wondered where she was going.

He heard footsteps approaching and almost tripped up the stairs but caught the banister in time. He hurried to his room and got under the covers. He couldn't stop feeling like he'd done something wrong. He turned on his bedside lamp. The book he'd checked out discussed southern India. When he found it at the library he'd thought of Uncle Eddie, who so often asked questions about Birendra's life before. He knew he wasn't supposed to talk about it, but he thought reading this book would be okay.

Uncle Eddie turned off the overhead light and came closer. He was smiling down at Birendra.

"Are you too tired? We can read some tomorrow if you are."

"No," he said. And scooted himself over. "I'm not tired."

Uncle Eddie picked up the book on the bedside table.

"Is this what you want to read?"

"Yeah. I got it for you."

"For me? Why for me?"

"I don't know. I thought you would like it."

Uncle Eddie opened it to the title page.

"And I do," he said. "That was very thoughtful of you. It's about your home."

He nodded. The front door closed downstairs, and he felt Uncle Eddie stiffen.

"Where's Mama Maddy going?"

"Oh, she's just going out with some friends. She feels like dancing." He was smiling now, but his mouth was pinched. "You're stuck with me tonight, all right?"

"I don't mind," he said and smiled at his uncle.

He scooched up a little more and took the book from Uncle Eddie, opening to the beginning. He paused to see if his uncle was ready, then he began to read:

Siva is one of the most important gods in Hinduism, the main religion of South India. Known also as Lord of the Dance, or Nataraja, this powerful god governs the universe by dancing and endlessly repeating the cycle of destruction and rebirth.

Uncle Eddie placed a finger on the opposite page to study the pictures of Siva.

"So this is one of the many gods?" He pointed to a painting of Siva, blue and dancing in the flames. "You know, you're a very good reader, Birendra. It's amazing how quickly you're losing your accent," he said. "Not that it's a bad thing to have one. It's not. But your English is so fluid now. They say it's much easier to learn languages when you're young. Of course, it must have helped you to have an aunt in London."

Bindi recalled how he and Aunt Nayana used to speak in English on the phone, usually to discuss whatever note or drawing he'd recently sent. Sometimes they talked about school. He remembered what his mother had said about his aunt and uncle when he was writing his report. They were *generous*.

"Yes," he said. "They paid for private school for me, and we spoke in English there."

"What? Who paid for private school?"

He repeated himself, then shifted to look at his uncle. His eyes were big, and he looked really confused. Birendra regretted talking about his aunt now. Maybe the book hadn't been a good idea. He'd only told the truth. And if he wasn't supposed to say anything, why did adults ask him questions in the first place?

"Were you and Mama Maddy fighting?"

Uncle Eddie took the book and set it on the nightstand. He pulled the covers up to Birendra's chin and smiled at him.

"No, not really. We just have different opinions sometimes. It's normal. Don't worry — we'll work it out."

After Uncle Eddie kissed his forehead, turned off the light, and left the room, Birendra pulled down Ganesh from his shelf, which he hadn't done since his first nights in America. He felt comforted holding it again and forgot about the angry voices he'd heard as he drifted off to sleep.

In the morning, Uncle Eddie made them scrambled eggs and toast for breakfast. Then they set up the Sega Genesis and played the game, but neither of them was very good. It was sunny and already warm outside, so they decided to swim. Uncle Eddie taught him a fun game called Marco Polo. After a few rounds, they each got on an inflatable bed and floated around the pool. Occasionally they bumped into each other, laughed, then floated apart again. The sun felt good. Uncle Eddie fell asleep for a bit and was worried when he woke up about getting a sunburn, so they went inside and decided to go see the movie that Uncle Eddie had worked on, the one about the dogs.

They tried calling the number for the little black phone Mama Maddy carried in her purse to tell her about the movie, but it was turned off, Uncle Eddie explained, and he left a not-so-nice message. He wore the same frustrated expression he'd had the night before.

"What's the point of carrying the stupid thing around if it's not on?"

They took Mama Maddy's car to the movies. Uncle Eddie checked Birendra's seat belt at a stoplight, even though they'd already been driving for a while. "You said your parents met in the north, right? In Delhi? And then they later moved to Kerala?"

"Yes. I was born in Trivandrum."

"That's in the south, right?"

"Yes."

He was getting nervous again and wished Uncle Eddie would stop asking so many questions.

"I'm sorry. It seems like you might not want to talk about it. I don't mean to push you."

He was torn. Of course he didn't mind talking about his mother and father and his life in India. He *liked* it. But Mr. Channar had said he wasn't supposed to.

"I just don't want to get in trouble."

"Birendra, why would you get in trouble?" He looked surprised that Birendra had thought he might. "I want you to be able to share anything with me, remember. Where you came from, what your life was like there. It's all part of you, and I'd love to learn about it."

"If I tell you, will you promise not to tell Mama Maddy?"

After a pause, when he was sure he'd seen his uncle's grip tighten on the steering wheel, Uncle Eddie said, "Can I ask why? Did Mama Maddy say something to you to make you think she didn't want you to talk about certain things?"

"No, she didn't," he replied. "Mr. Channar said that it would make her upset if I talked about it."

"I'm sorry — who's that? Mr...."

"Mr. Channar. Mr. Nair's cousin, at the orphanage."

"I see. And Mr. Nair is your uncle is London."

"No. He was my neighbor in Varkala."

"Ah, okay. And what is your uncle's last name?"

He could see it on the envelope, then it was gone.

"It starts with a *B*," he said. Why couldn't he remember? He could see the stamps and parts of the address in his mother's handwriting on the envelopes he used to bring to the post office in Varkala. And then he remembered his letter, the one he wrote with Mrs. Nair. And now he saw the name he had written. "I remember. It's Bhatia."

Uncle Eddie had him spell it, then asked his uncle's first name and why Birendra thought Mr. Channar told him not to speak of India. Birendra shrugged, afraid to say anything more but also realizing he'd never understood the reason himself, only that it might make him an orphan again.

"Well, I'm pretty sure, Birendra, that Mama Maddy wants you to be comfortable telling her anything as well. She was always a good listener when I was young. Did you know she's nine years older than I am? She took care of me when I was little." Uncle Eddie parked and turned off the car. "You know something, B? Adults aren't always right. Remember that, okay? Sometimes only you can know what's best for you. You know what I mean?"

Birendra had never imagined overruling an adult before, and he was grateful to his uncle for trying to help him understand. Mr. Channar had thought he'd known what was best for Birendra. But maybe he'd been mistaken.

They stopped at the pay phone outside the movie theater and called Mama Maddy again. Uncle Eddie hung up and swore when the phone took his quarter, then he apologized for swearing.

"It's okay. Mama Maddy says that all the time."

"Well, she shouldn't."

He tried calling her at home, but no one answered there, either.

"Is she okay?" Birendra asked, feeling his uncle's anxiety infecting his own.

"Of course she is. I just thought I'd catch her before the movie." He was talking the way adults do when they don't want you to worry or know the truth. "I'm sure she'll be home soon enough, B."

XXVII

If their previous losses had weakened the foundation of their marriage, this recent scare was a wrecking ball. Nayana had not lost the baby, but she hadn't come away unscathed. Its survival had a cost she was only beginning to make sense of in the days since leaving the hospital. There was too much relying on the fetus she carried, an insufficient mass to hold her there, on the ground, in her marriage, in England. She had simply been dehydrated and overly stressed; she'd worn herself out, according to Dr. Shah, and that, combined with natural changes in the cervix, caused an unfortunate confluence of events. Her doctor had been trying to reassure Nayana, but that wasn't possible. Nayana remained terrified, and Dr. Shah would only understand the reason when Nayana returned to request a paternity test.

In the meantime, she was moving forward with her plan. She would still go to India. No, it wasn't advisable, said Dr. Shah, but that was mostly because of Nayana's mental state; if she took care not to overexert herself, and to hydrate, she'd likely be just fine. The truth was Nayana couldn't rest in London. She couldn't rest in Ramesh's presence. In the presence of so much guilt and uncertainty. The results of the test would arrive soon enough and when they did he would understand why she'd left. Only then would he be in possession of all the facts. Only then could he determine whether he wanted her back at all. It was cowardly and one more reason to despise her own weakness in the face of someone so good. Her only justification was that he deserved the truth, except the words wouldn't come from her mouth, and she didn't trust herself to leave if they did; he would never let her, even if it broke his heart. And this, above all, she could not bear to witness.

Poor Ramesh tried to care for her in this state, but he was at a complete loss as to why it felt like they were mourning when there had been no miscarriage. He was the one averting his eyes now; Nayana was watching *him*. Really seeing him gave her the will she needed. She wanted to recover, if only to find the strength to set him free. But this is what scared her: being without him. Not just feeling alone but also being alone. And so she had forced herself to see Ramesh's suffering, to privilege it over her own. The best reason to leave him was also the most painful. It was his being there in front of her, day after day, wondering why they weren't quietly celebrating instead. This is what I can do for him, she thought. This is what I must do.

He was in the kitchen again. She heard cupboard doors open and close. What was he doing for her now? There was the sound of metal scraping against the iron burner grate, the ticking as he lit the range. His footsteps were quiet in the hallway as he approached. He stopped at their bedroom doorway. She felt him watching her from a distance. She pretended to sleep, on their new sheets. When she and Aditi were girls, they would pretend to sleep in an effort to put their telepathy to the test, but each always knew when the other was faking. If Ramesh knew, he didn't say. He retreated just as silently only to return a few minutes later, quietly saying her name. Like a question. As if he were asking the woman in his bed — *excuse me, miss* — if she had seen Nayana, his wife. He carried with him a tray of food.

"Please, *jaanu*, will you eat something?"

The pitch of his voice betrayed how desperate he'd grown. Maybe she was wrong. Maybe it was crueler to deny him the emotional support he needed now, regardless of what happened later. But she worried this would make her too weak, too dependent on him to finally walk out the door, which she honestly believed was the greatest kindness she could offer him. She could no longer see a way to happiness in their life together, not until he knew and perhaps not even then. She could eat. That was something she could do. Put his mind at rest, if only about her physical state.

She took the tray from him. It was plain broth and buttered toast again. She didn't want a sick person's food anymore. She wanted a rich and creamy fettuccine Alfredo from the Italian restaurant she loved. Perhaps it was what they both needed, to get out of the house. She could admit to him in that place of happy memories that she would still leave for India. He would be distraught, of course, terrified something would happen to the baby. Angry, perhaps, that she would even consider the risk. But she had no choice.

The phone rang, and Nayana felt a momentary spark. The broth swirled in its bowl. Was it a call from her sister? Aditi would have received her letter by now. Maybe even have had the phone installed. She'd be wondering when Nayana was coming. What day was it, anyway? Was it a Saturday? No, Ramesh was still in his work trousers. It was probably just Tahira checking in again. Besides, if Aditi had a phone installed, it would no longer matter what day it was.

She ate a piece of toast and sipped on the broth. She felt like having a cup of tea. She felt like going for a run in the park. She wanted to keep running and never look back. She lifted the bowl and drained its contents in two big gulps. She could hear Ramesh saying good-bye. It wasn't Aditi. In the room again, he couldn't hide his surprise that she'd eaten so much and so quickly. He even smiled, and she realized how long it had been, how unfair she'd been to keep him from smiling his handsome smile.

"Who was it?" she asked, though she didn't much care.

"It was Beth."

"Is she pawning off Felix again?"

"No," he said with a laugh. He'd like that, she thought. Perhaps he'd get a cat if she stayed gone. "Apparently she moved to Edinburgh. I take it you didn't know, either."

"No, I didn't. I mean, she left that bottle of wine, but you said it was just a thank you for cat sitting."

Ramesh removed the tray from Nayana's lap.

"She says she's found a letter from India. It got mixed up in her held mail while she was away."

"And she's just calling now?"

"She was apologetic. Extremely, in fact. She said with the holiday and moving, she'd only just found the time to sort through it all; she called as soon as she found it."

It was a relief of sorts to know Nayana had been wrong, that Aditi hadn't given up on her as she had supposed. That December's letter had just not found its way.

"So will she send it?"

"Yes. She promised she would drop it in the post first chance."

Nayana suddenly feared the letter would contain Aditi's decision to finally join them in London. Now, when things here were so precarious for Nayana. Once again, she would disappoint. Perhaps they could take Birendra to Delhi instead, return to their childhood home. Nayana could teach there, surely. At the graduate level, even. She pushed the sheets away, not wanting to be in the same room as Ramesh while imagining a future without him. He moved to help her when he saw she was getting up.

"No!" she shouted, louder than she'd meant to. He backed away from the bed. "I can do it," she said, calmly now. "Thank you, Ram. Thank you, but I can manage."

She walked to the bathroom and closed the door behind her. She was pale and gaunt. She'd paid a debt, anyway. A debt of beauty. The prematurely gray strands that she'd once thought highlighted her youth appeared dull to her now, foreshadowing instead her transition to middle age. She thought of the moment when she would see her sister again, how youth and beauty would have been preserved in Aditi alone. That was how Nayana had always known she was beautiful — because she looked like Aditi. She sat down on the edge of the tub and closed her eyes. She was ready to hear her sister's voice again. Ready to let it guide her. Maybe Aditi wasn't wanting to come to London. Maybe she was

saying: *Come home; I will save you. Come home; I need saving, too.*
In any case, it hadn't been the last letter in the end. How stupid Nayana had been to think Aditi would give up on her so
easily. She could hear it now, not in words but in the silence,
a repeated invitation, a song: Aditi calling Nayana home.

XXVIII

Madeline pulled into the pickup zone at Bindi's school, lining up with the other mothers and fathers — mostly mothers — and she marveled at the fact of being one of these parents picking up their children. Since she and Bindi hadn't had his first eight years together, it wasn't something she took for granted. It took these moments. His arms were full of books again, forcing him to waddle down the main steps. Between his schoolwork, the books he checked out from the library, and the damned encyclopedia set Eddie got him, she was lucky to ever find his head out of a book lately. There were worse problems, to be sure. Still, she worried. Kids could be cruel. He was already adopted from India. Could he afford to be a nerd as well? Maybe she should enroll him in a sport of some kind. Something that got him outdoors and active. He stopped at the base of the steps and was putting the books away. He must have noticed there was no taxi waiting in its usual spot. Madeline had sent Paige to meet potential clients, a commercial job she wasn't thrilled about. Madeline picking him up would be a surprise. When he heard her honking and saw her waving from the line of cars, his face lit up. She'd been waiting for that all afternoon, she realized. It was easy to doubt that she was doing a good job, doing right by him, especially after the tongue-lashing Eddie had given her the day after his party. She worried Bindi might not be happy, that he felt out of place in his new life. But the look on his face told her their connection was real and that she was clearly doing *something* right, at least some of the time.

Blondie's "Call Me" was playing on the radio. She turned it up and was already dancing in her seat. She had to shout over the music to be heard.

"What are you waiting for? Get in."

He struggled to hoist his bag into the back, then sank into his seat beside her.

"What have you got in that bag? A body?"

"No." He liked when she joked like this. "My *books*."

"Jeez Louise, did you already skip ahead to college?" He smiled. "Why are you out of breath?"

"I ran to the parking lot."

"Why were you running?"

"I didn't want to be late."

"Oh. Well, you made it!" she said and pinched his cheek, then pulled out of line.

She let Bindi put the top down when they stopped, then they zipped along Olympic. She heard Prince say "Dearly beloved" and turned the music up even louder, waving her hands at the open sky. Bindi loved it when she did her car dances and sang along to the radio. They stopped at the dry cleaner on Santa Monica, then she ducked into TCBY to pick up a frozen yogurt. He liked Oreo cookies and M&M's. She couldn't resist teasing him when he saw her holding it.

"Not so fast," she said, then tossed her dry cleaning in the backseat, next to his bag. In the driver's seat, she ate a spoonful and threw her head back as if it were the best thing ever. "Oh, you don't want this," she said, preparing to take another bite. "It's not very good."

"I do want it," he said.

"Are you sure? Wait." She hovered the spoon in front of her mouth. "Let me just make sure it's okay."

"It's okay!" he squealed, reaching out again. "Please — "

"Two bites is my limit anyway," she said and handed it over.

"Thank you," he said.

She started the car but didn't move. She turned down the radio and watched him eat.

"Is it good?"

"It's delicious."

"Good," she said and put the car in reverse. "You know what today is?"

"What?" he asked, chasing a blue M&M with his spoon.

"It's the day we celebrate! The lawyer called, and all the paperwork is done. It won't be long now, Mr. American."

He was trying to be excited, bless him, but she could see it wasn't quite computing. For him, it had all been sorted out back in India, no doubt, or perhaps upon arriving in California. For her, too.

The house was empty. And Paige wouldn't be back after her meeting. Madeline flipped through the mail and pulled out an envelope from Bindi's school. It was a letter from his principal, which shocked her but also — inappropriately, she realized — gave her a rush as she imagined Bindi misbehaving somehow. In fact, he was not in trouble. The letter was a reminder of a meeting that would be held in a week's time. It pointed out that parents were encouraged to attend in order to discuss suitable classroom reading materials regarding the subject of AIDS. Because of "the sensitive nature of the topic," the letter advised parents to consider making arrangements to attend the meeting without their children.

"Do you know anything about this, Bindi?" she asked.

"What is it?"

"A letter from your school." He shook his head. "Don't worry — you didn't do anything wrong. There's just a meeting for the parents. And a reminder about" — she read to the end and cleared her throat, hoping it might help her accent — "*les vacances de février*? You have another week off?" He shrugged. "A whole week? Okay, I guess I'll try to schedule work around it somehow. I don't know how people do it."

He stared at her a moment. When she saw he wanted to speak, she thought it might be to venture an answer, and she felt bad about it but also curious what he might come up with.

"May I make some rice?" he asked instead.

"You're hungry? Already?"

"No, I'm not."

She was confused, but decided not to probe. There was most likely a message in there she'd learn soon enough. It was often his way to be indirect. When he learned about Watts Towers, for instance. He'd wanted to go, but instead of just asking her to take him, he'd drawn her a picture and made her get it out of him. She'd finally had to sit him down and tell him it was okay to ask for things.

"I think there's some Uncle Ben's in the food drawer. Be

careful, and don't forget to turn off the stove when you're done."

"I won't."

As she read the letter again, the serious tone and subject matter hit Madeline. It would be her job to impart to this little person all the values she'd come to take for granted. The letter *was* serious. And this responsibility would require careful consideration. He was young and innocent, but what if he also came with preconceived notions from his own mother, or from his old school, or from India, for that matter? What if he'd been taught that AIDS was a punishment for homosexuality, as the idiot fanatics on the news said it was? How would she counter that? How could she tolerate it?

She should work a little before making dinner. But the house was quiet, aside from Bindi's rustlings in the kitchen. She moved to her chair in the sunroom. She would close her eyes, just for a bit.

The peel was lying on the counter, its brown spots spreading like a disease. She heard the front door close. Bindi was off for another day of school. Her eye moved now to the knife, still coated in peanut butter, the honey lid next to the jar. She ran to the front door, but the taxi had already left. She got in her car and chased after it. Up ahead, it pulled into the emergency lane at the hospital. A nurse had lifted Bindi from the taxi and was carrying him inside. Paige was crying hysterically, saying he couldn't breathe. Madeline followed the nurse into a hospital room. Her mother was lying on the bed in front of her, bloated and pale, asking for Madeline's help. The nurse took Madeline by the arm, guiding her deeper into the room. Her mother called after her again. Madeline pulled back the curtain. There he was. The skin of his skull had sunk and constricted around the dark circles that stained his eye sockets, like bruises, making his big brown eyes appear dim and small. The nurse was saying he'd gone into anaphylactic shock. Did he take any medicine that morning? Had he eaten something? Did he have allergies? She knew he did. So how did this happen? "Bananas," she said. The doctor and nurses struggled to revive him. Then she sat by his bed and watched his tiny body, already frail, dry up even more. She begged them to do something, anything. "Why is this happening? Why doesn't he improve?" But the doctor shook his head. Eddie shook his head. Even Paige — Simonetta had come, too — they were all shaking their heads at her. It was too late to do anything. Just like that, he was dying on a hospital bed right before her eyes. "But I won't forget ever again." She promised. She begged. They shook their heads. Then two more doctors entered. They spoke to Eddie, ignoring her. "The virus may have come from the mother," said one. "It's a miracle he lasted this long," added the second. And when she turned back to Bindi, she heard the steady beep, and she saw that life had already left his body behind. "It was your own damn fault." Who said that? She turned, but there was no one there. They'd all gone. The voice spoke again. "What were you thinking?" It was coming from the other bed. Madeline walked toward the voice as the beep grew steadily louder. She covered her ears, but it made no difference. She couldn't breathe. She awoke, gasping for air and still crying, half asleep. She sat up and listened for Bindi. Everything was quiet. The pot was there. The stove was off. The kitchen was empty. She tried to tell herself it was a dream, an awful dream, but it didn't help.

He was outside on the grass. He'd cut a leaf from the heliconia and placed it on the ground. She panicked. Was it in the same family as banana plants? The leaves were similar. She wanted to rush to him and make him wash his hands, but what was he doing? He placed a ball of rice onto the leaf, alongside two others, then stepped away. He clapped once. Then again. And a third time. It appeared to be a prayer or ritual of some sort, but she'd never seen him do this or anything like it before, and, after her dream, the sight disturbed her.

"Bindi, sweetie?" The sliding door stuck, and she left it open. "What are you doing?"

"Pind daan," he said, as if that meant anything. He seemed disappointed, his head hung low.

"I don't understand, Bindi. What does that mean?"

"I don't think it worked. I should have done it yesterday."

She approached and took his hand, leading him away from the leaf. They shared the center section of a chaise longue. She couldn't make sense of anything he'd said, and she questioned if she was still dreaming.

"What didn't work? What are you trying to do here? Help me understand."

"Yesterday was the sixteenth day. I counted earlier, when we were in the car, and you asked if I knew what day it was. I remembered on the sixteenth day we had to do *pind daan,* and I clapped three times and the birds came."

"Sixteenth day of what, sweetie?" she said, but suddenly she understood. "Oh, you mean since my mother died." He nodded. Was Bindi trying to set her mother free from purgatory or whatever the belief was? She wrapped her arms around him. "Why don't you think it worked?"

"No crows came when I clapped."

"I see." Feeling him so close, safe and in her arms, she finally felt able to breathe. "Well, shall we try it again, maybe a little louder and together this time?"

"But we're late and it might not work in California," he said.

"Well, it's worth a shot. Will you show me how?"

They returned to the grassy ceremonial site. Madeline put her hands out as he had and began to count to three, and, watching each other, they clapped three times. A small bird alighted on the fence. She pointed it out, and he nodded. It flew away, and she shrugged.

"Maybe they don't know we're here," he suggested.

"Could be. Or they're shy."

"Crows aren't shy," he said.

She didn't even have time to say he was right about that because one swooped down and stared them off. When they'd backed away a satisfactory distance, the black bird plucked a rice ball until it broke apart, the grains scattering over the leaf.

Later, when they were waiting for a pizza to arrive — she was still too frazzled to cook — she called Eddie and told him what happened.

"Well," he said, not at all impressed, "birds do like rice, and there are an awful lot of crows around LA."

Maybe he was right, or maybe he was still angry at her. In any case, she'd choose to think of the event as a minor miracle, the day Bindi set their mother's spirit free. She took the phone in her office and closed the door behind her so she could mention the nightmare she'd had privately. Just thinking about it brought back the sound of the machine flatlining, and she struggled not to cry. If she'd been incoherent in recounting the dream, Eddie still found a way to understand; she could hear it in his voice when he said, "I see." She knew she had to continue, to say the words aloud. She had to admit that in her haste and determination to adopt Bindi rather than one of the other children who were officially up for adoption, she had not obtained a health certificate for him. When Eddie remained quiet, she spoke for him, saying she knew she was blowing a bad dream way out of proportion, then she mentioned the letter from his school, which had certainly played its part, but the thought of anything happening was more than she could bear.

"But what *about* his school? You must have had to show immunization records."

"He didn't have any," she said. "So we got him all the shots he required, but I didn't think to get other blood work."

"And he's had a physical and all that?"

"I brought him to my nutritionist. She said he was in fine health. A little short for his age."

"That's okay, that's fine," he said gently. "But you should probably take him to a proper pediatrician as well. And you're smart to think about having his full blood work done."

She felt the constriction in her throat again, that feeling of not being able to breathe.

"Oh, Eddie. I don't even know how his mother died."

"Did you not ask?" He said it without judgment, but the words stung. "What about his school in India? Or his aunt in London?"

What was he talking about? And why was he suddenly taking that tone? She felt she both knew exactly and didn't have a clue what he was saying.

"His *what?*"

"You didn't know, Maddy? Honestly?"

"I have no idea what you're talking about."

Why did it feel like a lie? Silence. Please let him stay silent. Whatever point he was so intent on making, she would deal with it. But please not right now.

"I'm sure if you just explain the situation to your doctor's office, they'll know what tests to run, perhaps even rule out some potential health threats and put us that much more at ease."

She was so grateful he'd said "us."

"Thanks, Eddie. I don't know what I'd do without you."

"You know, Maddy, I've been thinking. A lot. And this just makes me feel more resolved. We need to contact his family in London." The words echoed back to Mr. Channar's office. "I told you I'm going there." The nape of her neck tingled with fear. What had he been planning? "It's not the only reason, but I do want to try to find his family while I'm there. They need to know where he is. And we need to be made aware of anything there is to know, for his sake. You see that, right?" She saw nothing clearly. "Madeline?"

XXIX

Birendra lay on his bed, clutching the book close to his chest. He felt he'd lived it, already been in War Drobe. In Spare Oom. Met those strange creatures and even finally knew what snow felt like. Mama Maddy had barely spoken a word to him all week, and no matter what he said or did, he was sure his presence only made her unhappier. It was as though she could not even look at him without frowning and walking away. What had he said? Something to Uncle Eddie, perhaps? Or had he done something to upset Mama Maddy? So many times he'd tried to say he was sorry, even if he did not know what precisely he would have been apologizing for, but her silence was contagious. He never found the chance. And so he waited for her to come to him, when she was ready, hoping she would tell him what he'd done so he might never do it again, praying each night that she had not changed her mind and that he would not be sent away.

Uncle Eddie had told Birendra that sometimes adults don't know what's best for him. It seemed to him that fixing things with Mama Maddy would be best for him. That way he could continue to go to his school, which would certainly be best for him. He got up from his bed now and put the book on his shelf. He could see Mama Maddy from the window in his room. She was outside working by the pool, in the chair where she often sketched. Maybe, he thought, if he just told Mama Maddy these things, what he wanted most, she would listen and understand. She had even told him it was okay to tell her when he wanted something.

If it didn't work, he would go to Uncle Eddie for help. But he'd have to hurry because soon Uncle Eddie would leave the country. He'd called and told Birendra he was going to London, and Birendra thought he meant forever, but he promised it was just a holiday. Birendra thought about all the days before meeting Mama Maddy when he believed he would be going to London, but this time he made sure not to say anything about that to his uncle. Then he remembered about Uncle Eddie's friend from high school, and he asked if Uncle Eddie was going to see her. He said he was going to try.

The sunlight reflected in quick flashes from the pool's surface below. Aside from Mama Maddy's big straw hat, he could see only the top of her sketch pad and a single foot, both of which escaped the hat's brim. She had been working even more than usual all week. Paige had picked him up every day from school, twice in Mama Maddy's car. Seeing it in front of the school the first day, Birendra rushed down ready to make up with Mama Maddy, but it was Paige, who told him that Mama Maddy had an important deadline, but he knew it was more than that. Paige stayed late most nights, and Mama Maddy was often away, avoiding him because she was angry, he thought, but he'd never found the courage to ask Paige if he was right.

He changed into his swim trunks now and took a towel from the laundry room on his way outside. The door to the backyard was open, but the screen was closed. He slid it open quietly, trying not to make it squeak. He didn't want to disturb her when she was working. He would wait until she acknowledged him, then go over and apologize. The pool water felt warm, like the sea in Varkala. He eased himself in as quietly as he could, one small step at a time. If she heard him, she didn't turn to look. She remained bent over her sketchbook, with her back to the pool. Normally he would have gone to her side to see what she was working on. He liked watching her draw and was always amazed how the quick lines became a recognizable shape that floated on the paper. He remembered how his mother would, just as quickly, turn a few scraps of fabric and some stuffing into a cow or a monkey, or his Ganesh. He'd once seen a man do something similar with a balloon at the beach in Santa Monica. He hoped someday that he would be able to make something as they all could, something out of nothing. Maybe stories. He liked writing down the stories he knew, but he thought he'd like to make up his own someday.

Holding on to the edge of the pool, with his chin bobbing along, he went hand over hand to the point where his feet no longer touched the bottom. If she looked up and over her shoulder now, she would be able to see him there. He continued to move himself around the edge. If she hadn't noticed him on her own and said something to him by the time he finished his loop around the entire pool, maybe he'd go and sit beside her, see what she was drawing, and wait until she spoke to him.

He felt the water ripple as he rounded the other side. He turned, but there was no one there. Mama Maddy's chair was empty, too. Then a distorted shape in the water became a head emerging through the surface. Mama Maddy's hair parted flat against her head, the red of it a dark auburn when it was wet like this. Her eyes opened and fixed on him, and he saw once again the Mama Maddy who'd gone away the week before. He was so relieved that he couldn't think what to say, then she disappeared again under the water. A moment later he felt a hand pulling gently at his foot, tickling him behind his knee, and finally giving him a few quick squeezes on his side. He was ticklish and couldn't help kicking his feet while holding on tightly to the pool's edge. His feet hovered above the pool's bottom.

"Stop, stop," he squealed, though she couldn't hear him while she was under water. When she surfaced, he was breathless but begged her once more to stop. She smiled at him, then pushed herself off the side of the pool and floated on her back, toward the center. Her eyes were closed again, and the sun was shining on her face.

"Maaaarco," she called.

He carried on toward the shallower part, calling "Poooolo" in the opposite direction, just as Uncle Eddie had taught him. But still she followed. He tried to move faster, but she was gaining on him.

"Marco," she said again, now just a few feet away.

"Polo," he responded, then inhaled a deep breath and pushed himself as hard as he could from the side of the pool, holding his nose tightly with one hand and paddling as hard as he could with the other. When he was able to right himself, his nose was just above the water, and he opened his eyes to see Mama Maddy reaching for him. He screamed and she laughed, with her eyes still closed and her arms outstretched. She called out once again.

"Maaarco."

"Polo," he said, and tried to run backwards against the force of the water on his heels in the direction of the steps, but he wasn't fast enough and she caught him by his waist.

"Gotcha," she said.

He stopped struggling and caught his breath, his head now completely above the water. Her eyes were a little red but sparkling from the light bouncing off the water.

"Your eyes look like diamonds," he said.

"My little poet," she said, beaming at him.

At last ready to apologize for upsetting her, he cast his eyes down at the water lapping his chest. He opened his mouth, but she spoke before he got the chance to say anything.

"Oh, Bindi. I'm so sorry."

"I'm sorry, too," he exclaimed. "I didn't mean to make you angry."

"Oh sweetie, *you* didn't do anything! You could never upset me," she said.

"You weren't mad at me?"

"Not one bit," she said, and pulled him close. "I just got so caught up and forgot to check in with you, too busy feeling sorry for myself and forgetting that my job is to take care of *you!* I'm still learning. Do you forgive me?" He nodded, smiling up at her, as though he were the one being forgiven. "Oh, how I love you, my little man."

He could feel it. It felt warm, like a hug, like the sun.

"I love you, too."

She did a little pirouette, splashing him in her wake. Then she took his face in her wet hands, gave him a big kiss, and swam away, ready for another round. He closed his eyes and began to count to ten, his smile so big he could hardly keep his eyes closed. Everything was quiet, the sun was bright against his eyelids, and it was her job to take care of him. The water lapped gently at his chest and shoulders. He got to ten and listened carefully for Mama Maddy. Then he called out to her.

"Maaaarco."

After lunch, Mama Maddy asked if he would like to see the big house in Los Feliz. She'd had an idea and needed to check something out. He was excited to explore the inside, because that's where she did all her *magic,* as she called it. At a stoplight on their way, she reached into a box in the backseat and pulled out a magazine. She handed it to him and said, "Look inside: your Mama Maddy's famous."

He turned to the table of contents and found her name near the bottom: *The Interiority of Madeline Almquist.* He tried to say the word to himself first so he could ask her if it was another way of saying "interior design." But he tripped on the word's many turns.

"Does this word mean 'interior design'?"

She looked down to the place where his finger pointed on the waxy page. She chuckled and said it was a play on words, but it essentially referred to how she thought about the way she works. He flipped through to the page indicated and began to read. It really was all about Mama Maddy. They had blocked off some of her quotations. He read them each twice, then once more aloud:

I love invading a big space. The trick is then collapsing it, forcing it into a display of intimacy without making it feel cluttered. It's what everyone wants: big and impressive on the outside, cozy and intimate on the inside.

If people want to say I'm not an artist, that I'm a designer because I'm not an architect, then so be it. But I've talked to enough artists to know we share a process. We all get lost in our canvases. My canvas is space.

"Like outer space?" he asked.

"No — the space here." Mama Maddy waved her hand between them. "And inside houses in particular."

"Something out of nothing," he said, remembering that this was precisely what he'd seen her do so often.

"Yes, that's exactly right. You really are clever, Bindi."

Inside the big hourse, it felt more like a palace, or many houses that happened to be connected by passageways and big doors that led not outside but to more of the inside. It was the largest house he'd ever been in. Though he'd gotten used to seeing big houses in many parts of the city, he still struggled to believe that each house was home to just one family — in this case, one person. He thought he would feel lonely there, but Mama Maddy said her client had many friends. She had told him that her clients had such big houses because they could and not because they needed to. He'd asked her why they would do what they didn't need to do, but it wasn't quite the question he meant. She said, "Do you need to eat frozen yogurt?" He didn't *need* to, but he liked it. "It's the same for them. It makes them feel larger than life." He felt small in the big house, following her this way and that. They went into one bedroom and then another. There were bathrooms as big as his bedroom. And a library with so many empty shelves that he wondered if it might be big enough to fit all the books at his school. She told him to have a seat or wander around if he preferred. She had a little work to do. He thought he would get lost on his own, so he climbed onto the giant leather sofa. Mama Maddy took a seat on the floor in the sunlight that was coming in from the window. He'd never seen her so quiet, so still. In the interview in the magazine, she explained that she was often guided to a decision by the angle of a window to the sun or the way an interior wall abruptly gave way to nothing: a line in the wood flooring suggested the placement of a piece of furniture, as did the shifting sunlight as it touched down throughout the day. She *listened* to what a room had to tell her. He looked at her again. Perhaps she was listening now.

Birendra might be an artist, too. Mama Maddy had told him so on more than one occasion. When he was younger, in Varkala, he and his mother talked about what he might be when he grew up, but they'd never come up with that possibility. She had told him he was like his aunt; if he worked hard, he could be whatever he set his mind to. They'd made a list after his aunt's last visit. His mother had written *Doctor* at the top to get them started. He thought that might be nice, helping people get well. He suggested *Engineer*, like his uncle in London. Then he'd asked, "Anything? Even a pilot?" Her eyes grew wide with concern, but she nodded and said, "Of course. Anything. But maybe something closer to the ground so your poor mother won't worry all the time." Because he liked writing, and his English class, he said maybe he could become a journalist. "A journalist," she repeated. "Yes, I think you would make a wonderful journalist."

Mama Maddy spun herself around, still seated in the middle of the room. She was smiling, and she stretched as though she'd just woken up from a long nap.

"So what did the room tell you?" he asked.

She stood and dusted herself off, even though the house was cleaner than any house he'd ever seen.

"The room told me it wants a rug, unfortunately. And a big one. And that you and I should go for another swim in the big pool. How about that?"

"I didn't bring my shorts."

"Well, lucky for you I came prepared."

She picked up the magazine and studied the cover, then set it down and took his hand. They wandered through the hallway, into the entry, then through the dining room and kitchen, where they stopped for something to drink. She said he could have an Orangina if he liked and could change in the bathroom by the door or in the one by the pool.

"Do you really think I can be an artist, too?"

"I think you can be whatever you want to be, Bindi." That she said it, too, meant it must be true. "Is that what you want to be?"

"Maybe. Or I might be a journalist."

"You can be both. In fact, being an artist isn't really a job. It's a way of viewing the world around you. Seeing it creatively. Finding what makes it beautiful, you add to the beauty of the world."

"I want to do that," he said.

"And you will." She caressed his face the way his mother used to. "You already do."

X X X

Nayana had an evening flight but was already packed and ready to leave the house as soon as the mail arrived. She was waiting for her sister's letter to come from Beth, watching for the postman from her office window. She'd written a note to Ramesh. Another impossible task, with only the wrong words to choose from. She'd hoped to express how grateful she'd been for his love and support all these years, but it felt trite. She attempted to express how much love she still had for him and always would have. She wanted him to know that she was leaving and unsure when or if she was coming back *because* she loved him. If he truly didn't understand already, he would soon. And she was so very sorry for everything — she couldn't seem to say that enough.

In truth, she had no idea what was going to happen in India or how long she would remain, and she wasn't convinced she'd never return to England, or even to Ramesh, if he'd have her back. But she didn't say this because she wanted to give him a way out, in case *he* wanted at last to be free of her. She wrote that she had been unkind to him in ways a man who loved her so well had not deserved. She knew this would hurt him deeply, but she hoped it would make moving on easier, if that was his choice. And also because she owed him the truth for once. She admitted that she had never had a home in England, only a home in him, and said this wasn't fair to either of them. Finally, she begged him to accept that she was gone for now and to refrain from following her; she'd broken her own heart slowly, painfully, and completely in the last year, and she needed all her strength to recover. It wasn't a long letter, and she didn't dare mention the baby. She hoped he would interpret its brevity as a sign of her difficulty writing it and not a lack of love.

Twice she'd run downstairs thinking she'd missed the mailman. Twice she took the lift back up. At last the mail arrived. She hurried to the lobby, forgetting the mailbox key in the windowsill. She had to ask the mailman for her mail as it was being distributed. He didn't refuse, but he was in no hurry. He handed her each piece as it came, continuing to dole out her neighbors' mail as well. She anxiously sought out the familiar envelope in his pile until finally he said there was nothing else. Confined again in the narrow lift, she sifted through the few pieces once more, in vain. There was still no letter from India, but there was something else for her. She tore it open and immediately knew what it was, though she had no idea how to interpret the columns and numbers. That is, she didn't want to. *Alleged father*. It was so cruel. She skipped to the bottom. A percentage anyone could understand: *Probability of paternity: 0%. The alleged father, Ramesh Bhatia, is excluded as the biological father....* She felt her knees buckle slightly, and she had to take hold of the handrail until the doors opened again.

Inside their flat, she gathered her things and made her way to the door, not stopping for a last look or to ensure she had everything. Of course she didn't. But there was no reason to wait any longer. Her bag's wheels skipped along the tile floors, heavy with a few key notebooks in case she felt like working again. She replaced the test results in the envelope, which she set beneath her own letter for Ramesh, hating herself but seeing no other way. How could she face him now, with proof? Finally he would have her full confession. She dropped her keys in the bowl on the small table and let the door lock behind her. There was a stop she had to make. One last act before she left London. She would call a taxi for Heathrow from the salon around the corner. She didn't want to deal with steps and trains and luggage. Nayana had to brace herself against the smell of peroxide. It had been years since anyone besides Aditi had touched her hair. The only other customer was sitting under a dryer with her face hidden in *Hello!*

"Have you got time for a cut?" Nayana asked.

"Let me see. Have I got time?" The woman was older than Nayana, someone's mother, maybe even grandmother. She looked around the otherwise empty waiting area, then chuckled to herself. "Yeah, love, I've got time. Nothing but time."

Nayana took a seat as instructed and pulled out the stick that had contained her hair in a heavy bun at the base of her neck. It draped the back of the chair. In the mirror, she could see the woman stop in surprise where she stood, holding a smock limp in her plump hand. Nayana's heartache renewed itself. The woman approached Nayana slowly, lifting the mass of hair, then letting it slip lightly through her fingers.

"Cut it off," Nayana said, indicating a place just below her jawline.

The woman was about to speak, to object, but stopped herself and set to work tucking a towel into the smock's neckline. Nayana sensed she'd understood, at least well enough not to get involved. She took careful hold of her scissors and looked at Nayana once again.

"Right, love. We'll give you a shampoo once we cut some of this off. You ready, then?"

Ramesh loved her long hair. She wasn't punishing him by cutting it; he may never know. But she was making it easier to let him go, cutting him loose in case that's the way it had to be in the end. Her face appeared gray under the sharp white light. She looked beyond herself, perhaps to her sister and a former version of herself, one who might begin anew. She nodded and already felt the burden of a great weight lifted.

"I'm ready."

At the airport gate too early, Nayana put on her headphones and was shocked once again at the feel of such short hair, as though she had lost a limb. She pretended not to listen to the conversation of the only other passengers waiting, an elderly English couple on their way to India for the first time. She imagined arriving and seeing a nephew taller than she was, with the cracking voice of a teenager. But she reminded herself that Birendra was still a boy of eight. No, he had just turned nine, she realized. She'd forgotten his birthday on top of everything else.

For once she would not be returning to India for monsoon season. Srikant and her parents had all died during the summer monsoons. And her most recent visit was only possible during her summer break from classes. Had it really been almost ten years since their parents' passing? Nayana and Aditi had both returned to Delhi from their respective homes, then they'd traveled together by train with their parents' commingled ashes to the Ganga to satisfy their last wish: to be sent together downstream by their daughters. It was slightly unorthodox, but so had they always been. The sisters stood up to their calves in the rusty waters of the sacred river, each with an arm wrapped around the other's waist, free hands clasping either side of the urn. They locked eyes and emptied the ashes under the heavy rain that had soaked their hair and clothes. Nayana had still been able to see herself in Aditi then: their long hair in wet dark clusters stuck to their faces; the damp petals of their floral wreaths clumped like golden fur collars around their necks, white cotton sarees clinging to their bodies. In the memory, Nayana suddenly struggled to distinguish between herself and her sister. And then she remembered the soft swell of Aditi's pregnant belly, through which Birendra was making himself known to the world for the first time.

It was hard for Nayana now not to associate a downpour with death. She had asked Aditi that day if she thought their parents felt abandoned. Aditi shook her head. "I think they were happy together, so happy they couldn't last two days apart, but mostly I think they were happy for us. I have Srikant and now this little one. You have your scholarship and a promising future in London." Nayana remembered the sense that so much was possible back then; was that the same as happiness? They'd stayed there by the river, standing in the rain, quietly remembering their parents. But without them to bind Nayana and her sister to a shared past, a place — a home — Delhi was all but lost to them in the years that followed, just a city to provide a backdrop for their memories. Still, the following evening, seated on opposite sides of their parents' bed, with hair still damp from the rains that had followed them back to Delhi, it felt like home. They sifted through their parents' belongings, occasionally showing each other what they'd found. Aditi lifted up a saree for Nayana to see, conjuring a shared memory that would hover there momentarily above the bed like a dream. They would each take two with them to their distant homes, north and south, but the others had no place in their futures. Under one of her father's jackets, Nayana found a small rectangular box. The cardboard lid collapsed as she attempted to lift it. Neatly folded inside was the paisley tie they'd given him for his fortieth birthday. A small golden clip was still pinned in place. Their mother had given it to him the same day. On the clip was a single rooster in profile walking along a path that had long since lost its gold plating. The sisters summoned their father's words that day, in unison: *A special-occasion tie.* "From his three hens," Nayana added nostalgically, and then they burst into laughter that brought them to their backs and once again to tears. It had been a decade of loss for both of them, but that was not the same as a decade lost. This isn't a visit, she thought. *Keep the lanterns lit, dear sister. I'm coming home.*

XXXI

Edward ordered a gin and tonic from the bar and sought out the nearest lobby phone. He felt underdressed in his T-shirt and faded blue jeans, under a chandelier as large and crystalline as the one above him and in a London hotel as smart as this one. It was his first time staying in such luxury as an adult, a huge step up from the shoe box he and Jane had found near King's Cross when they came to London years earlier. He gave his room number to the bartender and raised the glass to his mother, thanking her silently for the money to take this trip. The decor in the hotel actually reminded him of the time he'd come home from school to find their living room transformed for a photo shoot. Back then, he hadn't understood the extravagant costumes and set design. Redford and Farrow's *The Great Gatsby* had just come out, with a screenplay by Coppola, and his mother had been passed over as costume designer. She'd been determined to attach her name to the moment somehow. The photo shoot was her response. Months later, when it received a sizable spread in *Cosmopolitan* without a single photo of his mother, she'd flown into a rage. He sat on the stairs and listened as she had the same impassioned phone conversation with at least ten sympathetic friends and drank almost as many gin and tonics.

He took a sip from his glass, noting the irony with mild discomfort, then crossed the room to the pay phone. He'd brought the note down on which he'd written Nayana's last name as well as her husband's first name. He spelled both for the operator. She asked for a postal code, which he did not have.

"Sir?" She sounded annoyed to be kept waiting or perhaps to have to deal with an ill-prepared American.

"He lives in West London, if that helps."

"Please hold while I connect you."

Even if he hadn't just taken a sip of his drink, Edward would have been surprised into silence. He'd expected to get the number, not connected. And now it was ringing. A woman answered, and it might have been Nayana. She sounded neither too young nor too old.

"Yes, hello," he said, clearing his throat. "I'd like to speak to Nayana Bhatia, please."

"I'm sorry," the woman said after a moment. "You have the wrong number."

He was about to apologize for the inconvenience when the woman spoke again.

"May I know who's calling?" she asked.

"My name is Edward Almquist. Do you know Nayana?"

"Yes," the woman said. "I do. She's my sister-in-law."

He'd called Nayana's husband's family home, it turned out. Nayana and Ramesh lived somewhere else. Her sister-in-law was polite but understandably reticent with Edward.

"My sister adopted Nayana's nephew."

"Nayana's nephew in Kerala?" she asked.

"Yes, that's right."

"I'm sorry Mr. Almquist, but this is the first I've heard of any adoption. Is it possible you've got the wrong name?"

"Nayana and Ramesh Bhatia. Her nephew is Birendra. My sister adopted him in December after his mother passed away."

"Mr. Almquist, I hope this is some sort of mistake. Birendra, you say?"

"Yes." She seemed to gasp, then she covered the receiver and spoke to someone else in a different language.

"Please excuse me, Mr. Almquist. You're delivering a terrible shock."

"I'm so sorry." He felt light-headed and flushed. "You didn't know?"

She said they had no idea about any of it. And then she explained that Nayana was not in London at all. Edward would need to speak to her husband about meeting with Ramesh. She would have him call Edward back when he returned from work.

Where was Nayana, if not in London? And how long had she been gone? So long that her family had not learned of her sister's death months earlier? That seemed unlikely, yet there was no question: the woman hadn't known. He returned to the bar, easily able to justify a second drink, although it was not yet seven in the morning in Los Angeles. He had a few hours to kill, but he couldn't spend them all drinking at the hotel bar, especially if he was going to meet someone. But he didn't want to give in to jet lag and fall asleep. Feeling warm from the gin, he wrapped his scarf tightly around his neck and set off to wander the city center. He had meant to be walking toward Big Ben, maybe for some sort of closure on his time with Jane, but he must have misremembered the way and ended up carrying on along the Mall, then turning and eventually finding the Thames in sight. It appeared even larger than it had in his memory. He walked onto a footbridge, and the city on either side of him seemed amplified as well. Or maybe he felt himself growing smaller in a country full of strangers. Maybe that's what he'd wanted to feel anyway. Alone, as he had on the day Jane left him so many years ago. Alone in a place where no one knew him. Alone as he had been after his sister left home for college.

That house had sometimes been so quiet, so still, it was as if the air itself were locked in place, stifling. Before Maddy left, she would invite him into her room sometimes. Edward would watch as she flipped through a magazine or sketched in her journal. Mostly she drew houses. She'd wanted to be an architect then. The first time she told him so, he was six. Hovering by the side of her bed, he asked what she was drawing. She scooted over to make room for him and continued to sketch in quick strokes with her pencil. "It's the house I'm going to live in someday," she said. She had seemed so old in that moment to him. Maybe fifteen. He'd thought of her in her own house, a different house, and wondered if she would take him with her. "And that there," she said, indicating a structure with her finger, "is an iron gate so I can keep out everyone I don't want to come in." She must have seen the concern on his face, because she smiled. "I'll give you the key," she said. "You can come visit. I'm going to be an architect so I can build my own house, and I'm going to live there alone. Maybe with a dog."

She'd added the last bit about the dog while gazing out the window, imagining her future.

He thought of Maddy at Birendra's birthday party. Actually, he hadn't been able to shake certain images of her, which he found himself conflating with others of their mother. Can a child escape one's parents? He thought he had done this, though perhaps there were ways he was like his father, ways he would never know. Maybe Edward had never been single as an adult because he was trying to escape that solitude he felt growing up. And yet even with Jane, he had ended up on his own. The puzzles first, then the *Cheers* finale, which put an end to nights in front of the television together. It truly had been the end of an era. They'd stumbled along together for so long since, even the breakup hadn't felt final. But now, with the Thames rushing beneath his feet, on a quest that held so little certainty, there was no denying it: he was at last on his own.

Nayana's brother-in-law had called the hotel while Edward was out wandering. He'd left an address for a pub in Shepherd's Bush and a meeting time with the front desk. Edward paused at the pub entrance to take in the rich blend of ale, whiskey, and wood. He scanned the room and its handful of patrons for anyone who might be Mr. Bhatia. He was early. The bartender looked over briefly, then back to a soccer game on the television.

"Mr. Almquist?"

He was startled at the sound of his name behind him, so formally spoken.

"Mr. Bhatia. Please call me Edward. It's very nice to meet you."

"Raj," he said and took Edward's hand. He was tall and carried himself confidently. His features were sharp and striking. "Pleasure."

"Thanks again for meeting me, Raj."

"Would you like a beer?"

When Raj returned, Edward was still holding his wallet out.

"I'm sorry. I meant to offer," he said.

"Oh, you're all right. You might be buying the whiskey in a minute."

They smiled politely, tapped glasses, and found a seat by the wall. Edward's gaze fell to the wooden table between them, its unique pattern of scratches marking a particular history. Here he was, in London, with one of Birendra's relatives and little idea what to say.

"I'm really sorry to be the bearer of such bad news. I know it was an upsetting phone call for your wife."

"Yes, it was. I had just found out myself and hadn't had the chance to tell her. So your sister has adopted Nayana's nephew?" Raj said, though this was clearly not the question he wanted answered.

"Of course I didn't realize this would be news to you. I had only intended to reach out to you — well, to Nayana — in hopes of connecting her with Birendra."

Raj asked what had brought Edward to London. What could he say? That he wanted to feel anonymous in the place his relationship had been mortally wounded years ago? Or that he'd come all this way just to find Nayana? To find a high school sweetheart?

"It's a long-overdue vacation," he said. "And one of my favorite cities."

There was an awkward silence. They both drank from their beers.

"Where did your sister find the boy to adopt him?"

"In a place called Trivandrum." He wasn't sure he'd gotten that right, but Raj was nodding.

"Yeah, it's the capital of Kerala," said Raj. "And they never mentioned his relatives?"

Edward was stumped, embarrassed, even. He felt complicit and had no good answer. What *was* the story behind the adoption? How could it be that Maddy knew nothing, that they were never contacted?

"Look," Raj continued. "I'm not sure what to tell you other than that Nayana left London before learning about her sister."

"When?"

"Last week."

"But it's been nearly three months. How is it possible she wasn't aware of her sister's death for so long?"

"My brother just got the news. There was a letter sent in November, but it was delivered to a neighbor's house, and that neighbor was out of town. Anyhow, my brother has been making calls to India since he got it, trying to figure out what happened to Nayana's sister and her nephew. It's been a frustrating experience from the sound of it."

"So if Nayana left England before this letter arrived, you're saying she would have only found out her sister was dead when she got there?" Raj nodded gravely. "I'd love to talk to your brother, of course."

"Yes, I'm sure you would. But what you have to understand, Edward, is they've gone through a lot. My brother loves his wife very much." He hesitated before he went on. "I'm not sure that has always been entirely easy."

The door to the pub opened, and a black Labrador entered, followed by a blind man. They watched the man and his dog get situated at the bar, both clearly regulars. It was an opportunity to pause over all that was being said. Edward considered Raj's position, wanting to be sympathetic, but there was Birendra to consider as well. He felt he had to do just what Raj was doing: protect the interests of those closest to him.

"I understand, Raj. I really do. And I'm sorry about the timing and showing up unannounced. I am. I can't imagine worse circumstances."

"But you're here now, is that it?"

"Yes, precisely. Don't you agree that Birendra deserves the chance to contact his family, especially his aunt? As far as we know, she's his only surviving blood relative." He waited to see if Raj might have further information on this point. If he did, he gave no sign. "By the way, he's a wonderful boy; it's not like we're wanting to unload him or anything. He's remarkable, in fact."

Edward kept saying "we," which made him anxious on two fronts. It seemed to increase his own responsibility for Birendra while reminding him that his sister would be devastated when she found out that Edward had made contact with Birendra's family.

"Of course, none of this is his fault. But I have to say, Nayana has had a rough go of it lately."

Raj had come back to this point. As if he were warning Edward about something concerning Birendra's aunt. But what? They had reached the point in their conversation where they had heard each other's position. They were both invested messengers who didn't like the messages they had to deliver.

"I promise to be sensitive to your brother's situation," Edward said, unsure what more he could do or say.

"I'll talk to him. See what I can do."

"I can understand if he doesn't want to meet me," he said. "If that's the case, though, I would hope for a chance to reach Nayana."

"I'll talk to him," Raj said again, then emptied his glass with one swallow.

XXXII

"It's time to go, Bindi."

Madeline was leaning against the frame of the open front door, watching huge white clouds lit by a sun she couldn't see from where she stood. She was showing the Los Feliz house today and wanted to get an early start. She called for him again.

"I'm here." He appeared in the entryway, out of breath and carrying the particleboard model town he'd built for his social studies class.

"What were you doing?"

"I had to go back upstairs for my project."

"You forgot it? Silly boy, you've been working on that all week. Here, give me your backpack." He turned and let her remove the bag from his shoulders, helping him balance the base of his project as he slipped each arm out. She admired his work again, his imaginary town. Of course she'd helped, but she hadn't had to do much. He was so creative and resourceful in unique ways; he might just follow in her footsteps, she'd thought. Or maybe he'd be the architect in the family. "C'mon, let's go. I've got my meeting at the house today."

"It's all done?" he asked.

"Mostly. We're still waiting on some import pieces, but almost." She opened the car door and put his bag in the backseat. She scrunched her face and gritted her teeth nervously. "You-know-who's coming to see it."

"Are you worried?"

"Not really, actually. I mean, I hope she likes it, of course."

"Is she nice?"

"Yeah, you know. She's just a person, like you and me. Well, a very rich and famous person, but still flesh and blood." He nodded. "Ooh, I like that," she said, pointing to a small stand of trees he'd fashioned from green twist ties wrapped around painted toothpicks. "Did you add that last night?"

"Yeah. I used the extra toothpicks from the bridge." He fiddled with a tree next to the footbridge they'd constructed together.

"So it's a big day for us both."

"I hope Mr. Gruner likes it."

"Of course he will. It's beautiful. I'd live there."

"The famous lady will like your house, too," he said and worked to straighten one last tree. "You should be more confident. You're really good at your job."

He made these little comments, without even looking at her, as if they were the most mundane, axiomatic observations. He had no idea just how much they meant to Madeline. How much she needed to hear that, and to believe it.

At his school, she offered to hold his project while he got out of the car and put on his backpack. He leaned in and took the board carefully in both hands.

"Voilà, monsieur," she said. He almost hit the door's frame. "Careful."

"*Merci, madame.*"

"*Je vous prier.*"

She knew it wasn't right as she said it. She'd asked him to help her learn some French, and this was one of their little exchanges, in which they pretended to be strangers, but she never could remember the last bit.

"*Je vous en prie,*" he said, correcting her, and she repeated his words silently.

She was still repeating them when he disappeared over the top of the steps. She got lost in the words for a moment until she noticed the clock. If there was traffic, and there usually was these days, she was sure she'd arrive late. But she had a stroke of luck, and she zipped down Santa Monica, catching the lights until Vermont Avenue, a feat that grew daily more difficult with people avoiding the freeways to cross town. Maybe she *was* a little nervous. It wasn't about the meeting, exactly; she'd never been very starstruck. Though, true enough, she'd spent more time with the lawyers on this job than with her client. Mostly Madeline had been left alone, and she'd put more heart into this project than any before it, which was saying something. She hoped that would be enough in the end. Both assistants were waiting, leaning against their cars in the driveway, looking bored.

"Sorry I'm late. Had to drop the kid off at school. Is she here?"

"No, she's not," said the less pleasant one. Candace was her name. "But she wouldn't like to be kept waiting."

"Then it's a good thing she's not here," Madeline said and winked at the one she liked, Cindy. "I'll be inside."

While Candace and Cindy waited, Madeline got to work placing the custom cushions that had finally arrived by UPS with the drapes late the night before. Paige told her she'd had to stay at the house until eight to sign for them. She'd hung the fabric over the rods, as Madeline had asked, so the folds would come out. Madeline set to work hanging them properly and had fallen into one of her arranging vortices and forgotten all about the appointment when Cindy came inside and told her the meeting would have to be rescheduled for that afternoon. With both assistants gone and the extra time, Madeline moved on to the cushions she'd yet to place. It really was a magnificent house. She loved how it took full advantage of the natural light that Los Angeles had in such abundance. Sometimes she thought about leaving this city, but where would she go? New York was the obvious choice, but she'd lose two of the features that most often guided her in her work: space and light. Even the big city lofts didn't appeal to her; she liked rooms of various shapes and sizes, each serving a different function. San Francisco, perhaps? She was already receiving calls. For the odd job, maybe, but she would quickly grow bored of the Victorian and Edwardian layouts so abundant there, one on top of another. No, it wasn't perfect, but Los Angeles was home. And in any case she wouldn't make Bindi move again, not until he graduated from high school. She still had nine years, even if he caught up, and she was sure he would. She had to think this way, to will their future into existence. Her brother was in London, doing God knows what. But if she let her fear and imagination get the best of her, she didn't know what she might do. She got on her knees to arrange the excess fabric from the window treatments that fell to the floor. Madeline had warned her client that it was a trend that wouldn't last, but Apollah wanted it, and she could certainly afford to change it as often as she wanted to.

The patio furniture still needed arranging, and there were more cushions to be placed and light shades to be hung. She'd been waiting for the February rains to come and go, but they'd mostly stayed away this year. The days were even warmer than usual, like this one. Passing by the pool, she kicked off her wedge sandal and dipped her red-painted toes into the warm water, then watched the symbol, which appeared to float at the surface, retreat back in a ripple to its location on the pool's floor. The tile had worked perfectly and was perhaps even the touch she was proudest of in the end. She didn't always take on the outdoor areas of a home, but this house was going to define Madeline, and she wanted her mark on every inch of it. The sun was so warm on her neck that she contemplated taking off her clothes and going for a dip, but the last thing she wanted was for someone to walk in on her and send word to Apollah that Madeline had christened the pool in her birthday suit. No, she'd keep working, she thought, and when the lamp shades were hung, she moved on to the yoga studio.

Above a window that ran the length of the poolside wall, she held up various shades and types of sheer fabrics she'd bought to hang there. She hadn't been convinced by the evening light the day before and wanted to test them against the sunlight that filtered in before making a decision. Because the studio was set partially beneath a shaded section of the patio — the trellis would eventually be covered in creeping wisteria and bougainvillea with a backdrop of star jasmine — the room needed as much natural light as possible, but Madeline had wanted it to glow, giving the appearance of illumination, of enlightenment.

Her instinct had been right, and she went with the rose-gold silk muslin. The sun's tinted beams shimmered and danced around the room as the fabric moved in the breeze, and the light touched down on the giant face of a Buddha that she'd hung on the opposite wall. His knowing smirk seemed to invite Madeline to be still with him. She slunk down on the floor and watched his face glow. It really had been a good find. And it was all the more special because she'd bought it while shopping with Bindi after lunch in Chinatown. Of course, if asked, she would say she had it shipped in from Bali. And if the appointment were canceled again this afternoon, she might just take this one home with her and go back to Chinatown to see if there was another one or something similar to it. She wanted to hang this one on the fence in her own backyard, where it would patina with age and watch over Bindi and her and their home in the years to come. It had been silly of her to think of giving it up. The Buddha's face was so serene, so beautiful. She felt herself drifting.

It was the silence that brought her back; it was too foreign. They had all gone: the voices, the doubts, the feelings, the buzz of her mind. For a moment there, however briefly, she had fallen into peace. Into bliss. She was so grateful that she scooted herself across the glossy wooden floor and kissed the spiraling flame that rose from between the Buddha's eyebrows. At long last she had experienced what she'd always been seeking. No matter that she couldn't secure it: at least she knew it was something she could grasp, maybe fleetingly, but all by herself. She lay down before the Buddha and tried to re-create the sensation. She fell asleep still smiling. She was back in India, with Dr. Wright, sitting cross-legged, palms facing up and resting on her knees. She was meditating, actually meditating, repeating a mantra:

She would be kind. She would be confident. She would be loved.
Kind. Confident. Loved.

It was the end of a yoga class, and the boom of the instructor's "om" grew louder, then louder still, until Madeline knew she was awake, yet the sound was still filling the studio around her. She looked to the Buddha's mouth to see if that was where it was coming from. Was she still dreaming or finally losing her mind? She turned and found she was not alone. Was it afternoon already? Apollah was there in any case, eyes closed, mouth wide, hands in prayer. Striking a pose. The sound was deep and long, and her voice was more beautiful than it had ever sounded on the radio.

Madeline was embarrassed to be found sleeping on the job. This was no dream. She stood and waited for the hum to fall away and for her client to open her eyes. She didn't know whether to applaud or follow suit and put her hands together at her chest. She opted for silence and an admiring smile and waited to be spoken to. They took a silent tour around the studio together. Madeline watched as Apollah touched the walls, the Buddha's face, the floors. They looked out the window, resting against the soft touch of silk, at the pool. Her skin was luminous.

"It's perfect," she said.

The words, no matter that Madeline didn't agree — nothing was ever perfect, and she would always be the first to find a flaw — were just what she needed to hear.

"I'm so glad you like it," said Madeline. "Shall I show you around the rest of the house?"

"No. I've seen it. And I love it. I'll be moving in next month."

"That should work well. I hope to be completely done within a week or so. We're just waiting on two small pieces now."

She took Madeline's hand without shaking it. It was a tender, if brief, hand-holding. And just like that she turned and left Madeline alone once again. She could already sense the strangeness of the experience forming itself into a wonderful anecdote: the day she awoke on the floor of a yoga studio to the sound of no one less than Apollah herself, chanting "om" in harmony with the giant face of a Buddha. The day she found her bliss. And with this thought she felt the project itself coming to a close. She gathered the fabrics that would not find a home there and left the studio. There were no signs of Candace and Cindy. They were gone as well. For now, the house was still Madeline's, as were all the houses she designed, until she let them go, handed them over, almost never to return. She collected her purse and shawl and locked the house. On her way to her car, she saw the landscapers still at work. The garden was coming along as well. It really was almost complete. She dug her phone out of her bag and called home to see if Bindi might want to go to Chinatown for dinner. They had a Buddha to rescue.

At home there was a letter waiting for Madeline from her brother. He must have sent it when he left town. She considered whether reading it would disrupt the lingering peaceful hum she still felt within.

"What are you doing?" Bindi had found her standing in the kitchen with her eyes closed.

"Just thinking," she said and set the letter down. She went to the fridge and poured them each a glass of water. "How would you feel about a little shopping after dinner?" His eyes lit up. He loved Chinatown as much as he enjoyed Chinese food for dinner. "All right, then, because there's something we need to pick up for our home. Get your shoes on. We leave in five."

Dear Maddy,

First, I want to thank you. I'm grateful to you for so much, actually, but I'm referring here to my time with Bindi these past months. It's such a privilege to have him in our lives, but I know I don't have to tell you this.

I understand you weren't happy about my decision to look for his family in London, and we didn't discuss it as much as we should have. I'm not sure how much you know about them. I gather they were in fairly regular contact before his mother died. Did you know they paid for his schooling? I'm not sure what prevented them from going to India, but I can't imagine how painful that choice must have been for them. Whatever their reasons, I'm compelled to sit with them, to tell them that he is safe and well, and to connect them with you both, so that they might be in their nephew's life. I hope you want this, too.

I also need to apologize, Maddy. I've been unfair to you, and you've been such a support in my life. I'm not going to lie: I was disappointed when you left after Bindi's birthday party and when you stayed away as long as you did. It was unfair to both of us. But it was also only human. Sometimes I forget you're not the superwoman I've made you out to be in my mind, the big sister who succeeds in every endeavor, the one I've always looked up to. I hope you know what I mean. I know you make mistakes like anyone but also that you will do your best. What's more, I know firsthand how good that can be.

It occurs to me we may need to forgive each other, not for anything we've done but rather for the parents we had in common. And because they are both gone now, maybe we can truly move forward as adults, which it seems we must do, for ourselves and for Bindi. If this aunt and uncle in London are awful, then we'll forget them, right? But if not, well, couldn't we all, especially Bindi, use every ounce of support, and love, available to us? I hope you'll agree that it's worth finding out. For B.

With respect, and love,
your brother,
Eddie

XXXIII

As Edward left London behind for its western suburb, the winter sun was already setting, staining the white blanket of sky overhead here and there in blotches of purple and pink, a muted watercolor on the horizon. And when the taxi finally stopped it was dark and impossible to make out the house numbers on the doors from that distance. The street was a wall of brick, one house indistinguishable from the next, to Edward's unaccustomed eye. He left the taxi and found the house on foot, in the middle of the block. On the front porch, he could already feel the house's inner warmth against the cold night air, and when a little girl, smaller and younger than Birendra, opened the door, that warmth enveloped him, carrying with it a rich gust of spices that awakened his appetite.

"Are you Raj's daughter?" he asked, to which she nodded suspiciously. "I'm Edward."

"I know. I'm Jasmeen. You're from America. You talk funny."

A woman he assumed to be the girl's grandmother approached from a room off the hallway. She was drying her hands on an apron and nodding her head in a welcoming gesture. Her smile was free and wide and lacked any reluctance

Edward had feared might greet him given the circumstances. He had been trying to imagine the situation in reverse, and he wanted to intrude as little as possible while making every attempt to do what he could for Birendra.

"Welcome, Mr. Almquist. Come. Come. Excuse this silly girl."

She issued an order in another language to the girl, and they both watched her escape through the kitchen doorway. Edward followed the woman down the hall, past the kitchen, where the savory smells were strongest, and into the dining room. He handed her the bottle of wine he'd brought, and she looked at it, as though impressed and grateful.

"Mr. Almquist is here, Ramesh," she announced. "Look, a nice bottle of wine." Then, turning to Edward, she continued a rather solemn introduction: "Ramesh — my elder son."

Ramesh was seated alone in the room, at the far end of a long dining table, which was covered by an embroidered tablecloth the deep purple-blue of irises. He seemed to be admiring it, lifting only his chin to acknowledge Edward but letting his tired eyes shy away. He looked like a man who'd forgotten what sleep was. There was undoubtedly a resemblance to Raj, but Ramesh's features weren't as angular; he was perhaps the mellower, slightly less handsome, older brother.

"Thank you again for your willingness to meet me, Mr. Bhatia, and to you both for the kind dinner invitation."

"Please, join me, Mr. Almquist." He gestured to his right. "I hear you bring news of our nephew."

Mrs. Bhatia retreated from the room, in the direction of a man shouting. It took a moment before Edward recognized that it was a kind of shouting he knew, the shouting of someone watching a sporting match of some sort. It was something he'd often heard coming from the pubs he passed, and it was probably Raj. He took a seat beside Ramesh.

"Do you follow football, Edward? Or soccer, as you call it in America? May I call you Edward?"

"Of course. And, no, not really. I'm more into baseball."

"Is that right? Do you play?"

"No, I'm afraid I don't do much in that regard."

"Really? You seem fit. How old are you?"

"I'm thirty."

"Ah, still young. We Bhatias hold it all right here, front and center, where we can keep an eye on it," said Ramesh, reaching for his stomach. When he removed his hands, Edward noticed where the shirt gaped to expose a soft belly, covered in black hair. He averted his eyes, though Ramesh still wasn't looking at him. He appreciated the effort Ramesh was making to joke, though it was clearly the effort of someone in pain. He wasn't sure what to say to make their meeting any easier. "Speaking of," Ramesh said, "how do you feel about whiskey?"

"Whiskey is a great idea," chimed in Raj as he entered the room. "Arsenal, two to one. Your team will lose, brother." He gave Ramesh's shoulder a conciliatory pat, then turned and extended his hand to Edward. "Allow me," he said, and removed three glasses and a bottle from the hutch.

"Do you take ice, Edward?"

"However you're having it."

The drink helped loosen their tongues, and the conversation felt lighter with Raj in the room. They talked about what they did for work. Ramesh, like Raj, was in engineering and worked on the Channel Tunnel as well. He learned they had moved from Uganda to London as teenagers during the Asian purge there. Their father had been a banker but insisted on a more practical career in England for his sons. After their trouble in Africa, he wouldn't count on the majority of Brits to entrust their money to the Bhatia boys. He'd since passed away, but the family was already settled by that time, and London was home. Edward said he wasn't yet married. All this was a polite precursor to their meal. Raj's wife entered with Mrs. Bhatia, each carrying a tray topped with several bowls. Jasmeen trailed behind with a small tray, still eyeing Edward curiously. He stood and greeted Raj's wife. He looked for signs of his nephew in Jasmeen's face but remembered that there was no reason he would find any. The table was laid with a dozen bowls and plates, each containing something different: stews and curries and gravies that he had never seen, certainly never tasted. Naan, hot and succulent, to soak up the flavors. And bowls of fresh chilies that Ramesh and his mother popped as if they were potato chips. They had moved on to beer with the meal. Ramesh refilled Edward's glass after Edward made the mistake of eating a chili. He tried next to soak up the spice with more rice. By the end, he had eaten far more than he needed to and finally satisfied what he'd thought was an endless hunger. Only Raj was still picking at the food. And then his wife, mother, and daughter carried the empty plates and bowls out of the room the way they'd come. In his mildly intoxicated and deeply sated state, it felt theatrical, how efficiently they made everything disappear. Edward was alone again with the two men, and a sudden silence came over the room. Raj indicated, with a silent nod to Edward, that it was time. Ramesh's eyes had returned to the table. He was sweeping some crumbs into a small pile with his hand. Edward was moved by the scene and by the kindness he was being shown despite the difficult situation. He had to continually remind himself that, for them, this was all still so fresh, including news of the death. He didn't know if these men were even close to Birendra's mother, but there was something going on, and it related to Nayana's absence.

"So, brother?" Raj said, breaking the silence. "This man has traveled pretty far."

Ramesh looked at Raj. His eyes were glassy and unfocused when they turned to Edward, but his smile was sincere.

"Will you join me on the patio, Edward?"

"Of course," he said.

Ramesh didn't hurry to stand, nor did he hurry as he walked to the sliding glass doors off the living room. They left Raj behind to finish his beer alone, but he made no objection. Ramesh closed the door behind them.

The air was crisp but not as cold as it had felt when Edward was walking around the city center. There was no breeze here. He welcomed the cool sensation against his warm face. He was still sweating from the spice of the chili. Ramesh pulled a cigarette from a pack in his pocket and offered one to Edward, who refused.

"If you do talk to Nayana," Ramesh said, "please don't tell her you saw me smoking. I gave it up years ago, and I know it would displease her." Something in his tone indicated that Edward might not actually want to have the information he sought. Ramesh exhaled a cloud of smoke into the darkness. "Things are complicated."

Edward nodded silently.

"I've received a letter from Nayana." He looked back toward the house. "The others don't know the details, but I'm not sure she'll be back. Or I should say she's told me she won't be back, that she's left me."

"I'm so sorry," Edward said.

Ramesh let out another long billow of smoke. "Yes, well, the problem is that she thought she was going to be with her sister," he said. He was smiling, but it was a smile that indicated how deeply upset he was. "You see, Edward, she thought she had someone to go to. Someone to replace me, in a way."

"Aren't you able to reach her in India?"

Ramesh shook his head. His face was in shadow, but his kind eyes glistened and held Edward's gaze in the darkness. With the cigarette deep in the webbing of his fingers, his entire hand cupped his mouth, as though he were preventing himself from speaking. His face glowed briefly red with his inhale.

"Nayana almost miscarried a couple of weeks ago," he said. Edward was still murmuring apologies when Ramesh spoke again. "It would have been our third miscarriage."

Edward fell silent. He was tempted to reach out and put a hand on Ramesh's shoulder, but he didn't do that, either. He leaned against the railing and waited to hear whatever Ramesh was willing to tell him, perhaps needed to tell him. Ramesh put out his cigarette in a planter and reached in his back pocket. He handed Edward a folded envelope. It seemed strange that he would want Edward to read Nayana's parting letter, but it would have felt rude to refuse. He unfolded it and began to read. The writing was familiar. A child's. This wasn't

Nayana's letter at all. He glanced at the bottom of the page. It was signed from Mr. and Mrs. Nair, but there was a post-script: *Written by your loving nephew.* Here it was, his nephew's tragic tale, written in Birendra's own hand. *Your blessed sister is with God. She died 16 November 1993.* Edward looked at the date the letter was written. November 18. So much time had passed. And had Maddy really not asked about family? He felt like a thief and had to return the letter to its envelope, then back to Ramesh. They remained there on the patio a while longer in silence, the time it took Ramesh to light an-other cigarette. He cleared his throat and looked at Edward again. His sad smile was gone, and he just looked tired.

"I'm glad to know the boy has found a good family," he said sincerely.

Edward, still choked with emotion, nodded, understanding only that Birendra was the one blessing in all this. Maybe it wasn't too late for him to be a blessing to his aunt, especially. When he could, he said, "Won't it be a comfort for Nayana to have news of Birendra, even though her sister is gone?"

"I think it will be a great comfort ultimately. But I'm quite sure that returning to news of her sister's death and the boy's absence will have been more than Nayana could bear." Ed-ward could sense that the conversation was coming to a close. He still needed information, some way to reach Nayana. Ramesh must have read his anxiety. "I can give you her sis-ter's address. It's all I have. There's no phone."

"Will you go to her?" Edward asked.

Ramesh took a last long drag on his cigarette, then put it out. The smoke that had gathered was burning Edward's eyes. At last Ramesh shook his head.

"She's made that difficult just now. Perhaps we both need a little time. But I will be here for her when she's done blaming herself."

Edward felt the pressure of the note in his pocket all the way back to the hotel. It was, of course, the address in India where Birendra had lived with his mother, and it was the only hope he had of contacting Nayana. Feeling as though he'd traveled back in time, he wondered if a telegram would be possible. How did one even send a telegram? Someone at his hotel would know. But he was spent and wouldn't be able to find the words for that conversation just now. He carried on to his room, extracting a tiny bottle of whiskey from his minibar. From his window, his eyes went from one shadowy patch to another, treetops in Hyde Park below. He pulled the note from his pocket and studied the address. He said his nephew's name softly, as though a prayer, even though he did not pray. It was a reason, really, not a prayer, which is what Edward was seeking. A reason to carry on with the journey of a lifetime. Too much time had already been wasted. Birendra's aunt was already there, devastated and alone. And shouldn't Edward see where his nephew was born and had lived his whole life, if only to have a better sense of the place Birendra had called home? It would bring them closer. He would find Nayana and put a face to the awful situation, perhaps even provide a shred of the solace she needed to help her through this grief, perhaps even give her some hope. It was as he'd written to his sister. For wouldn't Nayana realize that Birendra needed her in his life as much as she needed him?

XXXIV

There was a house, and it was the right house, but it was also wrong. It was dark, and it was empty. And there were her sister's neighbors, and there were words, but they were the wrong words. Impossible words, yet they'd been spoken. And then there was anger, so much anger, and it was the one thing that was right in all this, the one thing that was maybe strong enough to overcome Nayana's grief. She harnessed it. She brought it with her to the police station in Trivandrum, where she was told it wasn't necessary, the anger, and to the orphanage, where a man told her he was sorry, but it wouldn't change the facts. The anger. And they all told her there was nothing to be done, with eyes that spoke a yet more pressing truth: she was an outsider there and a woman. What had she expected them to do for her? England, India — would this ever not be the case? And there were tears, some of which she shared with the neighbor woman but most of which she saved for Aditi's pillow, her mother's sarees, her father's tie, all of whose absorbent company she welcomed, until the tears were gone, the anger was gone. Nayana, too, all but gone.

Lions roar in the morning, sweet sister. I'm told they were marooned on an island at the center of the man-made lake that hugs this sanctuary in which I find no peace. They were brought here at some point from some other land, made a spectacle of. Each morning they roar at the water, at the new day, at their hunger, at their lost kingdom. Do they persist out of anger, I wonder, or desperation? Could it be boredom after so many years? And why do I carry on speaking to someone who is no longer here?

The bell rang throughout the ashram, as it did every morning at five forty. Nayana, as she had been the day before and the one before that, was awake for it. The mosquito netting that framed the unyielding single mattress on which she lay glowed softly in the moonlit darkness of predawn. She would have been content to remain in this temporary bed, quiet with her thoughts, but she was not alone, and she could not do as she wished. There was no privacy in the ashram, where even those in mourning had to abide by the rules.

The German Swiss woman with whom she shared this room slept only three feet from her. If they each reached a hand out while lying on their respective beds, they would be able to touch fingers through their nets. They shared, as well, the single desk, beside the door, and the single window above that desk. Judith rose promptly at the bell, with Swiss precision, and immediately left the room to take her shower. When she returned, she quietly asked if it was okay to turn on the light, though they followed this same routine every day. Nayana, with the sheet pulled over her face, mumbled her assent and listened to the sounds of Judith preparing for the day: hands moisturizing skin, the gentle scratch of the brush passing along her scalp, the snap of a band securing her ponytail, the pull of fabric against skin. Above them the whir of an overhead fan and the growing buzz of the fluorescent light.

Satsang began at six, and attendance was not optional. The path to the main hall was dark when she left her room. She disregarded the rows of matting that lined the hall and found a spot against one of the supporting beams to the side. In the darkness, she would merely be a shadow to those entering the room until satsang was over. Both sides of Nayana's mid-spine ached from the effort of so much sitting with a straight back. The pain prevented her from concentrating. The clarity of mind promised by the director shimmered in the distance like a mirage in her desert of hopelessness. Using the surface of the column, she massaged either side of her spine, pressing each ache into the wood. Then she tried to do as they told her, to shift her inner gaze to her third-eye center. When she finally succeeded in this, she felt a pulling sensation there and noticed a red light, like a backlit tornado, spiraling away from her, promising an escape. She wanted to be sucked into it, leaving her body behind, every part of it. But she could never hold the gaze. The funnel just as quickly fell from view. And Nayana remained anchored in her flesh.

There they were, on cue. The lions roared at a high hollow pitch that traveled across the lake's surface and through the gates of the ashram. She pictured three anxious lionesses pacing a tiny island at feeding time. Were they caged as well as stranded? Insult on top of injury. She imagined herself swimming to their shore, exciting their hunger on the other side of the iron bars, then lowering herself into their captivity and assuming this same cross-legged pose before them, eyes closed, no longer in pain, finally at peace. She would give herself to these beasts, leave her body for them — an offering — to be torn limb from limb, devoured entirely. Violently set free.

She opened her eyes and was crying again. Guilty after this vision, in which she held no regard for the future life she carried. There was more daylight outside the hall, and she could see their numbers had grown within. New guests had arrived, yet Nayana was still the only Indian in the room who wasn't working there. A man alone, not far from her, with hair as long as hers had once been and perfect posture was among the new arrivals, yet he was clearly a veteran of these places with posture like that, his hands in mudra. She tried to prevent the slouch in her own back. And then an extended guttural "om," repeated twice more, announced the conclusion of morning meditation.

"Turn to page three," the Italian director said with an accent that could have sounded Indian if she hadn't been looking at him.

He spoke from his seat on the wooden stage at the front of the hall, between two Indian swamis cast in bronze. His call: *Jaya ganesha jaya ganesha jaya ganesha pahimaam sri ganesha sri ganesha sri ganesha rakshamaam.* The room, a chorus, echoed its response. Even after days of repetition, it was the only line Nayana could recite without the aid of the pamphlet they provided, from which the director also chose supplementary mantras. "Jaya Ganesha," however, was a staple. It started and ended each day. In the morning, it loosened stiff bodies, and some began to sway now and pat their knees. A man at the front incorporated the beat of a tabla. There were tambourines being passed around. The woman to Nayana's right offered her one. She smiled and shook her head, then watched the woman tap it gently against her palm, her thigh, then alternate between the two, her head following along. It was still incredible to witness the mounting joyous abandon in the room as the chanting and beating picked up their paces. What were all these people looking for, so far from home, all the way in Kerala? What had they found that Nayana had not? None of it seemed real. Not that the others were faking anything; not that she believed this was an experience reserved only for certain spiritual Indians. It was unreal because she would never be able to tell Aditi about any of it. Then she noticed a woman who, like Nayana, was watching it all take place. Still observing, still reserving judgment. Perhaps it was being discovered that encouraged this woman to relinquish her role as spectator. She shrugged at Nayana, as if to say, *Why not, right?* and she looked down at her pamphlet and began to sing along.

After chanting, the director made the day's announcements, as he had each day since her arrival: there would be yoga after morning tea. Breakfast at ten thirty. New arrivals who hadn't been assigned karma yoga duty were directed to meet by the big tree at eleven to learn how they could contribute during their stay from Dario, who waved a hand above his wild curls. Everyone pitches in, said the director, as a daily reminder. At twelve thirty, there would be an optional yoga coaching class. Then tea again at one thirty, followed by the daily lecture at two. Today's lecture would be on *Bhagavad Gita*. How strange, she thought: all these Westerners learning the obscure scriptures she hardly knew herself. After the lecture, a second yoga class, then dinner at six. Evening satsang would be at eight, with lights-out at ten thirty. The strangeness of the ashram schedule made her time there a little more agreeable.

When this retreat had been suggested, Nayana had not objected. By that point, she'd all but given up. And she trusted Mrs. Nair's nephew. Benji had always been kind to her family. He was their translator, too, so they depended on him. She remembered him from Srikant's funeral. He might have suggested a madhouse and Nayana might not have objected. She simply wanted to disappear and didn't care where. If they'd left her at Aditi's, she might have spent the rest of her life in her sister's bed. He told Nayana she would feel like she'd left India, and that's what she wanted. He was right, too. Whatever was familiar was outweighed by all that was foreign. She was grateful for the structure provided by the ashram schedule in any case and even more for the silence. Meals were eaten in silence, and yoga was a mostly silent affair. One could even choose to take a vow of silence, wearing a sign around one's neck. If that would have silenced her thoughts, Nayana would have done it. Still, she spoke little to the others. Even with her roommate, Judith, conversation was kept to a minimum, and this seemed to suit them both. That Nayana was Indian and there among so many Europeans was a kind of sign she wore in and of itself, and she was mostly left alone. She avoided the social areas, such as the big tree where everyone gathered for tea and the communal tables in the Health Hut, where people went during the intervals of free time in the early afternoon and again after dinner. The only silence that she couldn't bear was her sister's.

For three days she hadn't been sure if the routine was keeping her together or simply delaying an inevitable collapse. She watched the whole procession each day, waiting to learn. Mostly she marveled as the white men and women before her worshipped two dead swamis, learned about Hindu gods, practiced yoga, ate vegetarian meals, and chanted in a language even she didn't know, finding their bliss.

During the lecture that afternoon, Nayana studied the paintings of gods that lined the hall while the others listened to their tales. She'd heard the stories growing up, and she knew them well, even if she rarely thought of them since leaving India. She tried to see them now as if through foreign eyes. Siva, a beautiful aquamarine, with his many arms, wielding a trident high in the air, dancing — a Hindu Poseidon; blue Krishna playing his flute, with his crown and peacock feathers; half-breed Ganesh's elephant head and trunk hanging around his big belly; golden Hanuman with his strong form and simian face; Lakshmi posed on her lotus offering abundance from her four arms; a raging purple Kali with a severed head in one hand and bloody sword in the other, wearing a necklace of shrunken heads; behind them all trailed eight-armed Parvati, riding her tiger. These were just a few of the gods and goddesses, and they appeared more fantastic to her than ever before in the context of these halls, where foreigners found refuge in a borrowed religion. What could they possibly hope to discover in these garish, often gruesome icons? For her, growing up Hindu meant being taught to understand these gods as symbols to be admired and feared; they were stories to teach lessons. Humans were not made in their image — Hindus didn't see themselves as anything like gods. Was this world of colorful deities simply an easier fantasy to escape into? These were characters in a grand tale meant to guide people to goodness, like all religious tales — full of beings that would never materialize to embrace her, or love her, or save her from herself. If she prayed, it was only to her sister, and, like the gods, Aditi was now silent.

XXXV

Leaving Varkala in a taxi as old as he was, Edward had the impression he had gone back to the beginning, his own beginning. He had started over and taken the fast track. He was so close. Almost to Nayana, as long as she hadn't slipped away yet again. If she had, he wasn't sure he could follow. This might have to be where his search would end. With the window rolled down, he breathed in the passing landscape in its entirety, the good and the bad. The sweet smell of burning coconut, which gave way to the noxious odors of melting plastic, black clouds of exhaust from unregulated vehicles, thick and metallic. A cluster of sacred cows as pungent as cattle on a ranch. He was leaving behind the green waxy leaves of coconut trees, wet with sea-salt air. He observed the passing motorcycles and scooters with their helmetless riders: a family of four, a family of five, two men transporting plumbing pipes twenty feet long — they all tested the center line of traffic as they bypassed whatever slowed them down ahead. In fact, the lines on the road served no purpose at all. And if there were two vehicles in any kind of proximity — and he couldn't imagine that there ever wouldn't be — their horns sang. As the warm wind blew against his face, stench and all, Edward embraced it with a stupid grin.

The farther he traveled, the denser the jungle grew. He hadn't known it would be so lush. So green. At a certain point, the asphalt road stopped and dirt roads continued, full of potholes, forcing the cars, trucks, and motorbikes to come to a crawl and choose circuitous routes, crossing the entire width of the road if necessary. The sign for the ashram at the last turn promised only one more kilometer. But Edward wasn't convinced his taxi was going to make it up this hill. He felt that he should offer to get out and walk the rest of the way. Or maybe get behind and push. The old car crawled and sputtered as they slowly climbed, as the trees grew denser, and the sun disappeared behind them. Edward leaned forward, scooting to the edge of the cracked vinyl bench seat, as if to urge them along the final stretch.

A lake came into view on the right. Across the road was an orange wall. He had to duck his head to see beyond to the temple gate. Bag in hand, he climbed out of the taxi and up the steps, passing under an archway. On the other side, he had the feeling he had left the world behind. Here, time itself moved slowly; a droning voice reverberated throughout the courtyard, the same two words repeated, though Edward couldn't decipher them at first through the elongated, nasal delivery. Then he understood: "Inhaaaale... Exhaaaale." It was coming from an open-air structure at the center of the complex: a yoga class in progress. He removed his sunglasses and could see the inverted bodies under the shade of the tile roof. He wondered if yoga was mandatory there. If one of those bodies was Nayana. No one seemed to be walking around.

A large metal rack stood to the side of the steps that led up to the reception office, but it was mostly empty, and many sets of sandals and flip-flops and two pairs of sneakers were scattered around the base of the steps. Edward removed his shoes and his socks, which he rolled up and slipped into the mouth of one sneaker, then placed them on the rack. His feet were grateful for the air and the cool earth and the even cooler tile floor at the top of the stairs.

A couple was seated at a table filling out a form, their burgundy passports at the ready. Edward felt for his own passport in his front pocket. A man with glasses and black curly hair approached him with his hands in prayer. He spoke with a strong Italian accent and introduced himself as Dario. When Edward was asked how long he would be staying, he answered that he was unsure. They had a three-day minimum stay, and yoga was strongly encouraged; there were mats he could rent or buy if he didn't have one. When he'd finished signing in, he took his rented mat and his suitcase and followed Dario to what was to be his bed in the men's dormitory. It was almost dinnertime, he was told, and he could join the others when he heard the bell.

He did as he was told, silently following the others into the hall where he'd seen the yoga class. He fell in line. The guests took their seats on the long woven mats that lined the hall, each finding a place behind one of the round metal trays placed in front of the mats. Two men in yellow shirts chanted at the front. There were six mats in all, stretching from the stage at the front to the middle of the room. And dozens of trays were already placed in front of each row. The trays looked like something from a hospital or military cafeteria, perhaps a camping store, with several compartments for food and a little metal cup off to one side. Were there this many guests? He looked behind him and saw a steady flow of people still entering the hall. If Benji hadn't warned him it was a place that catered mostly to Europeans, he would have been shocked to see so much white skin in one place.

A few of the guests walked along the rows serving food from one metal container or another — scooping or ladling their offerings onto the trays. There was a spongy white rice, a thin red broth with root vegetables and tomatoes, a sliced-carrot and purple-cabbage salad, and a white liquid flecked with green, which he assumed was some kind of yogurt sauce. The chanting finished, and a few prayerlike phrases were called and repeated. Hands were clasped together and swiftly raised to foreheads. Edward was too slow and uninitiated to follow along, so he watched. They were finally asked to eat in silence. There were no utensils. Those around him quickly and expertly set to work on their trays, using their fingers to create bite-size mounds. The servers circled perpetually, refilling as necessary. The steel cups remained empty, but he noticed a woman in the next row pouring an almost clear liquid he thought might be herbal tea. He reached for a carrot slice and brought it to his mouth. The woman seated across from him was smiling at him. He'd only seen her agile hands before, but now he saw her unruly frizz of hair, her tanned skin. She was young — much younger than Edward — and she looked like she'd probably been touring around India for a while, like her skin had resisted the sun until it could no longer do so. He returned her smile and felt suddenly very far from home and everything familiar. He was thirsty more than hungry. The teapot was slowly making its way up his own row now, and he tried again to determine what was coming out of it. When the person beside him reached out his cup, he thought maybe it was water despite its rosy hue. He'd been studying it so intently he forgot to lift his own cup when it was his turn, making it harder for the woman to reach, so she paused and waited for him. And then he looked at her, and he knew it was Nayana standing before him. It wasn't that she shared some feature in particular with Birendra, but somehow the whole of the relationship was immediately clear. Edward felt himself go pale. He must have had a horrified look on his face because she shrank away, visibly confused, ready to move on down the line if he wanted none of what she had. He thrust his cup forward.

"Thank you," he said.

She nodded once and looked around because, he realized, he'd broken the silence. Then she moved on. Now he flushed with embarrassment and grew nauseated. He sipped from the metal cup. It was an infused water, slightly herbaceous and warm but not hot. It quenched his thirst and settled his stomach, which was tied in an empty knot, both wanting food and rejecting the very idea. Edward watched Nayana carry on down the line. She was wearing the long sturdy white cotton pants that so many of the guests wore here and a thin long-sleeved shirt that revealed the outline of her spine as she bent to serve tea to each guest. He couldn't stop watching her. She was thin, perhaps even too thin for a pregnant woman, and this reminded him that she'd recently been in the hospital. He could see that she might be unwell, yet she remained absolutely beautiful. He didn't know if he found her so striking because she was his nephew's aunt and he'd gone through so much to find her or if she was simply a stunning woman. She reached the end of the row, checked her pot, and disappeared through a door.

Edward had barely touched his food. The woman with the hair across from him was being served rice yet again. And then more of the vegetables. She seemed to empty her tray just as quickly as the servers filled it. She acknowledged this, rubbing her belly, when she caught him staring in amazement. After he'd eaten his salad and a few mounds of the bloated rice, he brought his tray to the wash area outside, as he'd seen some of the others start to do. He hadn't touched the liquid yogurt, which filled a compartment at the tray's edge, so he had to be careful not to spill it as he left the hall. He wanted to lie down and sleep. He wasn't ready to talk to Nayana yet. Knowing she was there was enough for the moment. He would rest before they were called to come together again later that evening. Under the cover of darkness, he would find her and tell her who he was and why he had come. His head was spinning, and he felt slightly feverish. At the end of the dormitory, he found his bed again. His head touched down on the pillow, his eyes closed, and he slept through the night.

Nayana wasn't serving water or food at breakfast, and he hadn't seen her anywhere in the hall during morning yoga. He felt slightly less clumsy eating today and was able to sop up half his yogurt with a couple of the fried disks they were passing around. The woman with the hair and the big appetite was two rows over today, with her back to Edward, but he liked that she was there, that there were distinct individuals whom he had noticed and who had noticed him. And he felt rested after a long sleep. He thought of Jane, of his sister and nephew, of his life in Los Angeles, all so far away. What would they think of his being in this place? Not a single person, he realized, had a clue where he was, including Jane. He hadn't even told Nayana's husband in the end. His throat clenched, and he reached for his cup, but he couldn't swallow. He was going to cry, not knowing exactly why, only that nothing would prevent it. He picked up his tray and quickly walked out of the hall, the tears wet on his cheeks against a warm breeze.

After breakfast, he was to meet the Italian man who'd signed him in by the big tree in front of the hall. New guests would be informed of the duties they had to perform while staying at the ashram. Perhaps he'd serve food with Nayana in the evening. But what good would that do, being both silent and public? Dario was going around asking people what their professions were in their "other" lives. This apparently helped him decide what their jobs would be at the ashram. The nurse beside him would prepare and set up afternoon tea. The bank clerk would pick up trash on the road outside the gates of the ashram.

"A film scout, eh?" he said to Edward. "Then you are an important man."

"Not really," he insisted. But Dario ignored him and searched his clipboard. "It's very low on the totem pole."

Something about the exchange or the young man's mannerisms made everything seem suddenly comical to Edward. He was practically giddy as he scrubbed the tile floors and toilets in the men's dorm bathrooms. He was actually enjoying himself. Drinking the Kool-Aid, perhaps, or just happy to have a concrete task that didn't involve broaching the subject of Birendra with his aunt. He worked up a sweat and felt hungry again. He would see what he could find to eat at the Health Hut.

True to its name, the "hut" had a dirt floor and a thatched roof. The perimeter had no permanent walls but was surrounded by a thin bamboo matting that had been nailed to several wooden posts in order to secure it. A small food-preparation area was partitioned off by a double stack of the matting, and there were several benches under the hut's roof as well as a table with a parasol just outside, where Edward could see what looked like a valley and open sky. Despite his taxi's struggle to arrive, he hadn't realized how high up the ashram was. He wanted to see the view unobstructed and walked past his friend with the appetite and the hair behind the counter. She looked up from her book and waved as he passed.

The sun looked hot and white beside the gathering rain clouds that hung over a lush and vibrantly green valley. Exiting the hut at the other end, he closed his eyes and breathed in the open space, relieved to find the world again beyond the ashram walls. When he opened his eyes, he saw someone lying on the bench on the other side of the table and parasol, hiding behind a book. Nayana lifted her head to see who was there. She hadn't been visible from inside the hut. Now he had to resist the urge to turn back around.

"Sorry. I didn't know someone was here," he said.

"I'm here," she said.

He looked away, again at the view and the amassing clouds.

"A nice spot to read," he said.

"Yes, it is."

There was a nearly empty bowl and a spoon on the table. She must have skipped the morning meal and had her breakfast at the hut when it opened. In an effort to have something to say, he almost mentioned her skipping breakfast in favor of fruit, but realized that would be strange and demand the explanation he was suddenly at a loss to provide.

"Good book?" he asked instead.

She set the book on the table and looked up at him, either exasperated or indifferent — he couldn't trust himself to know.

"That's what everyone says. And, yes, it is. It's also long. I've been reading it for ages now."

"Would you mind if I joined you?"

She paused, then sat up on the bench.

"Feel free." She was even more striking in this light. "You're an American?"

"Yes. From California."

"I think you might be the first American I've come across here."

He could see their relation now — Birendra's and hers — in the nose and mouth. That face he'd come to love, the reason he was here. He felt himself relax some.

"I was getting that impression," he said. "I guess it is pretty far for us to come. So I'm the token American."

"And I'm the token Indian," she said, raising her eyebrow sardonically. "In India, no less."

That she made a joke seemed a good sign. He felt a sudden relief for Ramesh. Perhaps she was proving more resilient than he'd given her credit for.

"Will you excuse me? I'm just going to get a juice. I'm a little low on blood sugar. Would you like one? Can I get you something? Anything?"

He was being awkward, but she smiled politely.

"I'm fine, thanks."

"Would you mind if I came back and joined you?"

She regarded him, curious now. He'd already asked that. She simply extended her hand again in a welcoming gesture.

Staring at the handwritten list of fruit bowls and juices on offer, he contemplated telling the woman at the counter what he was about to do. She was watching him with a wry smile, probably wondering why it was so difficult for him to choose from among the four fruits that hadn't been crossed out. Why he kept looking back to make sure Nayana wasn't leaving.

"It's complicated," he said, and she laughed.

"Why is it complicated?"

It was a good question. There were answers, of course: because of Nayana's grief; her sister's death; Edward's fear that his own sister was never going to forgive him for what he was about to do; that she might hate him if it somehow led to her losing Birendra; the fact that he couldn't honestly say what had driven him to come all this way, despite knowing this possibility, and that this scared him most of all. But there was also the simple fact of Birendra, and now he had to walk over, sit down, and tell Nayana who he was.

XXXVI

The sun escaped from behind a mass of clouds and was once again warm on Nayana's face, the day's humidity building. Wet air lay like a blanket of quiet over the valley now. Some of the clouds had that dark backdrop, a promise they might break open. She would like it to rain again, to really rain as it did during the monsoon season. A reminder of times past. The table rocked slightly. She'd forgotten for a moment that the American was coming back with a juice. Something intrigued her about this man. His behavior was a bit odd, but he seemed harmless enough.

"You sure you don't mind?" he asked yet again.

"Not at all."

He was staring so intensely at her that she felt she might blush. She looked away, closing her book.

"So I actually have something — " He interrupted himself, looking back into the hut. Then he took a deep breath. It was all rather odd, as though he were preparing for some kind of performance. And then he spoke again, and he didn't stop. "My name is Edward. I know your name is Nayana. And I know about your sister." If she weren't seated on a bench, she would have backed away. "I don't want to upset you, but I've actually come here to find you. I was in London. I met your husband there and the rest of your family." Did Ramesh send an American to find her? "I have to tell you about your nephew. About Birendra. He is safe and well and living with my sister, in California. She adopted him late in December. I'm sorry to tell you like this. I'm sure this must come as a huge shock. I didn't mean for it to come out like this, but I wasn't sure how to tell you anything after all that you've been through." She could feel herself floating away again. "Nayana? Are you okay?"

Am I okay?

She wasn't able to process everything he'd said, but one note repeated in her mind. This man knew about her sister. This man knew who Aditi was. And Ram. And Birendra. After so much silence, after retreating so far, first to India, then to this place, and finally giving up on her search for Birendra. After all this, there was someone she could talk to again, someone who knew. For once she had no desire to hide.

"I think I've known for months now," she said. "Known and not known. I've been ignoring the signs, letting my own problems in London distract me from my fear that something really was wrong when I didn't hear from my sister for more than a month. I kept telling myself I was scared of my sister's judgment, but I knew better, that *she* was better than that, too good, too loving." He said he had met Ramesh. What exactly did he know? Was she, in his mind, the heartless woman who walked out on a loving husband? Who carried another man's child? She looked for evidence in his face but found only compassion, and this made her look away again, with shame. "I just didn't know it was this I had been scared of, or I didn't want to know. I couldn't let myself even imagine it. I still can't." She wasn't done punishing herself; she shouldn't let a stranger comfort her. And yet, looking at him, she felt relief, at least for her nephew. "But Birendra? You say he's okay?"

"He is, yes. And again, I'm just so sorry, Nayana." Was he tearing up? "Just know that Birendra is doing well. He's in school. He speaks of you so fondly. He's safe."

She released a breath she hadn't realized she was holding, then pulled the envelope from her book and placed it between them.

"She wrote me on the last day of Diwali. My sister. Do you know the holiday?" He shook his head. He hadn't even touched his juice. She gestured toward it, and he raised the glass to his lips. His hand was shaking. She averted her eyes, back to the envelope. "It's sometimes called the festival of lights. There are usually five days of celebration, and the last was always important to our family because it tells the story of twins, Yama and his sister, Yami. Yama brings gifts to his sister, and she lights his path with lanterns and guides him home with her songs. According to the myth, Yama is liberated of all his sins by visiting his sister on this day. This is what I was doing — trying to do — by coming back to India, back to my sister. I wanted her to wash me clean. But she was already gone."

"I'm not sure you can escape your past," he said. "Not that I haven't tried."

"No, you've got it wrong. I don't want to escape my past, I wanted to return to it. But it *is* gone. All of it." A small group of guests was leaving the hut. It was almost time for the afternoon lecture. "When did you arrive?"

"Yesterday, just before dinner."

"Well, there are lectures in the afternoons. Mostly stories from ancient Indian scriptures. The other day, the man referred to Yama as the Lord of Death."

She covered her mouth, afraid she might burst into tears, afraid she would not be able to stop.

"It's none of my business, of course, but I could see how much Ramesh loves you. And Raj. They all seemed extremely concerned for you. And I know Birendra loves you. He's not gone at all. Actually, I think he's still waiting for you."

There was no use holding it. She was crying again. It had been a few days since she'd last stopped. It felt good, like proximity to Adi.

"How did you ever manage to find me, Edward?"

There was a sudden shift in the light above them. Clouds had filled the sky, blotting out the sun. He took the last sip of his juice, then looked right at her as though he wasn't sure where to begin.

"As I said, I was in London. I only ever planned to look you up and arrange a meeting." She wanted to offer some excuse but said nothing, so he carried on. "I met Raj first, then Ramesh, and he told me about the letter from the neighbors." She acknowledged that she knew about it with a nod. Mrs. Nair had told her all about her nephew writing that letter, and it had taken every ounce of Nayana's strength not to scold the old woman harshly for such abysmal judgment. "Ramesh gave me the address where your sister lived in Varkala. I thought I'd send a telegram, but what could I say? I knew that you'd already arrived. I couldn't imagine the shock. I suddenly decided to come, to be here, and to tell you about Birendra in person. I also wanted to know where your nephew came from. Our nephew." He stopped and watched her, as though he wanted her permission to claim Birendra. She didn't know if she was ready to give it. "He's become very special to me. He is special." She nodded and wiped her face, having finally ceased crying. The lights went off in the hut. They were alone now. "I managed to make it to Varkala. But you were already gone. I had heard about the neighbors, the Nairs, from Birendra, but I didn't know which house was theirs. Mrs. Nair found me in front of the house. It was all a bit comical, really. We were both desperate to be understood, but the only word we had in common was *Birendra*. Fortunately, that and a little sign language sufficed. She took me to the cliff, to her cousin Benji's shop. The man who sold the stuffed animals your sister made." Nayana nodded again.

"Benji has been kind. He basically dragged me here. We first met at Srikant's funeral."

"Was that Birendra's father?"

"Yes."

"Srikant." He repeated the name, as though it were a character in some story. Of course Srikant was very real to her, but she could see how it must feel for this man, who'd come to a place he probably thought he'd only ever imagine, like visiting the setting of a novel that had always stayed with you. Except that these were the names and places from her nephew's story, and her story. Perhaps that's what she saw in him. It was becoming his story now as well. His eyes went glassy. She felt herself go rigid as a defense, for fear she might again fall to blubbering. "Sorry. It's all a bit much, isn't it?"

It was. Too much to make sense of but such a comfort to try. Even though she didn't know this man. It was like what he'd said about Mrs. Nair: they, too, had that one word, that one person, in common.

"I did my best when I arrived to find out what happened to Birendra. I went to the police, to the orphanage. They wouldn't even talk to me. My heart was broken. It *is* broken. And so I gave up. I even went to collect the money we'd wired my sister from London for Birendra's school. All I knew was that he was in America. I thought, how will I ever find him?"

Nayana looked at Edward for understanding, perhaps forgiveness. She found sympathy.

"I've been thinking that the farther away from home we get, the easier it is to love," he said, but he was immediately shaking his head as if the thought hadn't translated from his mind into words. She knew something about this. "I think I mean that expectations can make it harder to love, and the closer you get to home, the more you expect from those around you, and vice versa."

"That wasn't true of Aditi," Nayana said.

"Yes," he said. He seemed to be reconsidering. "Maybe it isn't true after all. Maybe it's just an excuse."

There was a story there, she thought, but she wasn't ready to hear it, and he didn't seem ready to tell. They sat in silence and in darkness until a tap on the parasol made them both look up. Then another. Gradually a random percussion became the steady beat of heavy rain. Nayana smiled. Still rain-ing on her after all these years. But now she welcomed the reminder of those she'd lost.

"Not long after college," he said, "my girlfriend got pregnant. My ex-girlfriend, I should say." He spoke as though he were surprising himself with his own recollection. "That child would have been a little younger than Birendra is now."

"You lost it?" she asked.

"No. We made a choice we believed was for the best. I mean it was. But how can you know, right? We assume that what's actually come to pass is what's right for us, but we never know. There's no going back. I guess that's what I was trying to say earlier."

They were both on the edge of their seats. This close attention was the only way to express such gratitude, perhaps. She would have said the words, except he seemed to already know, to feel the same. As if they could say anything they wanted to without being afraid of the big subjects. As if they'd found refuge from their very lives and could stay here as long as necessary, until they were ready to rejoin the world. After all, he'd come so far, and not without risk. For all he knew, she would try to take Birendra, but the more she sat with this kind man, the more impossible the thought seemed. Perhaps this was what she should do for Birendra; she should let him have this new life.

"Will you tell me about your sister? If you don't mind. I'd like to know about Birendra's new home."

"My sister is very successful in her work as an interior designer." He wasn't pleased with this introduction, and he shook his head at it. "Maddy's a good person," he said. The way he looked at Nayana, he seemed to want to implant this fact in her mind. "She's nine years older than I am, and she's got a really big heart. She's a lot of fun. A little eccentric." Nayana shrugged off his embarrassed expression; she wasn't in a position to judge. "Birendra is doing really well in school. He loves it, in fact. He's got this plan to read every English book in the entire library. He's at a French school — well, French and English. The Lycée Français in Los Angeles?"

Nayana's hand rose to her mouth, and she began to cry again. He was confused by this, but she waved it away.

"I'm just happy," she said through her tears. "Go on, please."

"She's not married. She's single." Nayana nodded, encouraging him to continue. "I, uh...should mention he goes by a nickname now."

"A nickname?" she asked, stifling her tears. "What nickname?"

"Well, he goes by Bindi?" He cringed, saying it as a question. It didn't make any sense.

"Bindi? But why?"

"So it is a name?"

"Yes. Well, Bindu, more commonly. A woman's name."

"I see. I was afraid it wasn't a name at all," he said. "Do you think he would know that?"

"I'm not sure," she said. "He would have said something, I suppose. Did he not?" Edward shook his head. "But what made her choose Bindi?"

"To be honest, I don't know why."

A wind blew the rain in a steady diagonal sheet now, but he didn't seem to mind that he was getting soaked. Nayana touched his forearm and motioned that they should go into the hut.

"We've missed the lecture," she said once they were inside.

"I'm okay with that," he said.

They took a seat, both dripping onto the table. He was smiling at her. He seemed to have the same question in his mind. What now? What would happen now that Nayana had been found? Now that she had a way back to her nephew? She honestly couldn't say. She hadn't even gotten as far as thinking about the child she was carrying.

"I guess I need to contact my sister," he said, suddenly quiet.

"I'd like to see my nephew," she said, and again she stopped herself from saying more. From admitting how little she feared she had to offer him now.

"Of course you would," he said. "Of course." His gaze fell to the puddle of water that was collecting at her wrist. "My sister," he said, then he fell silent. Nayana swept the water over the table's edge with a wet sleeve as Edward continued his thought. "She's been misguided at times. But she loves him, and I can vouch for the depth of that love." He seemed desperate to be believed, and he searched now for confirmation in Nayana's eyes. "I suppose she just needs a little help sometimes. Maybe I need some help as well."

If he was saying his sister was occasionally lost, Nayana thought she knew something about the feeling. As quickly as a flare of concern for her nephew sparked, another followed right behind it: Nayana didn't know if she'd be any better. And there was this man, who seemed genuinely to care for Birendra, and who'd traveled halfway around the world to find her. She had to believe that meant something. She felt the words she'd been so afraid to admit finally spilling out.

"I've no idea what will come of it," she said. "That is, what I can be for him right now. For anyone, actually."

She hadn't needed to clarify. Edward understood. Something had happened between them, a moment shared between two people equally at sea. A kindness they'd been able to show each other. An appreciation of one person's struggle by another.

"I don't think we ever know what we end up meaning in the lives of others — not for them, anyway," he said. He might have wanted her to convince him of an answer, but she said nothing at all. "Perhaps Birendra needs all of us."

Nayana wanted to believe this man, this unexpected uncle to her nephew. To believe that Birendra needed her, even as she was now. There was a part of her that wished Ramesh was going to be with her when she was reunited with her nephew, but she'd come this far; she knew she had to take the next step alone as well. One day Nayana and Birendra could visit London together, and she would introduce her nephew to Ramesh, regardless of how things turned out for Nayana and him. She wanted Birendra to know Ramesh's love, so big, so pure. It was the first time Nayana had thought of the future with anything like clarity since she'd arrived in this place. She stood and reached for Edward's arm now, then led him to the exit. They braced themselves for rain.

DIWALI 1984

VARKALA

Aditi was already lying on their bed when Srikant came in from turning off the lights. She was worn out after the week's celebration, but she was also taking a moment to miss her parents on this first Diwali without them. And this made Aditi miss her sister, too, for Nayana would feel especially alone on this day as well, far from home. They'd always felt a little alone without each other near. Srikant joined her now on the bed, and she nestled into him, wondering if it was at all similar for him, without his brother. It was worse, of course.

"Are you scared even a little?" she asked.

"Now, why would I be scared, Adi?"

"About the baby. Do you no worry that he will only have us? My sister is far away and may never come back. The others all with God."

"I don't know; there may be more," he said and, touching her belly, flashed a wry smile she could still see in the dark.

"You know what I mean," she said.

"You don't think we're enough?" She rocked her head, honestly unsure. "You know what I think?" he said. "I think we collect love and can never reach our fill, never have too much. He will have all the love I have ever known, and all the love you have ever known. And even if the two of us had only known our love for each other, I think it would still be enough."

"It's a very romantic notion," she said.

"You disagree?" She shook her head now. She'd like to believe that, too. "Well, then, that makes for a good pair." He kissed the top of her head. "I'll tell you what. Why don't we choose a strong name, for extra measure? How about Abhimanyu? A fierce and skilled warrior." She recoiled to see if he was serious. "I'm sorry. You're right. He dies. Not a good name."

He resumed stroking her hair, and they were silent for a moment. She thought she had it, a name, but wasn't sure she wanted to say. She believed she was having a boy but didn't want to jinx it or make a girl feel unwelcome if she was mistaken.

"Dabeet?" Srikant spouted suddenly, giving Aditi a jolt.

"Where are you getting these ideas from? Dabeet? Nobody is named Dabeet." She clicked her tongue, then paused, hesitant to discuss the baby's gender. "Besides, we don't even know we're having a boy."

"And yet you said 'he.'" She rocked her head again.

"I have a feeling."

"Ah, one of your feelings. It must be so, then."

She raised her hand to shush him, then poked his arm in jest. He took her hand in his and kissed the fading mehndi.

"Shouldn't we wait?" she said. "Or ask the pundit for guidance?"

"Paarthiv?" he blurted, then pretended to cower from her.

"You're not being serious." Now she gave his arm a little smack. "Besides, it doesn't exactly roll off the tongue." She shook her head, settling again beside him. "No."

She lay still for a moment, then turned on her back to relieve the pressure at her side. She said it as a whisper first, and he had to ask her to repeat herself. He leaned in close.

"Birendra," she said again.

"Birendra," he repeated with a contemplative air. "Like the Nepali *king. Oh, that's a very good name." He slid down and placed his face close to Aditi's belly, making her laugh. She rested a hand on his head, enjoying the feel of his thick hair, the vibration of his voice. "Hello, Birendra. Can you hear me? Do you like your new name? We're waiting for you, Birendra. A very happy Diwali from your amma and acchan, dear one."*

Les Vacances de Février, 1994

LAX

Birendra buckled himself in and lowered his tray table. The cup holder at the corner reminded him of the flight they'd taken from Delhi to New York on their way to Los Angeles — how there had been a bottle of water waiting for him then, how Mama Maddy had asked for a glass of Champagne for herself and orange juice for him. How she'd poured some of the orange juice into her glass and called it something else. Now there was no water, and Mama Maddy was holding only the monkey he'd given her on that same trip, twisting the tail with her finger, over and over, as she had been doing since they arrived at the airport gate. He worried that she was going to twist the tail right off, not because it couldn't be fixed — his mother had fixed his Ganesh's trunk more than once — but because he didn't know how to fix it, and he didn't know if Mama Maddy knew how to fix it, either.

"Aren't we going to order orange juice *et Champagne?*" he asked.

"See what good care you take of me, Bindi?" she said and placed her hand on his knee. "No, sweetie, we're not in first class this time."

"Oh. Why not?"

"Just in case," she said.

"In case what?"

"In case we're ever broke," she said, letting go of his knee and returning her attention to the monkey's tail.

"Are we broke?"

"No, sweetie. We're not broke. I'm being silly. In fact, I don't know what possessed me to tell Paige to book economy," she said.

He thought about it for a moment. "I think I was broke before, and it wasn't so bad."

This made her smile, which was good because he could see she was still worried. All week, she had tried to keep it from him, but he knew. Sometimes he heard her crying. And then she told him about the trip, and his aunt, and Uncle Eddie. And he thought, maybe Mr. Channar was right after all, but he didn't know what would happen. It didn't feel like he was in trouble. And Mama Maddy pinkie-promised she wasn't angry. She was more sad, maybe. Finally he'd asked her if Aunt Nayana wanted him to move to West London, but this just upset her more. She asked if that was what he wanted. When he had been with the Nairs, after his mother died, it was different; he thought he would go live with his aunt and uncle because they were his only family. Mr. and Mrs. Nair were not, even though he knew them better than he knew his aunt and uncle, really. But things weren't the same now. He had a family that he knew, in California. He had Mama Maddy and Uncle Eddie, too. He told her he thought he'd like to stay, and she said he made her "over-the-moon thrilled." She still cried, but they were "happy tears." She said she hoped he would never leave her. And that they would take care of each other forever. "Even when I'm old enough to take care of myself?" he'd asked. "Even then," she answered.

Mama Maddy had finally stopped playing with the monkey's tail and was now holding it still. She looked so peaceful, resting beside him with her eyes closed. He was going back to India, but it was okay. He was going back because Aunt Nayana had come after all. He hadn't been wrong to believe she would. He didn't exactly understand why Uncle Eddie and Aunt Nayana were in Varkala and not in West London. Mama Maddy said Uncle Eddie had gone to find his aunt. Didn't that mean that Uncle Eddie knew, even when no one else did, that his aunt would want to see Birendra again, that he'd never been an orphan after all? But how did Uncle Eddie know she was in India? Or did they go there together? Why didn't they come to Los Angeles instead? He would definitely ask them the story of how they found each other and why they ended up in India together rather than England. Even if they wouldn't tell him the whole story — adults can be so mysterious sometimes — he was glad they were all going to be there together.

He looked at the map in the airline magazine and traced his finger along the coast of India, where he thought Varkala was. It seemed so far away, and he'd been gone for such a long time already. He thought of his mother, almost forgetting that he wouldn't be seeing her again. Aunt Nayana would be there, though, and she was his mother's twin. It was funny that he never thought of them in the way he thought of other twins, like Kelli and Allison at his school. He couldn't really tell them apart, but his mother and aunt had always been different to him in his mind. Lately, though, when he thought of his mother, he struggled to remember every detail as he used to. What if the time that had passed since his mother died made his aunt seem less different somehow? He remembered the last time he'd seen her. They were saying good-bye at the end of her visit, at the airport. She'd bent down and kissed him and told him to be good, and he had been. She'd told him to take care of his mother, and he had tried. He knew it wasn't his fault she had to go away, just as it wasn't her fault for leaving. She'd been watching out for him in the end.

Would they all visit Mr. and Mrs. Nair in Varkala? Would they stay at his old house? He would like to see his neighbors again. He had so many questions he wanted to ask Mama Maddy. He leaned closer, trying to determine if she was asleep. A flight attendant stopped in the aisle and asked him to put up his tray. They would be taking off soon. He looked at the map again, now resting on his lap. The plane began to back up slowly. They were going back to Varkala. Maybe they could visit his old school on their way from the airport. What time would they arrive? He wanted to take them to meet Mr. Mon, who was sure to be impressed by Birendra's English now. And Birendra could ask for the family report he'd written and give it to his aunt and uncle to keep with them in West London. He would have to write a new one now. He wished he'd thought of it before leaving Los Angeles so he could have brought it along for Mr. Mon, to tell him about his new school and Mama Maddy and Uncle Eddie.

He loosened his seat belt and lifted himself up on the arms of his seat so he could look for the flight attendant. As quickly as he could, he unbuckled himself and retrieved his backpack from below. He pulled his *dictée* notebook out, along with his pencil, then replaced the bag and buckled himself in just as the plane began to move faster down the tarmac. Mama Maddy opened her eyes sleepily and smiled at him. He was safe, but he had to wait until the plane was in the air, flying smoothly, and for the bell to ding, before he could lower the tray again. He looked out the window. The plane pulled away from the runway, and he was soon trying to pick out buildings he could recognize below. The angle of the plane changed so fast that it was a challenge. When it leveled, all he could see out his window was the ocean, which he knew went all the way to India because he'd learned in world geography that all oceans are connected. When the bell rang and the flight attendant began to speak, he lowered his tray and opened his notepad to a new page. In his best cursive — much improved since he'd left Mr. Mon's English class the year before — he began to write.

ACKNOWLEDGMENTS

Bindi and I have benefited from many brilliant and generous advocates through the years. I trust you know who you are and that my gratitude is immeasurable. Additionally, support from the following institutions has been paramount: Iowa Writers' Workshop, McIntyre Foundation, Wall Creek, Wyoming Residency.

Paul Matthew Maisano is a graduate of the Iowa Writers' Workshop, where he was the third-year McIntyre fellow. *Bindi* is his first novel.